Sunset Lake Resort

Sunset Lake Resort

a novel by
Joanne Jackson

Stonehouse Publishing Inc. is an independent
publishing house, incorporated in 2014.

Cover design and layout by Elizabeth Friesen.
Printed in Canada

Stonehouse Publishing would like to thank and acknowledge
the support of the Alberta Government funding for the arts,
through the Alberta Media Fund.

Alberta◼
Government

National Library of Canada Cataloguing in Publication Data
Joanne Jackson
Sunset Lake Resort
Novel
ISBN 978-1-988754-56-7
First edition

This book is dedicated to Shelley Gregg, the woman who read the first words I ever wrote. And even as I was teaching myself to write, even when the writing was poor, she always had something positive and encouraging to say.

Thanks, Shell.

1961 – 2023

Other books by Joanne Jackson

The Wheaton
A Snake in the Raspberry Patch

In 2023, *A Snake in the Raspberry Patch* was shortlisted for both the Saskatchewan Book Awards, as well as Crime Writers of Canada Book Awards, where it won Best Crime Novel set in Canada.

1931

"Making a building appear out of a pile of wood," Cecelia says. "It just seems so, I don't know, magical." She opens her arms wide. "My cabin is going to be right here, looking into the sunset. Just you wait and see, Gerry. It's going to be beautiful. It's going to be the cabin of my dreams."

Chapter 1

"I can't believe what a witch she is." Aunt Marjorie, Mom's youngest sister says this so quietly, that Aunt Bernice, the second oldest, has trouble hearing.

"What?" Bernice says, cupping her hand around her ear.

"A witch," Marjorie says louder. "I can't believe what a witch she is. And I only say witch instead of," she whispers, "the b word because—"

Aunt Bernice takes up the thought. "—We're standing on consecrated ground and you wouldn't want a bolt of lightning to strike you dead."

Aunt Marjorie nods solemnly as the two of them look to the skies and make the sign of the cross. Both women are unmarried; Aunt Marjorie having been a widow for the past fifty years, and Aunt Bernice never having married. They've lived together since Aunt Marjorie's husband passed away in nineteen sixty-seven. Now, like an old married couple who've been together too long, though not always in agreement, they tend to finish each other's sentences.

Other than the usual childhood diseases, and a bout with pneumonia Aunt Bernice had thirty years ago, each has remained healthy well into their eighties, and they are able to walk across the lawn unaided, which is more than I can say for many of Dad's peers attending his funeral today. All around me I see bent backs, and gray heads hanging between slouched shoulders, pushing walkers towards the plot where the priest is already standing.

Having left the comfort of the air-conditioned church to venture to the cemetery in this oppressive heat, we are now following Julia, my father's second wife and my aunts' topic of conversation. Julia herself is so focused on not breaking a heel as she walks between headstones, that she's paying no attention to what's being said behind her.

"On second thought," Marjorie says, dabbing her top lip with a handkerchief pulled from her cleavage, "I can believe it. She had it all planned from the very beginning, didn't she?"

Bernice nods her head in agreement. "Had Arthur change his will the first week they were married. Cut Ruby out like she never existed. His own daughter. Even had the locks changed on the doors!"

"I wish Ruby were more assertive," Marjorie says. "But our brother-in-law," she nods at my father's coffin suspended over the hole we're approaching, "never gave his daughter anything. No self-confidence, no encouragement, barely any attention. Ruby grew up with such low self-esteem, she's never been capable of standing up for herself." She clucks her tongue.

"Our dear departed sister tried," Aunt Bernice says, "but Arthur ruled the roost in that family. Men," she says shaking her head, "they think the world will fall apart if they're not in charge."

"Remember when our father would lock us in our room to keep us from going out with boys?" Marjorie says. "You always snuck out the window."

"Of course I did!" Bernice says. "I knew Dad would never figure it out. He assumed females didn't have brains to think with. I got to be pretty good at shinnying down that drainpipe."

"Arthur always was arrogant; from the first time I met him, he thought he was better than women. He wouldn't cross the street to give me the time of day. You'd think growing up in an orphanage would have made him more empathetic."

"Why was he never adopted?" Bernice asks.

"Apparently he wasn't an attractive baby," Marjorie says. "Ears too big, and a bad case of eczema that didn't go away until he was two. As a toddler, he got head cold after head cold. Walked around with a snot-covered nose until he was six years old. By the time he grew into his ears, and stopped being sickly, there were probably too many newborns to choose from, and potential parents just passed him by. He lived at the orphanage until he was eighteen. It's surprising he became such a handsome man, considering how homely he was as a child."

"Likely the reason he was obsessed with money," Bernice comments and Marjorie scowls at her. "I don't mean being homely." She gently swats her sister's forearm. "I mean growing up in poverty. I remember the first time I met him; practically every word he spoke had something to do with making money. How he was going to become rich. How much he was going to make. How he would invest and get more money. That's all he could think about."

"I suppose his good looks, combined with his quest for wealth, were what attracted our sister to him. After all, a woman wants to be looked after when she's married."

"You're dating yourself, Marj. Do you know that many women nowadays make more money than their husbands?" Bernice says. "I wish I was still young; I'd have the world by the tail."

Marjorie pats his sister's hand. "I swear, dear sister, you were born in the wrong decade. You had so much drive when you were young."

"Thank you, Marjorie," Bernice says. "Unfortunately, back then, women with drive were called pushy, while men with drive were called ambitious."

"Arthur had drive," Aunt Marjorie says, returning to the subject of my father. "But that's all he had. He certainly didn't know how to be a parent. Likely because he'd never had one to guide him. Our poor niece. She was bound to rebel."

"Marj," Aunt Bernice says, "what I did was rebel. What Ruby did was look for a way out by marrying the first person who proposed to her, much like her own mother did. Not that being a wife and mother is easy, it most definitely is not. Why do you think I never waded into that pool? But Ruby really hasn't *tasted* life, has she? First, a prisoner in her father's house, her dad afraid someone would marry her for his wealth, then cooped up in her husband's house, no outside job, no real-world experience, waiting for her father to die so she could inherit his money. And now," Bernice whispers, "he's denied his daughter even that. Inheriting that money would have given her some independence from that husband of hers. And in the end, Arthur left it all to a gold-digger!"

Catching the last word, Julia turns her head and squints at the procession of mourners following her across the lawn. Bernice flaps her handkerchief at the woman, who attempts to smile, though with all the Botox injections she's had, her heavily made-up face remains a mask of insincerity. She turns back to the business of walking to her husband's graveside without twisting an ankle.

"You need to talk more quietly," Aunt Marjorie says. "Not that I care if she," she nods at Julia, "hears you or not, but our niece is within earshot."

Bernice turns to look at me not five steps behind, then gives me a sad little smile, and I count small blessings that my family is at the back of this procession, too far away to hear what's being said.

"It's not like he didn't leave her anything," Marjorie says. "He gave her a cabin."

Bernice snorts. "At a lake so far north, she'll be able to visit Santa Claus on the weekends."

"He also gave her three-hundred-thousand dollars."

"Of which that husband of hers will take control. And compared to the millions she was supposed to inherit, that's practically pocket change. Now Julia and her brats have everything." Bernice's voice is once again becoming loud and I begin to wonder if she's intentionally wanting Julia to hear. "What was our brother-in-law thinking?"

"Some part of his body was doing the thinking but it certainly wasn't his brain," Marjorie says as we watch Julia in her tight black dress place a rose on the shiny black coffin, then wipe away a crocodile tear.

"I wonder what Ruby's husband has to say about her getting so little?" Bernice says. "I've always thought that he and Julia would make a good pair; the two of them both after Arthur's money."

"At least the will said that he can't touch the cabin; that's one good thing Arthur did."

"Not unless he talks Ruby into selling, then wooing her out of the money," Bernice says. "And you can bet he'll try." She whispers, "Everyone knows that Arthur's money was the reason he married Ruby in the first place."

It's nothing I haven't heard before, my husband marrying me for my father's money. I even heard relatives whispering that at my wedding. If I'm honest with myself, I likely suspected it long before we were married, but at age twenty-eight, and anxious to get out from under my father's thumb, I convinced myself that Steve really did love me, and I him, so I accepted his proposal. But I knew; how could I not? I'd never had a boyfriend before I met Steve, barely even been on a date. My father was too afraid to let me out of his sight. Steve was charming and handsome and he convinced my father that he really did love me and wasn't marrying me for his money; so, Dad allowed the wedding to happen. I think Mom was suspicious of Steve's intentions and tried to tell me that maybe I was making a mistake, but I threw her own marital struggle back in her face and told her that she only thought it because that's what she did. In hindsight, I wanted out of my childhood home so badly, I didn't care how I got there.

For the past thirty-five years, I've tolerated my marriage for the simple reason I'm afraid to face the world alone. There have been joyful days, like when my mother held my babies for the first time, or when my own grandchildren were born, but more hard days than happy. Days when I couldn't stop thinking about what my life would have been like had I been more courageous, instead of settling for what I thought would be an easier life. Days when I wondered what it would be like to be independent, able to come and go as I pleased without having to answer to anyone. Days when I couldn't hide my disappointment in the path I'd chosen.

Steve, on the other hand, has been able to bury his anger at being trapped in this loveless marriage by assuring himself that each day he put in, he was one step closer to being a wealthy man. Then two days ago at the reading of the will, he found out exactly how much I'd inherited, and the veneer was peeled back. He couldn't conceal his anger any longer. He stomped out of the lawyer's office ahead of me and waited in the car. His knuckles white on the steering wheel, rage prevented him from saying more than two words all the way home.

I still haven't told the kids about the will. I know Robert in particular, has been keen on becoming financially secure when I die, and I'm not sure how he'll take the news. Probably much like his dad did. My plans are to tell them tonight, after the funeral.

I use the funeral card with Dad's face staring at me to fan myself as I pull my hair away from my neck, my thoughts turning to sitting on a beach, the breeze off the water cooling the sweat that's soaking my burning skin. For years I asked Steve if we could buy a cabin at a lake, but he always balked, saying we could barely afford the house let alone a cabin, and *Do I know how much upkeep is required to own a cabin?* Maybe now, with Dad's gift, I can finally have my dream of spending my summers at a lake.

"Did I tell you, towards the end, Arthur had regrets about marrying her?" Bernice says to her sister, snapping me out of my reverie. "Told me on my last visit at the hospital, during one of his lucid moments when the pain killers were wearing off, that she'd taken him for everything. But by that point, he was too sick to do anything about it." She pokes her chin in Julia's direction. "She knew that eventually the blush would wear off the rose, that's why she had everything changed in the first month of their marriage, before Arthur really got to know her and her conniving ways. Men just don't think. Didn't he wonder why a forty-something with a body like that, would be interested in an eighty-something who was falling apart?"

The women stop talking as we arrive at the grave and they stand with the other mourners on one side of the casket, while me, Steve, and our children, join Julia and her children on the other side. My eyes drift across the cemetery to where Mom is buried, towards the spot where she and Dad bought plots side by side more than fifty years ago. Julia, of course, said no to burying her husband there, and bought two plots on this side of the well-manicured lawn as far away from Dad's first wife as she could. I can practically hear Mom rolling over in her grave.

The minister opens his mouth to speak and a gust of wind picks up a dust eddy and swirls it directly at Julia, as if Dad is getting the last word before his descent below the surface of the ground. Bernice presses the back of her hand across her mouth and stifles a giggle while Julia waves her hand in front of her face, wafting away the dust and looking around, hoping no one noticed.

"Thank you for coming here today to celebrate the life of Arthur Daniels," the minister says. "A man who knew no boundaries when it came to giving of himself and his time. A man who accomplished greatness in his chosen field of architecture, and a man who shared his wealth generously with his family." He nods at Julia and her two adult sons. "A man, who in the autumn of his years, was fortunate enough to find the love of his life."

Aunt Marjorie snorts, then dabs her lips with her tissue.

I glance at Julia. I'm sure she gave specific instructions to the minister not to mention Mom. She hates it when my mother or myself are mentioned in front of her, preferring to pretend Dad was never married before, that I was never born.

"It was a lucky day when Arthur met Julia at the support group," the minister says.

"Stoney broke, that's what she was," Bernice says out the corner of her mouth. "Her husband passed years ago, went there specifically to troll for a rich widower."

"When they wed," the minister continues over Bernice's voice, "they didn't know that they'd have only three years together before Arthur passed."

"They may not have known," Bernice continues, "but everyone knew that's what *she* was counting on."

Marjorie elbows her sister.

"If anyone has anything to say," the minister says as Julia looks pointedly at Bernice, "please share it with us at this time."

There is nothing but silence as Aunt Bernice smiles innocently at the two of them.

"Then without further ado," he says as he sprinkles holy water on the casket, "ashes to ashes, dust to dust." The cemetery worker presses a button, lowering the coffin into the hole.

Chapter 2

"You let her take our inheritance, Mom?" Robert, my oldest child wails. "Out of millions to be had, all you got was three-hundred-thousand dollars and some mouse infested cabin?"

The funeral guests have left, and my kids, my husband, and I are having a drink in the kitchen of our twenty-two hundred square foot, two-storey house. Steve bought the house when I was pregnant with Robert. Thirty years old at the time, now, thirty-five years later, it's showing its age. I'd suggested to Julia that she host the gathering at her place since the six-thousand square foot bungalow my dad designed, then had built for her as a wedding gift, might better accommodate the large number of guests we were sure to have. She'd refused, saying that she was too upset to clean up after people; mopping up drinks spilled onto her hardwood floors, and wiping up food squished into sofas and smeared on end-tables. I could have pointed out that she uses a cleaning service, but true to my passive nature, I didn't want to rock the boat.

Platters of half-eaten sandwiches, plastic cups and plates litter every counter and table top in the kitchen, living and family rooms, and Jessica, my middle child, is cleaning up the mess. Of all my children, Jess is the most like me; a people pleaser. Robert takes after his father, a take charge personality, and Debby is more like Aunt Bernice; a bit of a wild-card. You never know what's going to come out of her mouth. Robert's wife, Sheryl, and my grandsons, have gone home, allowing the five of us to talk, and Steve has just informed them about the will.

"First of all, Robert," I say, "it is not *our* inheritance, it's *my* inheritance. And I didn't *let* her. You think I'd have allowed her to take all of Dad's money had I known?"

He raises his eyebrows as if to say *That's exactly what you would have done*, but instead says, "You should have asked if you were still the beneficiary."

"I told her to say something to him months ago," Steve says. "Years ago, even. When they were first married. But of course," he raises his hands telling me I did what he expected, which was nothing. "I should have said something to him myself."

Directing my anger towards Steve, I say, "He was my father and if anyone was going to say something, then it would have been me, not my husband. And I didn't say anything because I didn't think there was any need. I was made his beneficiary when Mom died three years ago, and he didn't tell me that the will had been changed when he remarried. I figured he'd likely made some provisions to allow for his new wife to live comfortably, but I certainly never imagined he'd give her everything. I didn't realize how tightly she had him wound around her finger."

"You're too naïve," Steve says. "You let people walk all over you."

I bite my tongue. "You're right, I do let people walk all over me. It's always been easier than standing up for myself. A fault, I suppose."

The five of us are quiet, the only noise, the sound of Jessica stuffing paper plates into the garbage bag. She leaves the back door open while she takes the bag to the can in the alley, and I can hear the neighbours on one side as they sit on their patio blaring their music, a nightly ritual all summer long. On the other side, Jimmy is screaming at his four-year-old sister to give him back his ball. I watch as the rubber toy sails over the fence and into my flower-bed.

"Where is the money now?" Robert asks. He's an investment banker and is always advising his dad on what to do with his money.

"I put it in the bank," Steve says. "I'll meet with you on Monday to discuss the best places to invest."

I cringe. Technically the money is mine, but for thirty-five years

I've allowed Steve to look after the finances, so I don't correct him. Deciding I'm just as invisible here as I would be in my room, I say, "It's been a long day, I'm going to bed," and I leave my family to talk.

The four of them head outside to sit on our deck, and with my bedroom window open, I hear my name pop up, but try not to listen, knowing that it's only my son or my husband complaining that I lost all their inheritance by being too docile. After the kids have left, Steve's voice continues to sail into the bedroom when he invites our neighbours to join him on our patio for a drink. Bob asks Steve what it feels like to be a rich man and Steve says he should divorce me and start dating the good-looking rich widow, then the two of them laugh. I pretend to be asleep when he comes to bed, unaware our marriage is coming to an end.

—

The following summer, I'm in the backyard, weeding between the tomatoes, when Steve opens the gate and stands on the patio watching me. He says nothing.

"You okay?" I ask.

He continues to watch without speaking.

"Did you want something?" I ask, feeling like I'm being judged on how I weed the garden. Steve has a habit of correcting things that I do, even if he never does them.

"I need to talk to you," he says, taking a few steps closer, and I brace myself for his critique.

He scuffs his feet on the grass and shoves his hands in his pockets. "I think Ruby, that we need to separate."

I spin. "What?" I say, confused because I was expecting him to say something else. "Separate? Is that what you said? You mean as in our marriage?"

"I do," he says. The same words we both spoke the day we got married.

"Why would you say that? What's happened?"

"Nothing's *happened*, Ruby," he says, emphasizing the word as if

I should already know what he means. "At least not recently. Surely you feel it too. We haven't been getting along these past ten months, hell, these past ten years. We barely talk to each other anymore and when we do it's only to say nasty words, or to correct one another, or to complain. I think we need to separate and cool down. Then we'll see what happens."

"I, I don't know what to say," I stammer.

"Come on, Ruby, did you think we'd continue on like this; being unhappy until the day we die? I don't know about you, but I want more out of life than that."

He enters the house, then returns carrying a suitcase he apparently has already packed. I'm still standing in the same place, too stunned to move. He opens the gate then stops.

"Have you talked to Julia lately?" he asks.

"Julia?" I say. "Why would I talk to Julia?"

"Just wondered if there's anything new on the inheritance front."

"There is nothing new, Steve, and there will never be anything new. Is that what this is about, you not getting your share of the inheritance? Is that why you're leaving?"

"I'm tired of being the sole contributor to this marriage," he says.

"You mean financially?" I ask, knowing full well that's exactly what he means. To Steve, money is the sun that our marriage orbits around.

"Bye, Rube," he says, then walks out the gate.

Surprisingly, I have no tears. I stand in my garden amongst the tomatoes, hoe in hand, my eyes dry. My first instinct is to get a job, contribute financially, maybe then he'll return, until I realize that even if I do, he won't come back. The only way he'd come back to me was if Julia gave us some of my dad's money. He's only suggested the separation to keep one foot in the door in case Julia has a change of heart. The divorce will come later, once he's either got his hands on half the money, or is positive that tap is dry.

As was prearranged when he invested my inheritance, half of the three-hundred-thousand is his. Of the other investments Steve has made, I get a small portion. Like the naïve person I am, I never imagined I'd have to make my own way in the world, and thought I'd always have Steve's money to rely on. I finish hoeing the garden as I contemplate my future, then go to bed and stay there for a year.

Chapter 3

"I made a decision last night," I say.

"And what's that?" Robert says.

I've invited my kids over for supper. Sheryl has the twins at mother/child swimming lessons and will join us later. She told me she wants to lose a couple of pounds.

"I've decided to sell."

"Sell?" he says. "Sell what?"

"The house, this house."

"This house?" Robert repeats.

"Since your dad left, it seems too big for one person."

"How can a house be too big for one person?" Robert asks. "You use only the rooms you need, the rest you stay out of. Problem solved. And Dad might still come back, you're not positive he's gone for good."

"Robert, the only way your father will come back to me is if Julia decides to give me some of your grandfather's money, or I win a lottery, neither of which is going to happen."

Jessica touches my shoulder. "I think selling the house is a good idea, Mom. You're right, it is too big for one person."

"Is the house in both your names?" Robert asks. "Because if it's not, there's no sense in selling. You would be no further ahead financially unless Dad gives you some of the money from the sale."

If Steve had his way the day we walked into the bank thirty-five years ago to sign the mortgage for this house, me six months pregnant with Robert, my name wouldn't have been on the deed. But the banker said it was common practice for both spouses to sign in case the one who owned the home was to die, then the other would be guaranteed a place to live. He ended his advice by nodding at my large belly and saying to Steve, *You wouldn't want your wife and child to be homeless, would you?* I could tell Steve was angry about being cornered, but I made sure I had my name on the form before we left the bank.

"Of course it is!" I say, trying to sound indignant.

"And where do you plan on living?" he asks.

"I haven't decided yet," I lie. "I should be able to find something smaller than this place."

"But if you stay here," Robert says, "you'll still have this place as your nest egg, and the house will only appreciate. Fifteen years from now, you could get ten, possibly twenty, hell, even thirty thousand more. That would be the smart thing to do."

"It would be one choice," I say, knowing what Robert really means is he wants me to save the money for him to inherit after I'm dead, "but not one I was contemplating. In the past year, I've been feeling like life is passing me by. I need to do something for myself. Like they say, I'm not getting any younger."

"Going into financial ruin is not doing something for yourself. How do you plan on making a living if you spend all your money? That investment I made for you is earning great dividends. And you don't get your old age pension for another two years."

"Robert, you may be the banker, and think me uneducated about finances, and I'm the first to admit I don't know much, but I assure you, I'm getting out of this house."

Looking like all is not lost, Robert says, "If you're committed to getting out of here, Mom, then what about moving to a seniors home? One of those Independent Living Facilities? You get your own suite, can come and go as you please, live your own life, but you're not alone. If something happens you have someone close by to help. You're never too young for that, are you? I could invest the money from the sale of this house, along with the inheritance money Dad gave you, and you'd have more than enough." I cut him off, my temper rising.

"The inheritance money your father gave me? Is that what you said?" Robert opens his mouth to defend himself, but again, I speak before he can. "It was *me* who gave your father half of *my* inheritance, Robert, not the other way around. Something that I regret every single day."

"Okay, okay, the money *you* gave him," he says as if this is an inconsequential point. "But really, Mom, a seniors home would be just the thing for you. Less responsibility, all kinds of people to talk to." He pulls his phone out of his pocket and begins scrolling. "No groceries to buy, no property taxes, nothing to maintain. Just your monthly rent. I'll bet you wouldn't have to spend a dime of your money, the interest from the investment would pay for everything." He slaps my kitchen wall. "This place must be worth five to five-fifty by now, maybe even six. You're sitting on a gold mine, Mom. Oh," he says, pointing at his phone. "Here's one. The Wheaton. Three blocks away. They allow you to book an appointment to view the place." He glances at me and sees the look on my face. "I know, Mom, you're still young and vibrant. But I'll bet there's all kinds of people who move to those places in their sixties." He touches my shoulder. "I know Dad's leaving was a real kick in the teeth, but you have to believe me, I'm only thinking of you. I could invest everything you have, and in just a few years your money would double. You know you've never had a job." I start to object. "Outside the house, Mom. You've never had a job outside the house. You won't get CPP when you turn sixty-five and old age pension isn't enough to live on. If you let me invest your share of the money from the sale of this house, you'll have a nice nest egg. You'll never have to worry about money again. And we," he points at his sisters, "won't have to worry about you, either financially or emotionally." He turns back to his phone. "I'll bet seniors homes in the country would be less expensive than ones in the city. Maybe even less than the interest you'll make once I invest the money from the sale of the house."

I smile at my son. In truth, I do know he is thinking of me.

As a boy, he was always doing things for me and for his sisters. Shovelling the snow when it was Debby's turn so Steve wouldn't get angry when he got stuck on the driveway. Helping Jess with her math so her dad wouldn't say she should be more like her brother. Vacuuming the house when I was too rushed to get it done before my husband, who didn't like to see me do housework, got home from work. Robert knew he could do no wrong in his father's eyes, but that his dad was always finding fault with his sisters, so he tried to help.

But as he got older, he seemed to change, become more aloof, more controlled by the thought of making money, more swayed by his dad. He still loved his sisters, loved me, but he pulled back, wasn't as giving of his time. He got two afterschool jobs and put every dime he made into a savings account. He rarely went out with friends, not wanting to spend any of his money frivolously. When the time came for him to go to university, he paid for the tuition himself.

So today, even though Robert says he wants what's best for me, I know, much like his dad, that money is his god. As long as I told him I was happy, he'd have me wasting away my years sitting on a bench outside the cheapest care-home he could find if there was a chance there would be money left over when I died.

I touch my son's arm. "I know you only want what's best for me, Robert, and I appreciate the help, but I'm only sixty-three, not ninety-three."

Debby, the baby of the family who hasn't stopped texting since she arrived, looks up from her phone and says, "Robert's right, Mom. There'd be all kinds of people to talk to in places like that. You wouldn't have to be alone anymore." She's my social butterfly child and has never understood my penchant for liking to be alone. There's never a day when she doesn't have something to do with someone. She practically has her cell phone duct taped to her hip.

"I like being alone," I say, as Jimmy climbs over the fence and stops to stare in the patio door at us. He disappears when I hear his mother screech at him to get home and have some supper.

"Mom," Debby says. "No one *wants* to be alone."

"I'll get a dog," I say. "You're making me out to be older than I am."

Robert waves his hand at me. "Once you've thought this over, you'll see that we're right." He taps the screen of his phone. "I'm going to start calling places tomorrow, set you up with a few viewings. It's too bad," Robert continues, "that Grandpa hadn't put his talent into designing seniors complexes instead of multi-million-dollar shopping centres and office buildings. Then you could probably get a reduced rate. Hey, remember about twenty years ago when he designed that resort on Turks and Caicos? I'll bet the owner would let you stay there for free if he knew you were Grandpa's daughter. It would be nice not to have to put up with our winters, don't you think?"

"Robert," I say. "You can talk until you're blue in the face, but I'm not living in a seniors complex, nor am I moving to a resort in some foreign country." I pause, knowing that at some point, I'll need to tell them what I've been thinking, but right now, I'm unsure how much I want them to know. Finally, I say, "I've been talking to a real-estate agent."

All three of them stare at me as if I've spoken a foreign language.

"I'm going to look at some property tomorrow," I continue.

"I'll drive you. I'll take the day off work and drive you," Robert insists as if he's doing me a favour. "Real-estate agents are notorious for taking advantage of people. And a woman by herself, especially one without a lot of worldly experience, they'd see as money in the bank."

"I'm driving myself," I say.

"But you don't like driving in unfamiliar places," Debby says.

"I'm tired of being dependant on you three. Whether you approve or not, tomorrow I'm going to look at some property with Mr. Strothers, a very nice real-estate agent from Modern Realty."

Chapter 4

I regret not having told my children that I've never met the real-estate agent so I'm unsure if he's nice or not. I also regret not telling them I wasn't talking about looking at property in the city. But I knew I had to put my foot down if I wanted to do this alone.

Having asked my sixteen-year-old neighbour to install Google Maps on my phone, and then teach me how to use it, I've arrived in the northern part of the province where somewhere in this vast wilderness sits the cabin my father left me.

Mr. Strothers told me he'd meet me in a town called Southside in front of Carnation's General Store on Main Street. I nose into a parking spot and a man gets out of the silver Cadilac parked beside me.

"Mr. Strothers?" I say.

"Call me Chip," he says shaking my hand.

He looks like someone who would be called Chip. He's young, or trying to look young in his tan blazer over a crisp white button-down shirt, top button undone, silver chain peeking between the lapel. He's wearing blue jeans with a frayed hole over one thigh, a rip across the other knee, and slip-on running shoes which probably cost him a week's salary. The beginnings of a paunch bulges over a belt that he's stubbornly pulling to the same notch he likely has for years, and the shadow of crow's feet are etched at the corners of his sky-blue eyes. He runs a hand through his thinning sun-blond hair, attempting to give himself that put-together disheveled look men of his generation seem eager to achieve.

"Nice to meet you, Chip," I say.

"I just need to run inside for a sec," he says. "Be right back."

"Before we go any further," I hold up a finger, stopping him from leaving, "there are a couple of questions I'd like to ask. I should have asked sooner, but I didn't think to say anything until I was driving up here."

"What's that, Mrs. Phillips?"

"Is the cabin lakefront? Because if it isn't, there's no sense in my even looking at it. If I can't hear the waves or stand in the front yard and dip my toes in the water, then I'd just as soon sell it sight unseen, and buy one that is."

"I think you'll be pleasantly surprised at the amount of lakefront you have. There are things about it you really need to see to appreciate. I do think it's worth a look."

"Second question," I say. "Is it a crowded lake? I'm looking for peace and quiet, not a lot of boats and partiers."

"It's a very quiet lake. You won't have to worry about loud parties, or boats on the lake, I can promise you that. Very secluded. Nestled into the pines with no one else around except the wildlife."

"Tell me, Chip, why is a real-estate agent showing me a cabin that I already own?"

"Our firm also does property management," he says. "I suppose your father knew he wouldn't be able to check on it all the time, so three or four times a year, a staff member drives up to check on the place, make sure it's still standing. And since it's a large property, I imagine your dad wanted to make it easy for you by having an agent lined up in case you're more inclined to sell than to stay." He pats his pockets and glances at the store. "I just have to run inside; I'll be right back." He disappears inside, passing a man who looks older than God, sitting at the entrance.

It's near the end of summer, and a hot wind blows down the deserted street. I close my eyes and imagine myself sitting on the beach in front of my cabin, a frosty glass of wine in my hand, the breeze off the water cooling my skin and all around me, nothing but peace and quiet. Perhaps this will all work out after all. Maybe, after all these years, I will finally get that cabin at a lake that I've always dreamed of. I open my eyes and look at the store. A sign with two carnations, their stems crossed, are pictured at each end of the name, Carnation's General Store. I look through the screen door.

Chip is tucking his wallet into his pants pocket as he talks to a woman. She hands him what looks like a package of gum, then steps out from behind the cash register. They exit the store together. She's tall and lean and wearing a white apron covering her pink and white plaid blouse and blue jeans with white running shoes. Her face is bare except for a touch of light pink lipstick, and her dark hair is tied into a bun at the nape of her neck. She appears to be in her late sixties or early seventies and I wonder if she's the owner. The two of them walk down Main Street, stopping where the highway meets the road, and she points, then bends her arm indicating a turn. My agent nods his head a few times. She returns to the store, while Chip returns to his car.

"Haven't been out for fifteen years. Not since the last appraisal. The previous agent was showing me the ropes. Thought I'd better make sure I remembered the way," he says, nodding towards the highway. "It's not difficult to find, but after we leave the asphalt, the rest of the way is in rough shape. Store owner said they spread gravel three times a year, but right now, it's a washboard road."

I follow Chip back to the highway while the man sitting outside the store waves goodbye. We turn left at a sign that says, Sunset Lake, 2 kms, then drive along this asphalt road for a short distance, before making a sharp right, then a left, the hamlet still visible across the field. We make another right leaving the asphalt, and the town, behind. A sign, partially hidden in the ditch, says, *Sunset Drive*, in faded lettering on a green background.

The dirt road is rutted and narrow, and we're only able to go about ten kilometres per hour. To my left, overgrown trees that are keeping the air cool and the sky dark, sound like ghostly fingers as their branches brush the sides of my ten-year-old Honda. I get glimpses of water, but the foliage is so thick, the lake is just flashes in my peripheral vision.

We bounce along this rutted path for another minute then pass between two columns made of stones set in concrete, one on each side of the road. A sign, which at one time was likely strung across the top of the columns, lies in the dirt, its surface too weather-worn to read. In the distance I see the boreal forest which surrounds the lake.

Chip pulls in beside a building that could be anything from a shed, to a boathouse, to a garage. A wooden sign hanging above the double doors says *C. Johansen 530 Sunset Lake.* I am sincerely hoping this building isn't the cabin. Chip gets out of his car, and I follow suit.

"What is this place?" I ask.

"It's private property. One-hundred acres of private property. Come on, let's take a look."

The two of us walk up the side of the building we're parked beside, and emerge into a large yard.

"As you can see, most of the property around the lake is forest, but these six acres," Chip faces the land in front of us, "were cleared and commercialized close to ninety years ago."

Cabins dot the shoreline, each one facing the lake, with tall pine trees lining the perimeter between the cabins and the lake. Smaller trees, scrub, and bushes have filled in the land that was once cleared, making it difficult to see the buildings between the branches. An above ground pool, its sides caved in, stands in the middle of the cleared land between the washboard road and the cabins, a tree growing out of the middle. A pad of crumbling paving stones that must have at one time served as a patio, circles the pool.

I look at the run-down buildings. "Which one is mine?" I ask.

"All of them," Chip says.

"What?"

"He waves his arm like Vana White. "All of them. They belonged to your dad, now they belong to you."

"That can't be. I'm here to see a cabin. One cabin. Not all of these." I too wave my arm. "There's been some mistake."

"I'm afraid there's been no mistake," Chip says. "Everything you see is yours."

"But," I say, looking at the buildings, "did Dad run a motel?"

"Actually," Chip says, "you're not far off. Back in the day, this was a resort. Quite a successful resort for many years, or so I've read online. I'm unsure if your dad ever ran it, I only know that when he died, he owned it and left it to you."

"I find it hard to believe that my father owned a resort, especially this resort. He was more of a five-star hotel kind of guy."

"He owned more than this," Chip says. "He owned all one-hundred acres."

"No, that can't be." My laugh is contrived, almost panicky. "Dad was not an outdoorsy kind of guy. He would criticize a place like this, not purchase it. Maybe in Hawaii, or some Caribbean Island, something glamourous, something sophisticated with swim up bars and white sand. I can guarantee you he would never own a place like this." My eyes pass over the derelict buildings and yard that hasn't seen a groundskeeper for decades.

Chip is blushing. "I'm sorry to disappoint you," he says, "but your dad really did own this. I have the deed right here." He tugs a paper out of his breast pocket and hands it to me. "As soon as we passed those stone columns, the land between the road and the lake belongs to you. And then in that direction," he points south, "for another hundred acres, all the way around to the other side of the lake, that's your property as well. It was all part of the resort, though only this cleared section was used for guests."

I look at the paper and see Dad's signature at the bottom. "This is crazy," I say.

"The sign you saw lying in the dirt said *Welcome to Sunset Lake Resort.* This cabin," he points to the cabin we're closest to, "was built and lived in by the woman who ran the resort. I've been told that it's in better condition than the others. Are you still interested in looking at it, like you said on the phone?"

"When I called," I say, my voice halting, "I assumed it was simply one cabin I was going to look at, not a whole slew of them. This, Chip, is a lot to take in."

"But you're here now," he says, holding his hand in front of him, inviting me forward. "What's the harm in looking? After you see it, we can put it on the market today if you want. But for now, I think we should go inside and take a look around; see what your father left you."

I gaze across the yard, thinking of the long drive home, and how it will be made even longer wondering what I missed if I don't at least look inside. "I suppose you're right," I say with a sigh, then Chip and I wade through weeds up to our knees, to stand behind the run-down cabin.

Craning our necks back, we look at the structure in front of us. I'm unsure if you could even call it a cabin, it's more like a shack. A second storey appears to have been begun and abandoned with wall studs tilting in all directions and barely supporting the partially built roof. Plastic, which at one time must have been there to protect the new wood from the elements, is hanging in filthy shreds and blowing in the wind.

"That must be the wood for the second storey," Chip says facing a pile of rotting lumber with water stains as dark as tar dripping down the sides. "Shouldn't take much to finish."

I scowl at him with one eye closed.

"Let's go around front," he says. "Take a look at the lake."

We circle the property, keeping our eyes on the ground so as not to trip on tree roots, while pushing branches and cobwebs out of the way as they reach for our legs and faces. In the front yard I hear water lapping, but the shoreline is so overgrown with bushes, reeds, and scrub, I only get glimpses of the lake through the brambles.

"At least it's lakefront," Chip says, nodding in the direction of the hidden water.

"Something to be grateful for, I suppose," I say, turning to face the cabin.

The split-log siding on the first floor is lifting in places, with trees growing so close to the windows, there must be branches cracking the glass. The beginnings of the second floor, which extends straight up from the first floor at the back of the cabin, is built in the A-Frame fashion on this side with an open space in the centre where a window would have been installed if it were finished. A balcony, hanging on by a wish and a prayer, is under this open space, and posts, which were likely going to be installed to hold the balcony up, lie on the ground at our feet. The rafters and roof are tilting forward on their studs, and the entire structure appears to slope from back to front. Broken lumber and rusty nails litter the ground and we have to watch where we step so as not to get a nail through our shoes.

"A real do-it-yourself project," Chip says following my gaze to the second storey. He points towards the lake. "I believe this is west, so that balcony will be a lovely place to sit and watch the sun go down." He tugs a package of Juicy Fruit Gum he bought in town, out of his pants pocket, pulls out a stick and pops it into his mouth. He offers me a piece; I shake my head. "Remember," he says, chewing the stick into a wad, "you can always sell. Unless your dad stipulated in the will that you couldn't?"

"He didn't," I say.

"Then selling is always an option. Might be more up your alley. No workmen to hire, no plans to make as far as what you want to do. You don't even have to come back here; you can leave everything to me."

Stepping away from the smell of the gum, I ask, "If I were to sell, what's this property worth, do you know?"

He takes some papers out of his inside jacket pocket. "This," he slaps the pages with fingers stained yellow from cigarette smoke, "is the appraisal that was done fifteen years ago. I'll read it to you, then give you today's value." Again, he shakes the papers. "There's no cell service here, so I printed everything off last night. It's difficult to find comps being as this is such a large piece of property, but I found one on the other side of the province."

"Comps?" I say.

"Comparable prices. Keep in mind, selling this much property is difficult, but one could conceivably sell it in pieces, which might be more realistic, not to mention, affordable." He looks down at the paper in his hand. "If you were to find a buyer who wanted to buy the entire package," he begins, then glances up at me. "You understand, you'd basically be selling the land, most buyers would consider every one of these buildings," he cracks his gum, "as tear-downs."

"I understand," I say.

He slides his hand down the page. "If you were to find a buyer who wanted to buy the entire package," he repeats, "including the resort area," he flips the page, "and the one-hundred acres of forest," he chews loudly, "at current market value, it would be worth," again he looks up from the page, "remember, this appraisal was done fifteen years ago."

"I remember," I say.

"One million dollars," he says.

"Pardon me?" I say, my legs going weak.

"One million," he repeats. "But after comparing this property to the one I found online last night, I came up with a slightly higher number." He swallows. "I believe that the current market value of the resort area and the one-hundred acres that has also been bequeathed to you, is now one and one-half to two million," he says. "But," he holds up a yellowed finger, "if this land were just a few kilometres south of here, the price would be double. This lake isn't as popular as some; doesn't have the amenities cottagers want, plus, as I already said, there is no cell service. And demand is what drives prices up. So, if the lake ever becomes a popular tourist destination, and the province puts up cell towers, which they would likely do if the place became popular, the value of your property would double, if not triple."

"My father left me a resort that's worth one and one-half to two million dollars?" I say. "And his new wife didn't get it in the will?"

"I know nothing about what his wife got or didn't get in the will," Chip says. "All I know is that he left this to you. But like I said, the value is in the land, not the cabins."

"Why would my father leave me something so valuable?"

"He loves you?" Chip says, his voice raising on the last word, as if it's a question.

"Seems unlikely," I say.

Again, Chip's fair skin turns red. "He bought the place in nine-teen-sixty-five and paid seventy-five thousand. The price of proper-ty was far less back then; you could get a nice bungalow in the city for fifteen to twenty thousand in those days, though I imagine that seventy-five-thousand for all this land was still on the inexpensive side. My guess is that either whoever was selling it was in a hurry to be rid of it, or they didn't know what the place was worth. I have no information as to whether they had an appraisal done originally; I suspect not."

"He's owned it for—" I do the math, "—fifty-two years? I was nine when he bought it?"

"That's what it says. Though of course, it doesn't say how old you were."

I say nothing. Clearly, Dad must have had something else in mind when he purchased the property. He would never have been generous enough to buy this with the intention of gifting it to me when he died. And it couldn't have been his intention to flip the place or he'd have done that and gotten rid of it long ago. He certainly didn't let Julia know he owned it, or she would have had her claws into it long before he died, and as far as I know, Mom knew nothing about it, or she'd have brought me up here when I was a child. So, if it wasn't purchased with the intention of giving it to me, or for him to sell and make a profit, and he didn't let either Mom or his new wife know he owned it, I've no idea why he would buy something so rundown and then let it sit and rot for five decades. In all the years I knew him, he'd holidayed in five-star hotels in Hawaii countless times, gone to the Riviera and a few other exotic places a couple of times, but never once, to my knowledge, did Dad ever stay in a cabin at a prairie lake.

Chip shuffles the pages and I see a picture of a cabin. "What's that?" I ask, stopping him from turning the page.

"History of the place," he says. "Would you like me to read it to you?"

"Why not, we've come this far," I say.

He spits his gum into the bushes then shakes out the pages. *"In 1907, a husband and wife by the name of Vereschuk arrived from Ukraine to homestead in this province. They acquired farmland and built a house on the homestead where they raised two sons; one born in 1910, and one in 1915. Other homesteaders also settled in this area, eventually forming the town they named Southside. Mr. Vereschuk's farm made a profit and using his newfound wealth as collateral, he borrowed money from the bank and bought one-hundred acres of land at Sunset Lake, clearing a site by the beach to build a small cabin."*

Chip points south of the cabin and I squint between the bushes in the direction of the beach where I can make out water lapping against sand, and the outline of a dilapidated roof.

"His wife and their boys enjoyed their summers at the lake," Chip continues, *"while he lived in town working his farm. For many years his farm profited, then in 1929, when the stock market crashed, the price of grain dropped so low that Mr. Vereschuk couldn't pay his bills. The bank took both the land at the lake, and the farm, which they put up for sale. Except for the youngest son who stayed behind to finish high school, the family moved away, never to return. The land sat on the bank's books for a year. Then in 1931, everything was purchased by a woman named Cecelia Johansen."*

"That's the name on that shed in the backyard," I say.

"She built herself a cabin," he points at the cabin in front of us, *"where she resided, then renovated the Vereschuk cabin,"* he again points to the cabin nestled into the bush closest to the beach, *"and rented it out for income. Over the course of the next few years, Miss Johansen built eight other cabins,"* he waves at the other buildings spread to the north, *"renting them out during the summer and even in the winter. She turned it into her business. Called it Sunset Lake Resort."* He looks up from the page, pointing and counting. "It says there should be ten cabins, but I only count seven. I wonder what happened to the other three." He reads further on. "Oh, here it is. *In 1949 lightning struck a tree near a cabin north of the original,"* Chip points to the empty land on the far north side of the once-cleared

property. *"It caught the tree on fire, which in turn caught the nearest cabin on fire. Two of the cabins burnt to the ground, the third was partially destroyed and later demolished because of structural damage."* He looks at me. "I guess that accounts for the missing three cabins." *"Cecelia Johansen lived at the resort from 1931, until 1965."* Again, he pauses, reading ahead to himself. "Oh my," he says.

"What?" I ask.

"In 1960," he reads, *"the provincial government made outhouses illegal at all lakes in the province. Cabin owners were given five years to add indoor plumbing and septic tanks, or they'd be fined and their cabins padlocked. By the end of the summer of 1965, Miss Johansen had finished the bathrooms on all the cabins except the original one."* He points to the unfinished second floor. *"She began the renovations that fall and had the walls and floor framed, and the roof on, when the first winter storm of the season forced her to quit. She was attempting to cover up the new lumber with plastic to protect it from the elements, when she slipped and fell over the edge. She hit the balcony,"* we look up at the balcony that's barely hanging on, *"slid down the pitch of the first-floor roof, sailed through the air, finally hitting the ground beneath the balcony."* We look at the ground near where we're standing. *"The coroner concluded that she died of blunt force trauma, likely having hit her head on something during the fall or when she hit the ground."*

"Well, that's gruesome," I say taking a step backwards.

"Crazy, heh?" Chip says. *"Because she died intestate and never married or had children, her family was located and the land and cabins were given to them, which they, in turn, put up for sale. Mr. Arthur Daniels purchased all one-hundred acres in 1965. He never lived at the resort, nor did renovations to any of the cabins, causing them to become decrepit. If the cabins aren't renovated or torn down within the next three years, or at the very least, have a plan for renovation or tear down, the town will tear them down and send the bill to the owner."* He looks up from the page and meets my eyes.

"Do you know what my father's plans were?" I ask. "Or why he didn't tell anyone about this place?"

"I don't. Hey," he says, "you should renovate them all, bring the place back to its old glory. You could open a resort."

"Don't think I'll be doing that."

"I suppose it would be best to sell. With the sale of this property, you'd be able to afford whatever you want in the city, or even at another lake. One in better shape and with more amenities."

I look at him, wondering if that's what I want, or if that's what he wants me to do. He'd make a nice commission on a two-million-dollar sale. "Are there other cabins besides these on the one-hundred acres?" I ask, pointing at the rundown cabins.

"There are none," Chip says, turning the page and scanning the text. "Neither Mr. Vereschuk, Miss Johansen, or your father, cleared any more land other than these six acres, or built any other cabins anywhere else around the lake. There are a few, once you get off your property; fishermen, hunters, that kind of thing; pretty rustic places. Because of the lake's remoteness, most vacationers don't venture this far north. If it's peace and quiet you're looking for, then this is the place for you."

"Not sure how I feel about that," I say. "Being totally alone."

"Would take some getting used to. Have to enjoy your own company. But the town's close by," Chip says. "If it's going to be a summer getaway, not your permanent residence, you don't have to worry about driving the road in the wintertime." He crosses the yard and climbs the rickety front step. "But like I said, selling might be the best route for you, buy something closer to people. It just might take a few months. Now, be warned," he says, "it won't be much to look at inside."

"Okay," I say.

He's patting his pockets when he feels the need to caution me for a second time. "Don't let appearances discourage you. It hasn't had anyone living in it since Miss Johansen died in '65, but as you can see," he slaps his palm against the exterior wall; a shower of dust and cobwebs fall onto the shoulder of his blazer, "the building has potential. If you plan on renovating then it's the bones of the building you're here for, not what's visible."

"Bones of the building."

"And if you do sell, buyers might want something they can renovate, or at the very least, something to live in while they're building their own cabin. The place is yours to do with what you want. Damn," he says, as he stops patting himself down and rattles the lockbox the real estate agency put on the door knob. "I must have left the key in the car. Be right back."

Chip leaves me standing on the front step wondering if I should simply sell and not even bother going inside. He certainly seems anxious for me to put the place on the market, I suppose property management doesn't pay as much as the commission on a two-million-dollar sale.

But perhaps he's right; with the outside being in such poor shape, I'm sure the inside must be the same, if not worse, and do I really want to take on such a massive renovation project? With this place valued at two million dollars, I could get the cabin of my dreams and still have money left over to live well the rest of my life and leave some to the kids. Before I can decide what I want to do, Chip returns, key in hand. He faces the cabin, then with a sigh, and, I imagine, a silent prayer, he twists the key and pushes open a door that looks like it's been beaten with an axe.

Chapter 5

I peer around his shoulder through a tangle of cobwebs crisscrossing the doorway and into the darkened cabin. The scent of mould and decay fills my nose. One large room faces the lake, lit by the dim light filtering through two dirt-caked windows flanking the entrance. Chip picks up a rock to prop open the door and allow some light inside, but the door seems to want to sag open on its own, and he tosses the stone back to the ground. A mouse, disturbed by intruders, runs out from under the couch, zigzags across the floor, finally squeezing under a closed door on the other side of the room. We step inside.

Even though it's still summer outside, it's cold in here, and I wrap my arms around my body for warmth. There's a light switch by the door.

"The place has power; it's just not turned on," Chip says, not flicking the switch. "All you have to do is call the power company and they'll reconnect you. Probably for a small fee."

At first glance the room looks as if time has stood still. Couches and chairs are arranged in conversational groupings next to walls with end tables between, and a dining table is in front of a buffet and hutch in the far corner of this small room; all the places you'd expect them to be if you walked into anyone's living room. Until you look more closely. Mould, like a living thing, has crept its way across the floor, eating up the wood and fabric, shrouding everything with its ghostly fingers. The couch, upholstered in what at one time might have been green velvet, is coated in an inch of dust obscuring the colour until it appears gray, the cushions torn, with stuffing oozing out like flesh in an open wound. The fabric on the arms is worn away by time and dirt, as if invisible hands have been rubbing them raw. Wooden legs of the chairs have been gnawed down by rodents, and the coffee table balances on three legs, with sawdust and dirt piled on the floor beneath. A wood burning fireplace, ashes still in the firebox, its stone façade laced with cobwebs, flanks one entire wall. A braided rug covered in what looks like mouse droppings, lies on the floor in front. A broken light bulb dangling from a socket in the ceiling would be the only source of illumination in the room, and sagging plaster, stained by water damage completes the picture.

"All of this furniture comes with it as well?"

"Everything you see is yours." He reaches down and wipes his fingers across the dust and mouse droppings on the top of the coffee table, then rights a tipped over end table. "Not that you'll likely keep any of it," he says, pulling a tissue out of a pocket and wiping his hand. He shuffles the papers. "There's something about the contents mentioned in the contract your dad signed when he bought the place in '65." He flips a couple of pages, searching for what he wants. "Here it is." He reads: "*The house and the belongings are to be sold as one. Everything in view or out of sight, if it is within the boundaries of the one-hundred acres of property, upon the sale of said property, or the transfer of said property to another family member either by will or as a gift, will automatically become the new owner's possessions, no questions asked.*" He lowers the paper. "I suppose Miss Johansen's family wanted to get rid of it, that's why they added that clause; they wanted nothing more to do with the cabin after it was sold. Probably reminded them too much of their dead daughter. I guess that means if you find hidden treasure anywhere on the one-hundred acres, it would belong to you."

"By the looks of this place, I sincerely doubt that's going to happen." I cross the room, stepping on broken dishes, and peer into the hutch; the glass in the door is spotted and gray with age. A sugar bowl stands alone on the dirt caked shelves, sugar still in the bowl, and mottled with mold and insects. A desiccated mouse carcass lies beside the sugar bowl, and I look away, the bile rising at the back of my throat.

The dining table is covered in mouse droppings, and tiny pawprints criss-cross the top. Two chairs remain pushed up to the table, the other two, smashed into pieces as if thrown against the wall. The interior walls that were at one time finished with lathe and plaster, are now either stained by damp and mould, or broken away, leaving the insulation, which appears to be nothing more than rags, visible against the studs. In a few places I see daylight where the exterior siding is gone. I pick up an empty Doritos bag.

"Teenagers," Chip says. "Store owner said they come out here to make out, break things. One of the reasons the town wants these places either renovated or torn down... Unless it's the ghost."

"Ghost?" I repeat.

"Rumour is the place the place is haunted, if you believe such things."

"I wonder how they get inside?" I say. "The teenagers, I mean."

"There's a staircase the other side of that wall," he points towards the wall behind the hutch. "Goes to the unfinished second storey. All they'd have to do is climb a tree and hop onto the sub-floor upstairs, then walk down the stairs."

I open the door the mouse squeezed under and step into what used to pass for the kitchen. An ancient refrigerator that would be considered retro-stylish these days, sits to the left of the door, and a cookstove, something that, along with the fireplace, was likely used for heat when the cabin was in use, sits near the back of this room. As it stands, the stove couldn't be used for cooking let alone heating, its black iron top is coated with dust, and the pipes that were meant to take the smoke out of the house are disconnected and lying on the floor next to its cast-iron feet. Most of the cupboards don't have doors, and plates, cups, glasses, and other mismatched dishes lie in shards on the countertops. I shake my head at the destruction some people cause just for fun. A rusty sink is under a window covered in cobwebs. I reach to turn the tap, and a large spider crawls out of the spout. I quickly pull my hand back.

"How would I get water?" I ask Chip.

"I was told some businesses in town left their cards here in case the place was ever sold. Should be a water company card mixed in with them."

One by one, we peer into the dusty cupboards. Across from the stove, Chip pulls out a stack of cards. He rifles through the pile looking for the one he wants, then, glancing down at his jeans now shimmering with cobwebs and streaks of dirt, wipes the card off on his pantleg and hands it to me. "You call them and they deliver water right to your door." He looks out the kitchen window, scratching off a spot of grime with his finger. "That's the water reservoir," he says, pointing at a blue tank settled into the weeds. "It's plumbed into the kitchen taps and there's a pump against the back of the cabin by the step. The septic tank is that large tank behind the shed we're parked beside. This company," he points at the business card, "will empty that for you as well."

The name at the top of the card, printed in gold lettering, says *We-R-Pee,* along with the slogan, '*We take care of all your water needs.*' At the bottom of the card it says, 'to book an appointment for water delivery or waste removal, inquire at the General Store.'

"You'll need a bathroom built if you decide to move in since outhouses are illegal," Chip says.

A black rotary phone sits on the counter and I pick it up. There's no dial tone.

"Store owner said there is landline service out here, which is a good thing since there is no cell service." He nods at the ancient phone. "Just give the phone company a call and they'll come out and hook it up."

I step into the porch and open the door to look into the backyard. "You said that's a shed?" I ask, pointing through the screen door at the building our cars are parked beside.

"Could be," Chip says. "Or a boathouse. Could even be a garage. Don't know for sure and I don't have a key. Must have been misplaced after all these years. If you want to look inside, I can drive into town and get a pair of bolt cutters. I'm sure they sell them at the General Store."

"No, no," I say, not relishing the idea of being left out here alone. "Not today." I stand in the porch and let my eyes wander around the kitchen, then through the door into the living room. The wall between the kitchen and living room appears to divide the cabin neatly in half. Another wall running perpendicular, cuts this part of the cabin in half and I imagine a bedroom is on the other side of the kitchen. "Everything would have to be gutted," I say. "Start from scratch. Do you think a contractor from the city would come up here?"

"Doubtful," Chip says. "Not unless they charged you an arm and a leg for gas. You're thinking about renovating?"

"At this point, I'm not thinking about anything."

"There are often contractors who live in towns adjacent to lakes. People are always wanting to build decks, add onto cabins. They're probably already booked solid all summer, but you never know until you try. If nothing else, they could give you the phone number of someone else." He thumbs through the stack of business cards. "Pizza Palace," he mumbles, "Noodle King, babysitting service, farmers market, boat sales, here's one for square dancing if you're ever interested." I narrow my eyes at him. "Ah-ha," he says lifting a card in the air like he's found gold. "Here we go, and he lives in Southside." He squints at the card. "Company is called *W. V. Contracting. For all your building needs*, and a local phone number." He hands me the card. "Might be easier than getting someone from the city. Just remember, I'm here to help you sell if you choose to sell rather than renovate."

I stick the card in my back pocket along with the We-R-Pee card, wondering if I'm really thinking about taking this on, or if I should sell as Chip has suggested. I open a door in the back porch and step into the room on the other side of the kitchen. A bed, its comforter and pillow torn to shreds and thrown on the floor, the mattress slit with springs popping out in all directions, dominates the small space. A dresser with a smashed mirror is pushed up against the back wall, and the drawers have been pulled out and shattered on the floor.

"Why is everything broken?" I say. "It's almost as if someone was searching for something?"

"All I can think is that it's the kids who come out here to fool around."

I look towards the staircase in the far corner; the point of access for the teenagers.

"I imagine Miss Johansen's plan was that once the bedroom and bathroom were added on upstairs, she would turn this room into part of the living space, perhaps a dining room. I was told we're welcome to go up, but at our own risk. There's a board at the top," he points up the stairs, "covering the hole. Are you interested in going up?"

"I don't know," I say, stepping onto the bottom step then pausing to look up the darkened staircase.

"I'm sure it's ok, Mrs. Phillips. Just watch out for nails and don't step too close to the edge. It's been standing for over fifty-years; it's not going to break the moment you go up."

Chip sidles past me on the stairs, then slides the board away; a breath of fresh air wafts down the stairs. He steps back down, allowing me to go first. I grab the handrail to begin my assent, but it pulls off the wall and I fall backwards into my agent's arms.

"Gotta watch yourself around here, Mrs. Phillips," he breathes into my face and I pull my head back at the smell of Juicy Fruit Gum. "Lots of hazards in old places like this." He lets go of my shoulders, setting me upright on the bottom step; it squeaks. "You go on up, I'll just get rid of this thing." He takes the balustrade I'm still clutching out of my hand and unwedges one end of it from the wall where I swung it when I was falling. He then maneuvers it past the dresser and towards the back door, where he exits the cabin pointing the railing in front of him.

Again, I look up the steep rise, thinking, *Do I really need to see the rest of the place*? I shrug, figuring I've come this far. Except for the squeak on the bottom tread, the steps seem to be in better condition than the rest of the cabin and I emerge onto the sub-floor at the top. Rafters, dark with age and weather, comprise the underside of a sagging roof which has a post wedged in the middle to help hold it up. Studs ring the perimeter, some contacting the edge of the eves, and some swinging free. A gust of wind blows through the space, and I tell myself to hurry before I share the same fate as the previous owner.

The first room I encounter is cordoned off by two-by-fours where a sink, toilet, and tub lie uninstalled on the plywood floor. Cardboard that was wrapped around the porcelain has disintegrated into scraps and dust, and beneath the dirt caked on to the fixtures, I get glimpses of pale teal; a popular colour choice for bathroom fixtures in the sixties.

Across the hall another room is framed. I step into the small space which I assume to be a bedroom, and cross to the framed-in window which faces the backyard. I see Chip sitting in his car, scribbling in a notebook.

The final doorway is situated at the end of the hall facing the lake. It's the only room that has plywood nailed to the wall studs and a door installed. I push it open and the wood, swollen from years of being exposed to rain and snow, squeals against the floor. This room is much larger than the other one and takes up the entire front of the second storey.

I cross the floor to look out the empty space where a window would have been installed, hoping I might get a glimpse of the lake from up this high. I can't imagine working up here when it was snowing or blowing; falling over the edge seems to be a real possibility and I shiver thinking how Cecelia must have felt when she slipped. I'm looking across the treetops when my eye catches movement on the ground below and I look down to see a woman in the yard. She has her hand to her eyes as she lifts her face to the balcony, and her body is encircled in an aura from the sun's glare. I wave but she continues to look at the cabin without waving back. By the time I rush down the stairs and out the front door, she's on her way out of the yard.

"Hello," I call from the step. "Can I help you?" I run up behind her and reach for her sleeve, but she's moving too quickly and the material slips easily through my fingers. "Did you want something?"

She stops and turns to look at the front yard. "Seems like yesterday, not fifty-two years ago." Her diction is perfect, as if she attended an expensive school as a girl.

"What seems like yesterday?" I ask.

"She was found right there," she points.

"You mean when Cecelia Johansen died?" I say.

Either this woman has spent her entire life outside, or she is, in fact, very old. Her face is furrowed in wrinkles so deep they're like ruts in a road. Her hair is shiny, gray, and braided down her back, and she has on a weather-beaten sunhat that apparently has done nothing to protect her skin. She's wearing denim overalls with a white t-shirt underneath, and a plaid jacket like a man would wear, is draped around her shoulders. Her feet are clad in workbooks that look as old as she does, the soles so thick, it's as if her feet aren't touching the ground. She smells of smoke and water; the way you'd smell on a summers day after you've come home from a wiener roast on the beach.

"October fourth, 1965. Terrible winter."

"Do you live close by?" I ask.

She absently waves her hand in the direction of the beach.

"My name's Ruby," I say and hold out my hand.

"Missy," she says without extending hers. She studies my face. "You look a little like him."

"Like who?"

"The man who bought the resort after the accident."

"Oh, you must mean my father," I say. "He died and left this place to me in his will. We weren't close. I didn't even know he owned it until after he died."

"Some people find it difficult to express their love, and giving you this was the only way he knew how." she says. "Perhaps being here will bring you closer to him."

"Perhaps," I say, surprised at her insight. "I only came up today because I thought I might like to live here, but it isn't suitable in the condition it's in."

"It was a pretty cabin in its day. Be nice to have it looking good again."

I lift my eyes to the run-down cabin. "I suppose I could hire someone to renovate, it just seems like so much work and so much money to make it liveable. I wish I knew what to do."

Again she searches my face, then shifts her gaze to the treetops. "Sometimes the secret lies in taking the first step, but we fail to recognize it so as a consequence, don't move forward."

"That's true," I say, thinking that's an odd way to phrase it.

She looks at the cabin one more time, then turns to leave. I ask her to stay and talk a while, but she disappears without answering, barely making a sound as she tramps through the thick foliage. I turn and face the lake, then push my way through the undergrowth, until I break through to the shore. I find myself looking across a span of water free of boats, towards the other side of the lake where a golden strip of sand lines the edge of the water. A group of ducks swim past and a loon calls in the distance. I have my eyes closed listening to the silence when I smell cigarette smoke.

"Mrs. Phillips," Chip calls. "You in there?"

I'm tempted to remain quiet, but then decide he might worry I've gotten lost, and he has been trying hard even though he's been hinting I sell rather than stay. I'm sure my father's estate is paying him next to nothing to show me the resort. "I am," I say.

He follows the path I took through the bush, then stands beside me. "Your property ends there," he says, pointing at the sand on the other side of the water.

"Did you see Missy?" I ask.

"Who?" he says brushing at his jeans and picking leaves out of his hair.

"A woman named Missy. I had a long conversation with her in the front yard. Well, more like at her than with her. Not the most talkative person. She lives over there," I point in the direction Missy pointed.

"You mean here, on the resort?"

"Not sure. I assumed she meant the original cabin. She just waved in that direction. She could have meant the other side of the lake, I suppose."

"There's supposed to be no one else living out here so if she is staying on this land, she's squatting. Do you want me to go and talk to her? I can bring the cops in, roust her out."

"No, no," I say. "I'll look after it."

"When you talk to her, don't be too lenient. She'll take advantage of you if you let her. I've come across people living in abandoned cabins before. It's not easy getting them to leave unless you bring in the authorities. So," he says, jumping back from a wave that was just about to wash over his designer shoes, "is this close enough to the water for you?"

—

"You sure you're not biting off more than you can chew?" Chip asks, this time with real concern on his face. This morning he's at my house in the city taking pictures for the listing. He opens a kitchen cupboard, then turns on a tap, looks in the pantry, and knocks on a window frame. "It's one thing spending your summer holidays there, but to live year-round in the wilderness is another thing altogether. Perhaps you should reconsider selling and find something not so—"

"Like something out of *The Shining*?"

He shrugs.

"Growing up, my father didn't allow me much freedom. I was sheltered and innocent when I met my husband. We had a family right away, and I stayed home to look after them, my husband taking control much like my father had. And because I'd been dependent on others all my life, I allowed it to happen. I didn't get my driver's licence until after the kids were grown, never even paid a bill until after Steve left me. I think it's time I became an adult, don't you?"

"You're not afraid?"

"I thought you didn't believe in ghosts?" I say.

"I was thinking more about the work involved to make it liveable, the remoteness, and being stuck out there during the winter. It's not like living in the city with all the amenities at your finger tips."

"I can't explain it; it's like this cabin has been waiting for me to come along. Like it's giving me a chance to do something other than what people expected I would do with my life. Cecelia built that cabin, built them all to make a home for herself, to become independent. I feel like that's what this cabin is telling me to do. Maybe that's why my father gave it to me."

I doubt Chip has ever had a client talk to him on such a personal level and he's looking uncomfortable.

"Well," he says, picking at some invisible lint on his sleeve, "you don't have to decide right now. If we reassure the town that you have plans to renovate, then the cabin's not going anywhere."

"I don't want to wait," I say. "I want to sell this place now. I want to live at Sunset Lake."

Chapter 6

"You're doing what?" Robert says.

"I'm moving," I say. "To a lake."

I've invited the kids over for supper to tell them the news.

"You're moving to a lake? I thought you were going to look at some seniors complexes? I've already got three lined up for you to tour next week."

"I never said any such thing, Robert. That was your idea. I'm moving to the cabin your grandfather left me in his will."

"You're going to...." He stops talking, shocked at the idea I decided to do this without consulting him.

"You know I asked your dad for years to buy me a cabin, you know it was my dream to live at a lake. But he always said we couldn't swing it. Well, now that I have my own cabin, I'm selling this place, and moving to the lake."

We're sitting outside on the patio, trying not to listen to the neighbour's music, enjoying what is likely the last barbeque of the season. I can't wait until next summer when I can have everyone to my cabin for a wiener roast with no neighbours to bother me. Sheryl, Robert's wife, is filling my twin eight-year-old grandson's plates. She picks up a plate for herself and takes only some salad.

"Is that all you're having?" I ask. "I thought barbequed hotdogs were your favourite."

"Trying to lose a couple of pounds," she says, glancing at Robert.

I put my arm around her waist. "I love you just the way you are.

And if someone says differently, they should try and carry two babies inside their bodies for nine months."

"You're so sweet, Ruby. What's the name of the lake?" she says, changing the subject then taking a bite of salad.

"It's called Sunset Lake." I pick up the tongs and load a bun with a wiener then hand it to her. "It's about a five-hour drive north of here. You should see it. No boats, barely any cabins."

"Never heard of it," Robert says, scowling at his wife enjoying her plain hot dog while he smears mustard and mayonnaise on his own.

"You wouldn't have. It's not what you'd call a tourist spot."

"What's it worth?" he asks.

"Robert!" Sheryl says. "That's none of your business."

"I don't know," I lie. "I didn't ask."

"Sell it and buy something in the city," Robert says. "With the sale of this house and that cabin combined, you'd be sitting pretty."

"I'm not going to sell; I'm going to live there. I like it *because* it's far from here. No traffic, no neighbours on top of me. There's no cell phone connection, but there's a landline so I'm not totally incommunicado. It was part of a resort from the mid-thirties to the mid-sixties. Dad bought it in '65, just after the resort shut down. The other cabins are standing, but they're very run-down, I'll likely have them torn down at some point. I'm going to renovate the one the owner lived in, it's not in as poor a shape as the others. She was trying to give herself a life, trying to make her own way in the world without help. I kind of feel, I don't know, a kinship to her."

"A woman, especially a woman who's never done anything by herself, shouldn't be living alone in a place so remote that there's no one to help if she gets into trouble. I can't believe you made this decision without me," Robert says. "I should have gone with you."

"What do you think I've done since your dad left?" I say sharply. "I've looked after myself."

"And who had to show you how to do things, Mom? Selling this place and living somewhere far off the beaten trail is a lot different than paying a bill."

"Give your mom some credit," Sheryl says. "She's a grown woman with a mind of her own. If she says this is what she wants to do, then you need to respect her choice."

"Yeah, well," he says nodding at the hot dog in his wife's hand, "it's been my experience that sometimes women don't make the best decisions." Sheryl blushes.

I'd love to give my son a piece of my mind but know it's not my place to interfere in their marriage.

Debby asks, "When can we see the cabin?"

"Not for a while," I say. "It's not much to look at right now. Been empty for fifty years," I say.

"Sounds lovely," Robert says, his voice thick with sarcasm.

"You know, Robert," I say turning to face him. "If I'd let you come with me, you'd have taken over. You'd have told me it was a bad idea and talked me into staying in the city. I'd have been, as your father said so eloquently the day of my dad's funeral, walked all over. I needed to do this by myself."

"Have you listed the house then?" Jess asks softly.

I turn from my son and try to calm down. "Just today." I look out the window and see Chip pounding a For Sale sign in the front lawn. "Before you leave, take any mementos you want. I'm going to put some of the furniture into storage until the cabin is finished, and the rest will be sold to an auction company or included with the sale of the house."

—

Six months later my house still hasn't sold and I'm worried it never will. The main concern, Chip has informed me, is it needs too much work, and I can't help but see the irony. In the years before Steve left, he did a few things; windows, storm doors, new furnace, but nothing aesthetic. As I look at the worn beige carpet, and oak cupboards with the laminate trim, walls that need painting, and stippled ceilings, I see how dated it is. It never occurred to me that it wouldn't sell, and I've been feeling lately that the universe is trying to tell me something.

Chip keeps telling me not to worry, that *for every house on the market there is a buyer,* and that the right buyer just needs to come along. My house is in a good neighbourhood, he says, and while it's not perfect, it's in good enough condition to attract buyers. We just have to keep trying. On an afternoon late in March, he calls.

"Ruby," he says. "Can I show the house? I've someone here who's interested."

"Is it a serious buyer or a tire-kicker?" I ask.

"Serious buyer. It's today or not at all for these people." I hear him talking to someone else. "Be right there," he says. His voice is muffled as if he has his hand over the receiver. "They've moved here from Vancouver and all their furniture arrives the day after tomorrow," he says to me. "They need a house like yesterday. If they don't buy yours, they'll be buying someone else's today. It's a cash sale. If they say they like the place, that's six-hundred thousand in your bank account this week, Ruby! I think this might be the one."

"Okay," I say. "I'll go out for coffee. Give me a call when you're done." I hang up, grab my purse and a book and leave, my expectations for anything to come of this, low.

I'm sipping my coffee and trying to concentrate on reading my book when the door to the coffee shop opens and Steve enters. He's with a woman who appears at least twenty years younger than him, whom he directs to a table on the other side of the shop, then stands in line for the both of them. I quickly turn my head hoping he hasn't spotted me. He looks around and sees me hiding behind my book.

"Hey, Rube," he says sauntering over in that arrogant way of his, with a cup in each hand.

A few months ago, when I called Steve and told him my plans of selling the house, he said it was fine by him as long as he got his share. He said he would contact a realtor and get back to me. I told him I already had someone I was working with, and didn't need his help. I could hear him breathing on the other end of the line, wanting to tell me no, but he said nothing, probably figuring I'd fail soon enough. He did not ask where I was going to live once the house was sold.

"Surprised to see you here," Steve says. "You were never one for going out for coffee when we were together."

"House is being shown. Had to get out for an hour or so."

"Been a few months. It should have sold by now. I'll stop by when I'm done here, talk to your realtor. Just out for coffee with a friend." He waves at the woman seated on the other side of the room. "Perhaps I should take it off the market for a while, wait until there's more demand for houses. I'd rather do that than lower the price."

"No," I say quickly. I smile. I don't want him to think I'm incapable of doing this by myself. "Thanks for the offer, but we're doing fine. If I need your help, I'll ask."

"Just don't give it away, Ruby," he says over his shoulder while walking away. He sits at his table and I see the woman he's with give me the once over as he talks quietly to her.

God, please let the house sell today, I pray. The last thing I need is Steve's help, which means pushing me aside and completely taking over. I do not want to be sitting in that house for another two years waiting for it to be a seller's market.

Fifteen minutes later Chip calls. "Guess what?" he says. "They loved the place. Give your husband a call then get back to me about when the both of you can meet us at the bank. If he's available now, we can have this deal signed and finished today."

I hang up then stand and cross the room to talk to Steve.

Chapter 7

After collecting the six-hundred thousand, paying the real-estate agent and lawyer bills, then divvying up the remainder of the money with Steve, I've been left with just over two hundred and seventy-five thousand. That, combined with half my inheritance, has given me a grand total of four-hundred and twenty-five thousand dollars. I'm hoping to be able to keep a minimum of two-hundred thousand to invest, leaving me with just over two-hundred to use for renovations.

In the past week I've tagged everything in my house, from the largest to the smallest, with coloured sticky notes. This morning the movers are coming to pack up my things and take those marked with red sticky notes into storage. Those marked with blue are being included in the sale, and those marked with orange are being picked up by the auction company to which they've already been sold. The things I'm taking with me, I've already packed into boxes, suitcases, and bags, and stowed in my car.

The day my house sold, I called the power and phone companies to reconnect the cabin, then I called the contractor on the business card Chip and I found in the cupboard to see if he'd be interested in meeting me at the cabin to give me a price on renovations. He paused when I told him the address before agreeing to come and look. I can hear reluctance in his voice though I don't know why.

As soon as the movers have loaded their trucks and driven away, I go to visit my aunts. Shortly after I made the decision to sell the house and move to the lake, I went to their house to tell them the news; they were happy and sad. Happy because I'm striking out on my own, but sad because I won't be able to visit as often. This evening, as we sit at their kitchen table, sharing a bottle of wine, the tears are flowing.

"I'm going to miss you so much," Bernice says, mopping her face with a tissue. "You've been like the daughter I never had."

"I'll come and visit, I promise. And I have a phone, I'm not totally out of touch. Just call me anytime you want. I stuck the number on your fridge."

Marjorie pats my hand. "We're both so proud of you, Ruby. You know that, right? Your mom would be proud of you too."

"Hopefully I won't make a complete fool of myself," I say.

"You're going to do great," Bernice says, "I had a dream."

Aunt Bernice is known for her dreams. There was the time, when I was a child, she'd dreamt of me in a hospital, helping other people and said she suspected it meant I was going to grow up to be a doctor. Years later, when that didn't come to fruition, she dreamt of Mom in the hospital getting treatments. For what, she was unsure of, but she suggested the dream was a sure sign that Mom ought to go to the doctor. Believing her sister, Mom went to the doctor and was diagnosed with cancer. I drove her to the hospital for all her chemotherapy treatments then stayed and talked to the other patients also taking treatments, to help them take their minds off what was happening to them.

"What did you dream?" I ask this evening.

"That you were going to live by a beautiful body of water. That you were going to be happy and successful."

"See," Marjorie says. "You know your Aunt Bernice is right about these things. I can't wait to see the place."

"As soon as it's done, I'll have you out," I say. "Right now, it's not in good shape."

Worried about the long drive ahead of me tomorrow, I stand and kiss and hug both of them. "You two take care of yourselves. And the kids will help if you need anything."

"We'll be fine," Bernice says. "Don't you worry about us. Just go," she gently nudges me towards the door. "Have yourself an adventure. It's about time."

I head back to the house, then snuggle into my sleeping bag, willing myself to sleep.

Come morning, I'm out of bed before the sun rises, anxious to get this day started. It's been years since I've felt this alive, if ever.

I've rolled up my sleeping bag, and am now sitting in my car, ready to leave my home of thirty-five years for the last time, looking at the empty house and remembering.

Even though my marriage didn't turn out as I planned, there are parts of the life I spent in this house that I remember fondly. The kid's birthday parties, especially when they were little and wide-eyed with delight. Christmas mornings when the kids and I sat under the tree looking at the gifts Santa brought, peaceful moments before Steve got out of bed. Planting the garden each spring with Jess and Debby.

I remember one year, near the end of winter, when the temperature had soared and the snow was sticky. The kids and I had built a snow fort in the backyard. I served tea and cookies inside the fort. Eventually Steve came home, and seeing us sitting outside laughing and giggling as we had fun in the cold, he asked why we wasted our time doing such a stupid thing since it was going to melt the next day. I sometimes wonder if Steve was jealous of my relationship with our children. I think he believed that if he played with them, they would lose respect for him, so he never did.

This morning, after a lifetime of changing diapers, dealing with teenagers, making meals, scrubbing floors, celebrating birthdays, Christmases, and everything in-between, it's surprising how easy it is to say goodbye.

Five hours later, with the naivety of someone new to home renovation, I pull into the overgrown yard and get out of the car with a spring in my step and a smile on my lips. To my surprise, Chip has offered to give me a hand today talking to the contractor. I told him I was alright on my own, and perhaps, as my realtor, that was above and beyond his duty. He said he knew I was capable of talking to a contractor, and that helping me was more than he would usually do for a client, but to his surprise he'd found he loved being at the lake. He found it peaceful. I said he was more than welcome to come out here and I was grateful for the help.

I'm a few minutes late and Chip and the contractor are already standing on the back step. It's mid-April and colder here than in the city. I zip my coat up to my chin.

"Ruby," Chip says as he approaches me. "Good to see you." He gives me an awkward hug as if the two of us are best friends, then whispers in my ear. "His name is Wilson Vereschuk. Says someone else must have put his business card inside the cabin because it sure as hellfire wasn't him."

I lift my suitcase out of the trunk, leaving the bags and boxes stuffed with items I thought I might need, until after Chip and the contractor have left. "Mr. Vereschuk," I call. "Good to meet you. Thank you for coming out today." I tug on my gloves. "Are you by any chance related to the Vereschuk family who used to own this land?"

"He was my grandfather," he says. "And call me Wilson. No Mr., just Wilson. My father was an ornery SOB who made everyone call him mister. I'd rather not be linked to him."

Wilson is a thin man, not too tall, not too short, with a head of thick black hair, brown eyes, big nose, and thin lips. He looks at his watch, reminding me I'm five minutes late.

"Freezing my balls off out here, do you think you could make it snappy?" he says, and I wonder if he isn't more like his dad than he admits.

"Sorry," I say. "Guess I didn't get on the road as early as I thought I had."

He taps his foot on the step and again looks at his watch.

"Let me get that for you," Chip says as he exchanges the handle of my suitcase for the key to the cabin. He winks at me then says quietly, "Don't let him scare you. We've only been here ten minutes. I didn't want to go inside until you arrived. Honour goes to you," he says.

I stick in the key, open the back door, and step into the porch for the first time since last August; it's not much warmer inside, but at least we're out of the wind.

I know, in my practical heart of hearts, that the place looks the same as it did last summer, if not worse, but this morning I'm seeing my new home through the rose-coloured glasses of ownership, and can't help but be happy. I take a deep breath of the musty air and smile. Wilson bustles in behind me, zipping his parka higher on his neck and tugging his toque lower over his ears. He stops to look around, his mouth agape, his breath foggy in the cold air.

"You're going to live here?" he says. "Year round?"

"That's the plan," I say.

"And what would you have me do? Bulldoze the place and start new?"

"No," I say, surprised at his abruptness. "I want you to renovate it."

"You want me to renovate it? This place?"

"I do," I say.

"You young people and your renovations," he says, even though he and I are likely close to the same age. "Watch too much television. Be cheaper to build new. Not everything's worth fixing up."

Undeterred, I plow ahead. "I'd like this room gutted," I say. "I won't say right down to the studs, because as you can see," I rest my hand on a section of wall where the plaster has broken away, "the studs are already visible." He does not smile. "I'm going to need new cupboards, a new sink, new countertops, new light fixtures, and all new appliances, except for this," I step further inside and tap the cookstove. "I want to use it but it needs to be vented. I also want a regular stove to cook on. And I want this wall removed," I say pointing towards the wall at the far end of the kitchen dividing the cabin in half.

"Can't," he says.

"Can't? Can't what?"

"Take out the wall. Load bearing. Only thing supporting that," he points his thumb towards the ceiling. "Unless you're planning on not having a second storey. Otherwise, you take this wall down and the whole shebang," again, he points his thumb skyward, "ends up down here. And if you aren't planning on having a second storey, then we'll have to change one of these rooms into a bathroom. Government outlawed outhouses over fifty years ago."

"No," I say. "I mean, yes, I know I can't have an outhouse. I want the second storey rebuilt with a bathroom and two bedrooms and a balcony at the front of the cabin so I can sit outside and watch the sunset."

"'Course you do," he says with a sarcastic edge to his voice. He steps into the porch then opens the door to the bedroom on the other side. Chip and I follow. More nimbly than I'd expect a man of his age to move, Wilson runs up the stairs, sliding the wood away at the top and disappearing into the second floor. When he returns, he says, "That'll come down in a day. Wood's rotten right through. Can't believe no one has fallen through the floor yet. The stairs are in good shape. Squeak in the bottom step, but I can fix that. No sense spending money replacing something that doesn't need fixing. I could cut out the wall on the side of the steps so you could use the space underneath the staircase for storage, but am hesitant to fiddle with something that seems to be so well built. Don't want to weaken the entire staircase just so you have someplace to put your vacuum."

"That's fine," I say. "I can use the back porch for storage." I tap the wall separating the bedroom from the kitchen. "I want this wall out as well, and then this half of the room turned into the dining room."

Wilson shakes his head. "Might get away with the one wall down, but not both."

"What about beams?" I say.

The man looks surprised, as if he can't figure out how I know to suggest beams, probably thinking I watch too many home renovation programs. He takes off his toque, scratching the scalp under his thick hair. "I suppose you could, but it'd have to be steel to support the entire upstairs. Cost a fortune."

"That's fine," I say and his eyebrows go up. "As long as I get a quote first," I say quickly.

Chip and I follow Wilson back to the kitchen. "What about that?" he asks pointing out the dirty kitchen window.

"What about what?" I say.

"That. The water tank. What are you going to do about that?"

"Um, fill it?" I say.

He sighs as if I'm the stupidest person he's ever met. "Not now," he says, "for the winter? If you want running water next winter," he turns on the dry tap and I secretly hope a spider crawls out, "then you need to do something about that," again he points outside. "It'll turn into one big popsicle sitting out there in forty below."

"What do you suggest I do?"

"You need to bring it inside."

I turn in a circle. "I need to bring it inside? Where inside? It takes up too much room. And it certainly won't fit under the stairs."

"You do own all one-hundred acres?" he asks. I nod. "Then there's no reason why you couldn't build an addition. More'n enough room."

"An addition? For the water tank?"

"An insulated addition. Put the pump and water heater in there too. Deep freeze for extra groceries, if you're so inclined. Make it out of cinderblocks with a cement floor, and big enough for storage. Hold the weight of the water tank and last for decades. Have to take out a couple of trees, but it could be done. Trees are in danger of falling on the cabin anyhow. You staying out here by yourself or is there a significant other?"

"I'm alone."

"Then three thousand gallons would last you a month if not more, ten thousand would be a better choice. I'm sure city women want their dishwashers, not to mention showers every damn day." He slides his foot across the floor. "Cabin slants east to west," he says, waving his hand from the back door to the front. "Place likely needs new footings, and if you get a bigger—"

"Can you just tell me," I say, interrupting his critique of the cabin, "if you can do it or not and perhaps give me a ball park estimate?"

He rubs his red nose. "Well, like I said, it would be cheaper to tear the whole thing down and start new."

"That's not what I want to do," I say.

"If you get a bigger water tank," he continues, "I'll have to replace the septic. Likely have to replace it no matter what you do." He sniffs. "By the smell of this place, it's probably cracked. I could bury it; no more tank above ground. You gonna use this to heat this whole cabin?" He taps the top of the cookstove.

"I'm not sure," I say. "I'd like an electric fireplace installed in place of the wood burning one in the living room."

"So, you'll need a propane furnace then. Electric heat isn't enough to keep the cold out."

"Please," I say. "Can you just tell me if you're able to do it and what you think it will cost."

He pulls off a glove and counts quietly on his fingers. "Roof, walls, floors, insulation, water heater," he pulls of his other glove, "pump, and tank, second storey, addition, and furnace. How much do you have to spend?" he asks.

"To heat the place?" I ask.

"No," he shakes his head, "for everything. How much money are you planning to waste throwing at this place to make it liveable for you?"

"Well," I say, trying to not take offense, "I was hoping under two-hundred thousand."

"Cost you a hundred seventy-five," he says quickly, and I'm wondering if I'd said under one-fifty if his estimate would have been lower.

"A hundred and seventy-five?" I say. "You mean a hundred and seventy-five thousand?"

"Already she's arguing." He lifts his hands in the air.

"I'm not…."

"I suppose I could cut the cost by not putting in new windows," he says. "But in my opinion, there's no sense keeping these old things if you're getting a new furnace. May as well just throw your money out the window."

"I need new windows?" I ask.

"You can see here," he picks at the frame, slivers of soft wood come off in his hand. "Everything rotten. A bear could break in here with one swipe of its paw. Tear this place apart."

"A bear?" I say.

"Black bears everywhere in this province," Wilson says. "Once they figure out there's people living here, they'll gradually leave, as long as you don't do anything stu…, that would attract them," he corrects himself.

"What would you consider something that would attract them," I ask, a little worried about the answer.

"Leaving garbage out," he says. "Black bears can smell food from miles away. There's a bear-proof dumpster at the edge of town for you to use. If you're going to save your garbage for a few days, leave it in your trunk, or in the shed with a good padlock on the hasp. I've seen bears open doors you'd think they could never figure out."

"Okay," I say.

"And the front and back doors need replacing," he says. "Bears could walk in through those things without even knocking. I think even with windows and doors, I can still come in close to one-seventy-five, maybe one-eighty. So," he says. "What have you decided? You hiring me or not?"

"Let me think about it for a day. Would that be okay?" I say, feeling overwhelmed.

"Think about it for as long as you want," he says. "You're not going to get anyone else to take on this job. It's me, or no one." He moves towards the back door.

"Okay," I say quickly before I change my mind.

He turns but says nothing.

"I'll hire you." I glance at Chip.

"You sure?" Chip says.

"I'm sure," I say. "Is it a deal?" I ask Wilson.

"As long as you know that an estimate is just that, an estimate. Most jobs you should add on another ten percent."

"Is it a deal?" I repeat figuring a hundred and ninety-two is far cheaper than buying a house in the city. And this, when it's done, will be the cabin of my dreams.

"It's a deal," Wilson says.

"When can you start?" I ask.

"Hang on there, young lady. First thing you need to do is buy yourself some insurance. You're going to have all kinds of workmen here for the next few months. And summer's coming; wouldn't want to lose everything in a lightning strike. Could install a lightning rod for you if you like. Storms sneak up on you round here; it's being surrounded by trees. You don't know the storm's here, until it is. I'll send my crew out with a dumpster in the morning to haul away furniture, so you've got to be here to let them in or they'll leave. Have you looked in the shed?"

"It's padlocked and I have no key," Chip says. "Forgot to pick up a pair of bolt cutters."

"I have a pair in my truck. Might be good to use as your garage but it would have to be emptied. Cecelia kept it filled with tools and things that she needed to keep this place up and running. Probably all rusted beyond recognition by now." Wilson pushes open the screen door and we head outside. He drops to his knees and peers under the cabin. "Yup," he says, "just as I suspected. She used stones for footings and they've slipped. Common practice back then, using rocks dug up from when the land was cleared. Not the best choice, but free, and I doubt she imagined the place would still be here, let alone be being renovated, close to ninety years later."

He jumps to his feet and grabs the bolt cutters out of his truck then cuts the lock off the shed.

Chip steps forward and opens the double doors. "Whoa," he says. "The motherload."

The three of us stare at the multitude of picnic tables, lawn chairs, lawn mowers, tools of all shapes and sizes, furniture, and countless articles crammed into the space. There are things hanging from the walls, the rafters, tucked into every corner, and stacked to the roof.

"Want my advice?" Wilson says. "Toss the whole shooting match."

I sigh, touching a chair hanging on the wall nearest us. "There might be some things I could use," I say. "Guess I know what I'm doing tonight."

"You're staying here?" he asks. "Tonight?"

"From now on," I say. "My house in the city sold."

"Can't," he says.

"I can't stay here? I've had friends in the city who've lived in their houses while they were being renovated. I might not be as comfortable as in my house in the city," I say, thinking he's criticizing me for not being tough enough, "but I think I can manage."

"Did your friends have the floor ripped out from under them, or the house jacked up? Not to mention I'm going to be digging a trench around the cabin and knocking down that second floor. It'll be unsafe to live in there; insurance wouldn't cover me, or you for that matter."

"Is there a hotel in town?" I ask.

"There isn't. Burned down in '63." His eyes wander to the decrepit row of cabins. "What about one of these places?" Wilson suggests. "Have you looked inside any of them?"

"We haven't," Chip says. "I was told this cabin was in the best shape, so it's the only one we looked at."

"Worth a peek," Wilson says, picking up his bolt cutters.

The cabins aren't close together, the space between each, comparable to the distance of half a city block, and the underbrush is thick and prickly, so it's slow going. We stop at the first cabin on the north side of mine. While I'm pulling burrs off my pant legs, Wilson cuts off the lock, though with the way the weathered planks are sagging on its hinges, I don't know why it's even locked. He tugs on the rusty knob and the door falls to the ground.

"Don't worry about that," he says, "I can fix it in no time. Go ahead, see if it suits you."

"Me?" I say. "You want me to go in there first?"

"You're the one who's going to be living out here, not me."

I look back at Chip, who smiles encouragingly, then I step over the threshold. The first thing I notice in the dim light is the sharp smell of something acrid in the musty air. My foot slips and I look down; the floor is covered in smears of white. I hear a rustling noise, and when I look up, a flock of birds, which have been perched on the exposed beam across the ceiling, take off in one group. Wings flap in my ears as they make their way out the door, feathers, and dirt raining down onto my shoulders. I cover my head and run outside, screaming.

"Birds," is all I can manage to say.

"Okay," Wilson says, as he and Chip watch the birds make their escape to the treetops. "So, this one's a no?"

I nod as I pick feathers out of my hair.

"On to the next," he says. Then, like Paul Bunion, lifts the bolt cutters over his shoulder and moves towards the next cabin.

"What about that one?" I say, pointing over my shoulder at the Vereschuk place.

"Too old," he says without meeting my eyes. "We should look at the others before we resort to having you stay in that place."

We push through the brush and weeds to the next cabin, where Wilson cuts off the padlock, opens the door then holds his hand in front of him inviting me inside. I shake my head. "I'm not going in there," I say.

"I'll go," Chip says. He steps in, but doesn't get very far before he returns, covering his nose and shaking his head.

"Why not?" I ask.

"Trust me," he says. "It's not liveable and you don't want to be going inside."

The next cabin doesn't even have the door attached; its warped wood, lying in the weeds. I peek inside without stepping across the threshold. The centre of the floor has a large, ragged hole in it, as if someone has had an indoor wiener roast. The part of the floor that isn't burnt is littered with God knows what. I turn around and shake my head.

Wilson cuts off the lock on the next and I peek inside, take a whiff, then say no.

We've come to the last cabin in the row, and the smallest of the group, likely meant for only two people. My thoughts are confirmed by the aged wooden sign hanging above the door that says Honeymoon Suite in faded letters. Wilson opens the door and this time, goes inside himself. He's gone for only half a minute. When he returns, he says, "This'll do."

"Are you sure?" I ask, hesitant to look.

"I'm sure a city girl like you probably wants a three-piece bath and cable television, that's what I'm sure of," he says. "But there are no animals, no fires, and no sh….," he looks at Chip, then at me. "Trust me. It's better than any of the others we've looked at."

Chip steps up to the doorway and sticks his head beside Wilson's. "She can't live here," he says, his voice subdued in the gloom of the building.

"Nonsense," Wilson says. "I've lived in worse places. And compared to the others, this is heaven." He looks over his shoulder at me shivering in my not warm enough winter coat, leather gloves, and knee-high winter boots. "Oh yeah," he says. "I forgot who we're talking about."

"Oh, come on, you two. It can't be that bad." I join them at the doorway, trying not to touch the rotting frame. The inside is as disgusting as the outside, with spider webs and mouse droppings everywhere. A rotten quilt covers a mattress resting inside a broken bed frame. A plate, with things too old to distinguish, sits on a broken coffee table, a dead mouse lies on what passes for a countertop and a very large spider scuttles across the floor, burying itself under the moth-eaten mattress. On top of everything else, it smells like the boot room in the elementary school my kids went to. "I can live here," I say quickly, not wanting Wilson to criticize me again for being a city girl. "Obviously you two men have never raised kids. I've cleaned out teenager rooms that smelled far worse than this. Wash it down, buy a new mattress, a few rolls of shelf liner, a bar fridge, and hot plate, and this thing could be liveable in a couple of hours."

"Okay, then," Wilson says, brushing his hands together. "You have a place to live." He clears his throat. "Not to be indelicate, Miss," he says, turning to me, "but have you given any thought as to where you plan on using the, uh, facilities? Because, if the smell in these cabins is any indication, I'm quite sure all the septics," he points to the hulking tanks beside each building, "are cracked, and you won't have a bathroom in the cabin I'm renovating for quite a few weeks. And," he says pointing to the outhouses standing sentry between each cabin and the road, "I'm pretty sure you wouldn't want to go inside any of these."

My cheeks turn red.

He pulls his notepad out of his jacket pocket. "I'll rent a porta potty and add that to your estimate. Need one for the crew anyhow. I'll bring it out tomorrow."

"Thank you," I say, feeling overwhelmed.

"And buy yourself a pair of work boots. Louise'll have 'em at the store in town. Those things you have on your feet won't do you any good out here in a construction site. Have a nail through your foot in no time. Hope you brought a warm sleeping bag and a space heater," he says, continuing his critique of me and my belongings. "Gets cold at night until the ice goes out."

"There's still ice on the lake?"

"It'll be there for another month, three weeks if you're lucky," Wilson says.

Chapter 8

The first thing I do after the men leave is call the insurance agency Steve used for the house in the city, and purchase insurance on this property.

I'm now standing by the shore in front of my new home, looking across the thinning ice, trying to decide what to begin cleaning first, the shed, or the Honeymoon Suite, when I see Missy standing on the beach. She looks the same as she did last August with her wrinkled face and sunhat. The cold wind is blowing her clothing, and her braid is whipping around her head in the wind, but she makes no move to wrap her arms around her body to keep warm, or stop her hair from blowing across her cheeks. She has on no winter coat, toque, or gloves. I lift my arm and call her name, but she doesn't turn around and acknowledge she saw me. Instead, she walks behind the Vereschuk cabin and disappears into the forest on the other side of the road.

"Well," I say to myself, "I guess she's a loner. We should get along well."

—

Instead of cleaning, I decide to procrastinate and drive into town to see what I can do about water, pick up a few groceries, and buy a bottle of wine to christen my new place with a toast.

In the ditch where the highway turns onto Main Street, there's a sign announcing the population of Southside. The number written at the top of the battered wood says two-hundred and forty-seven, but has been x-ed out, and another number is written below. That number has also been crossed off, as has the next, and the next until now, near the bottom of the sign, a six, which has been scratched off and a three written above it, puts the final tally of the town at seventy-three. The streets are not paved, and there are no sidewalks, just the occasional piece of wood thrown over a pothole or puddle. I stop at the gas station to fill up. The building next door has its windows boarded over and a faded sign hanging above the door that says, *Tony's Tailors*. Across the street, an ice-cream parlour called *A Scoop Above*, also sits empty, though it looks in good repair and I imagine it's still in business, the weather just not yet conducive to opening its take-out window. The building next to the ice-cream shop is empty however, with a For Rent sign in the window. Except for the occasional car at the gas station, or parked in front of a restaurant called *The Golden Sheaf* which has an attached bar aptly named *The Kernel*, the place could be a ghost town.

I nose into a parking spot in front of Carnation's General Store where Chip and I stopped when he asked for directions. A mailbox stands on the sidewalk outside the store, and a gentleman dropping in a letter, tips his hat, then turns to watch me climb the steps—a stranger in town. I turn at the top and look towards the windows of the restaurant across the street, and can't help but feel I'm being watched.

Outside the store, baskets of toques and mitts, as well as a rack of winter boots, are all on sale for half price. What appears to be the same man I saw last fall, is sitting in a chair to the side of the door, his walker parked next to him, and he's looking at me as if I'm an alien from outer space.

"Dad," a woman says as she emerges from the store, "close your mouth. You'd think you'd never seen another human being before." I look up and see the woman who gave Chip directions last summer. "Hi," she says. "Name's Louise. Louise Carnation. I own this place. This old man is my dad. You must be Ruby Phillips? Bought the Johansen place? Saw you in your car last year when you were here with that real-estate agent."

"Word spreads fast. I just arrived today."

"We don't get too many new people moving in around here, so even when it's at the lake, it's big news. And Wilson may have mentioned something about the crazy city lady who thinks she can make it on her own out there."

I follow her inside. The store is empty of customers but crammed with merchandise. T-shirts printed with *Southside, the biggest little hamlet in the north*, hang from a rack in the far corner. Baskets filled with dog treats sit close to the floor near the cash register, and shelf upon shelf of dry-goods and canned goods, dominate the space. A Canada Post banner hangs from the ceiling in the back and a pile of packages waiting to be picked up are stacked on the counter.

"Where is everyone?" I glance at the empty street.

She looks at her watch. "This time of the day? The Golden Sheaf, though a couple of 'em have likely already wandered into The Kernel. I'm sure they're talking about you right now, trying to figure out why you decided to move into that old rundown place. I'm surprised they aren't crowding through the door, falling over each other to be the first one to interrogate you."

"I thought it felt like I was being watched."

"What did make you decide to move to our neck of the woods, if you don't mind me asking?" she says and I smile to myself. "Don't get me wrong, I totally understand, I was born and raised here. Dad owned this store before me." We turn to look at her dad who's waving at a car driving down the street. "Neither of us would be caught dead living in the city. Just some people are suspicious when a city person moves here."

"The resort belonged to my father."

"Your father is Arthur Daniels?"

"Was," I say. "He died just about two years ago now."

"I'm sorry," she says. "And he left the resort to you?"

"He did," I say.

"I was a kid, but I remember him," Louise says. "The whole town was surprised when we heard about this city-slicker who bought Cecelia's resort. He came out, looked around, and we thought maybe he was going to keep it running. But he left and never came back."

"I haven't figured out why he bought the place, haven't figured out why I decided to move here." I shrug. "Felt like the right thing to do."

"It's a nice lake," she says. "Clear and clean. No algae. Just too far from the things tourists want. Maybe when the cabin is all fixed up nice, you could sell it and buy something closer to civilization." She shakes her head. "Listen to me, chasing away business."

"There must be enough people around here to keep you up and running," I say, "if you've been in business all these years."

"Winters can be tough, but Dad and I live simply. No holidays to far off places, no expensive cars. No cable. Have a satellite dish on the roof so we can watch our shows. Lots of farmers around these parts who support us so we can make it through the winter. And business picks up come summer. As soon as school's out, that highway will be whizzing with cars. People stop to fill up," she points towards the gas station. "Own that, and that as well," she says pointing to *A Scoop Above* across the street.

"Wow," I say. "You're a busy woman."

"They pop in here to buy candy, drinks, magazines, then cross the street for a cone."

I look at the baskets of butter and rum flavoured Life Savers, and Cracker Jacks stacked by the cash register.

"They call our town quaint," Louise continues. "Say how they'd love to live in a place like this, get away from the hustle and bustle of the city. Then they pull out their phones. When I tell them there's no cell service, they look shocked, then get in their cars and race out of here like we're some kind of cult." She begins sorting magazines into the rack beside the cash register. "People say they want seclusion, say they want to get away from everything, trouble is, they don't want to do it alone. They want restaurants, movies, shopping, technology, everything they have in the city." She shakes her head. "You're planning on renovating, Wilson said."

"I am."

"Be nice to have that old place looking good again. Was a pretty cabin in its day."

"That's exactly what Missy said," I say.

She spins. "You saw her?"

"I did, last fall. Had a long conversation with her in the front yard. Well, mostly I did the talking. She commented on how long it had been since Cecelia's death, that kind of thing. Seems a little eccentric, but nice enough. And I saw her this morning after Wilson left. She was standing on the beach near the Vereschuk cabin. I called and waved at her, thought I'd tell her I'm moving in, but she didn't seem interested in visiting with me this time."

"She's a bit of a recluse. Doesn't usually talk to anyone. You were lucky you spoke with her last fall."

"I wouldn't mind talking to someone who knows more about the history of the resort. Maybe I can get an inkling as to why my dad bought it."

"That would be Dad. He knows more about that cabin than anyone around here. He helped Cecelia build it, and the others; the whole resort, actually. Worked for Cecelia for years, right up until she died. When you're done shopping, I'll ask him if he'd like to talk to you. Nothing he likes better than to reminisce about the good old days." She drops a stack of magazines into a slot. "How did she look?"

"Missy, you mean?" I ask.

Louise nods.

"To tell you the truth," I say, "she looked the same as she did last fall, right down to the clothes she was wearing. Didn't even have on a winter coat or gloves. Must be a tough old girl."

"She is that," Louise says. "So," she slides the last magazine into its space in the rack, then wipes her hands on her apron and places them on her hips. "What can I get for you today?"

"I was wondering if you know what I can do about water? There is a tank outside the cabin, but I'm getting a bigger tank installed inside the cabin and that won't be ready for a couple of months."

"Too early to fill outside tanks," she says. "Still going below freezing at night. Pipes'll freeze. We start delivering water in four weeks or so, shortly after the ice goes out on the lake and it's not going below freezing at night. If you have your new tank by then, Wilson will let me know."

"You own that business too?" I ask.

"I do. My cousin's son drives the truck."

"What'll I do for water until then?"

She points at a display of water jugs. "You use those," she says. "Spigots on the wall."

"Wilson said I should pick up a space heater, some work boots too."

"You're staying out there now?"

"I am. I've got the power and phone hooked up. I'll be sleeping in Cecelia's cabin tonight, then tomorrow I'm cleaning out The Honeymoon Suite to stay in during the renos."

"Watch out for ghosts," her dad calls from the doorway.

"Pardon me?" I say, not realizing he was listening to our conversation.

"Ghosts," he repeats. "You do know she was murdered, right?"

"Cecelia, you mean? She was murdered? I was told she fell off the second floor," I say.

"Don't believe a word of it. She'd lived out there for over thirty years; she knew better than to go up there in a snow storm. You're too far away from medical care to take chances." Tears fill his rheumy eyes and he wipes them away. "As sure as shootin' someone killed her. Now her ghost wanders around out there; least that's what I've been told. Not been out for years."

"Okay, Dad, that's enough of that," Louise says. "No sense scaring the poor woman to death before she's barely even moved in." She waves towards the back of the store. "Space heaters are over there. Right beside the work boots. Grab yourself a couple of extension cords too; I doubt the ones in Cecelia's shed are still working. Mice probably chewed through 'em years ago."

I gather up what I need and pile it on the floor by the cash register.

"Don't let Dad scare you with his talk of ghosts," Louise says.

"I have three grown children," I say. "It takes a lot to scare a woman who's raised kids through their teenage years and beyond. As a matter of fact, a ghost would be a pleasant change from a sixteen-year-old screaming he hates me because I won't let him borrow my car. Or another one trying to sneak out the window to go to a concert."

Louise laughs. "Don't have kids myself, but I can imagine."

I pull a grocery list out of my purse. "My real-estate agent said there was a liquor store near by?"

"Next door. Not a big selection of brand names, but there's some wine, beer, whiskey, the usual," she says taking the paper from my hand. "Go and pick something up while I get these things together." She places a jar of peanut butter on the counter.

"That's very kind of you," I say. Ten minutes later I'm back with a couple bottles of pinot grigio. "Just met another cousin. Your family's got a monopoly on business in this town. Does your husband run the gas station?"

"Someone's got to keep the place on the map," she says. "And no, my ex-husband does not run the gas station. That particular union from hell ended many years ago. I see you're still a member of the marriage club." She nods at my hand. "Your husband joining you later?"

I look at the wedding ring still adorning my finger, and wish I had the courage to take it off. "Trying to decide what I'm going to do. We're separated, his idea, though I'm sure it will end in divorce. Don't know why I haven't taken the ring off."

"Took me all of two seconds to remove mine," she says. "Left his house and moved in with my dad the next day. I was lucky. House is right across the alley." She points out the back door. "Born and raised right there. Mom died years ago; lung cancer. So," she shrugs, "Dad and I keep each other company. It's good. We seem to live together well. I'll help you take this to your car, then we can talk to Dad."

My groceries are packed in a box and sitting by the door with my work boots and space heater. "How much do I owe you?" I ask.

"One eighty-five, thirty-nine," she says. "Had everything on your list except that jam you asked for. Substituted a jar of my homemade Saskatoon berry jam. Hope you don't mind. I'll start stocking the raspberry if you like."

"I'm sure your jam is far better than anything I could buy."

"Made from berries I picked on your land. Sell it in the store year-round." Louise loads the three jugs of water, and the space heater onto a dolly, I pick up my box of groceries and boots, and the two of us head to my car.

"Ruby, this is my dad, Gerry Carnation," she says after we've loaded my groceries in the truck. "Dad, this is Ruby Phillips. She inherited Cecelia's place."

Gerry smiles, his blue eyes sparkling with life. "Aren't you a sight for sore eyes," he says. "Saw you last fall. Hoping you'd be back. You look a little like her. Cecelia, I mean. Not quite a chip off the old block, but a little around the eyes. Don't you think so, Louise? Thought I was seeing a ghost when she walked in."

"Sorry," Louise says to me. "Dad likes to talk in clichés. Don't know what that's all about, started a couple years ago, but it's surprising how easy it is to get used to." She pulls up two chairs, placing one on each side of her dad and patting the seat of one for me to sit. "Dad," she says, "Ruby's wondering if you'd mind talking to her about Cecelia, or the cabin. Whatever you can remember, I imagine."

"Love to, as long as I don't buy the farm before I'm done." He winks at me.

"He's also a joker," Louise says. "Don't take him too seriously."

I sit, thinking of all the work I should be doing at the cabin. Louise sits the other side of her dad and places her hand on his arm.

"It was nineteen-thirty-one," Gerry says. "I was fifteen, and we were at the beginning of that cursed depression. Got a job building that cabin you're restoring."

"Wait a minute," I say, interrupting him as he leans back in his rocker, ready to regale me with his tales. "That would make you," I count to myself, "one-hundred and one?"

"That it would, my darlin', that it would. My eyes are dim, my hearing is weak, and my bones complain every time I stand." He taps his temple with a gnarled finger. "But the years I spent with that woman are still here, as intact as if they happened yesterday."

Louise kisses his grizzled cheek.

1931

"I wanna help," I say. "I'm just about sixteen."

Dad puts his hand on my shoulder, the black dust from working in the coal mine, worn into his knuckles like creases in a leather glove. "You're too young to be worrying about supporting a family, Gerry."

"But Dad," I say. "We could use the extra cash, and you know I'm a quick learner. I could do most anything."

Dad nods. "Yes, an employer would be crazy not to hire you." He rubs his hands down his face. "Okay. But just a few hours a week." He gives my shoulder a squeeze. "No twelve-hour shifts, you hear me?"

I fling open the front door, yelling over my shoulder as I run outside. "I'll be back with something; I just know I will."

After trying at two different stores and being told there's no jobs available, I'm passing the window of Garret's Hardware and see the owner, Mr. Garret, inside talking to a lady. I enter the store and stand near two men who are watching the owner and the woman talk. Mr. Garret is holding his palm towards her, as if trying to stop her from saying any more.

"Now just hold on, Miss. Like I've told every woman who's come in asking for work," Mr. Garret says, "the most I can give you is sweeping up and making coffee. Five dollars a week, that's it, I can't hire a woman for anything more than that. I'd have rocks through my window if I gave you a decent paying job when I have a list of able-bodied men the length of my arm who are looking for work."

"I think," she says, "you have me confused with some other woman who's trying to put a roof over her children's heads and feed her family. I didn't ask you for a job, I asked if you know of a man who would be willing to work for me. I've bought some property at Sunset Lake and want a cabin built, so someone familiar with construction would be preferable."

"Work for you?" Mr. Garret says. "You're looking for a man to work for you? Well now, that's a different story. Here's a couple of men, why don't we ask them."

The man closest to me speaks up. "It'll be a cold day in hell before I have a woman boss." He slaps his buddy on the shoulder who nods in agreement.

"The only way I'd work for you, little lady," the second man says, "was if you understood that I'd be the one in charge."

I step out from behind a basket of nails. "I can do it," I say. "I know how to build stuff and I do what my mom tells me all the time." She waves me over.

"You know," Mr. Garret says as the woman pushes open the screen door and ushers me outside. "These men are more qualified than that lad. Men who need the job to support their families. This boy's daddy already has a job."

She turns. "Then they should have taken the opportunity when it was handed to them. I asked if anyone wanted to work for me, and this boy," she turns to me, "how old are you?"

"Fifteen," I say.

"This fifteen-year-old boy," she continues, "was the only one man enough to step forward. Perhaps next time they're offered a job, they won't be so picky." The screen door bangs shut behind us. "Or so stupid," she says under her breath. "Men, think they own the world." She sticks out her hand. "Name's Ceclia Johansen."

"Gerry Carnation," I say placing my hand into hers.

Chapter 9

"I was surprised when she hired me, being as how I was only a boy, but I was glad for the work. Best decision, other than marrying your mother, I could have made, working for Cecelia." He touches his daughter's hand. "She was so proud of her land. We started clearing the property the day after she hired me."

"He didn't know how to build a thing," Louise says.

"I didn't," Gerry says. "I was a town boy; I knew next to nothing about how to build or fix things. And I was scrawny. More of a bookworm that a labourer. But I'd always been good at watching and learning, figured how hard could it be to build a house? She told me she'd pay me seventy cents an hour. I couldn't believe it; that was more than my dad was making working at the coal mine. Rumour was she'd paid cash for that land. Ten-thousand dollars. Next to nothing by today's standards, but in the nineteen thirties, ten-thousand dollars was a fortune. She never seemed to bat an eye when a sales-person told her what the cost of something was, just whipped out her wallet and handed over the money. She did tell me once that she'd come from money, and that she'd had a privileged upbringing, but she was no longer a member of that family."

"Where did she get her money?" I ask.

"Mom and Dad were suspicious of a woman who wanted to hire a boy to help and was willing to pay him such a generous salary, so they went out to the lake to talk to her. She explained that her family was helping her financially. Dad asked why she wasn't living with them and she said that there had been a rift, so now she was living on her own, trying to make her own way. Said she had plans for the land and as soon as she made some money, she was going to pay her family back."

"And that was enough for your dad?"

"It was. In a way, I think he was proud of this young woman who was striking out on her own. After my parents left, Cecelia told me her father was wealthy and each month, as long as she didn't discredit her family with her sordid reputation, her dad sent her money. She said she couldn't bear to live with her parents anymore, because it didn't matter how it happened, being the woman, she would always be the one who was blamed. She told me it broke her heart the day she had to leave him with the nuns, but she figured he'd have a better life than she'd be able to give him."

"Sounds like she had a baby out of wedlock," I say.

"I was only fifteen, and already embarrassed by being told such intimate information, so I didn't ask anymore questions. But that's what I took it to mean. About a month later, Dad and I were in the city to buy a new bike with some of the money I'd earned. We were driving by a building and I saw her standing outside, watching nuns wheeling baby carriages around the yard. Dad told me it was a home for unwed mothers. It wasn't until later that I realized it was likely the place where she'd given birth."

"That's so sad," I say.

"It was nineteen thirty-one. Women who got pregnant without being married were ostracized and they certainly didn't raise their babies alone. Not like these days when women want to have a baby without even having the man in the picture!" He shakes his head with a sorry look on his face as if the world has gone to hell in a handbasket. "I'm sure the money her dad sent her was a pittance of what she would have inherited if she'd not been kicked out. But it was either take his money or live on the street."

"You've never told me this before, Dad," Louise says.

"I was never sure that's what happened; it was just a guess. Not something I could talk to anyone about. My mother would have been shocked if she knew what Cecelia told me.

"We started our venture by going to the lumberyard. Back then, a woman buying that much land for cash, stuck out in a small community like ours and every person in town knew exactly who Cecelia was. Eric Prentice, owner of the lumberyard and all-around bad egg, raced over as soon as he saw us step foot in his store. Told Cecelia he'd be more than willing to build her cabin for her. Said a construction site was no place for a woman or a boy. Cecelia thanked him for his offer, but declined. Said if we ran into trouble, she knew who to ask, but for now, if he could answer her questions about building, and she was sure, being a woman, she'd have many, that she'd bring all her business to him in the future."

"She was a clever woman," I say.

"She was," Gerry says. "Her self-deprecating manner seemed to change Eric's mind, though I imagine it was more the thought of spending time with her that agreed with him. Over the course of many visits, he taught us how to do everything we needed to know. Through every lesson, he would keep one hand on the small of Cecelia's back. I don't know how she stood it, but she never said a word. She was a striking woman; I witnessed many men make passes at her that summer, but she always took what she needed from them without giving in to their advances."

"I don't know if I'd be able to hold my anger in check," I say.

"Women are different today," her dad says. He holds up a hand. "Not saying it's wrong, just saying it's different. Don't misunderstand, she stood her ground when she had to, but she had this uncanny ability to remain even-keeled. She may have taught me how to pound a nail in straight, but she also taught me to stay calm, a lesson I've never forgotten."

"I've never known you to lose your temper, Dad," Louise says.

"People listen to you if you get your point across without getting angry," Gerry says. "Cecelia taught me that." He massages his gnarled fingers. "I never had a better summer." He leans his head back and his voice gets quiet, remembering. "I can still taste those fried eggs, hashbrowns, sausages and coffee she made."

When he starts to snore, I decide it's time to leave.

1931

"My Dad is in construction," Cecelia tells me as we pull away from the hardware store in her beat-up truck. "I was around workmen all the time when I was growing up." She turns onto the highway that leads to Sunset Lake. "When I was a child, I'd listen when Dad would take me to a worksite; managed to pick up tidbits here and there; how to mitre a corner, lay flooring straight and sure, measure twice, cut once, that kind of thing, so I'm not totally in the dark about building. Probably absorbed some things I don't even realize I know. Being his daughter, Dad never actually taught me anything; that privilege was given only to my brothers. But it's always intrigued me. Making a building appear out of a pile of wood; it just seems so, I don't know, magical. I know how to do some things, but I'm hoping that when we buy the lumber, there'll be someone who will show us how to do things I don't know." She pulls off the rutted track and parks. We get out of her truck. "You understand I don't just own the land you see in front of us, Gerry, I own it all." She opens her arms wide. "I bought all one hundred acres." She rests her hand on my shoulder and gives a squeeze. "You and I are going to build a cabin. Right here, looking into the sunset. It's going to be the cabin of my dreams."

—

"I can't believe they let a woman purchase such a large piece of property," Eric, the owner of the lumberyard says. "If you were mine, I wouldn't let you out of my sight." He slaps the side of Cecelia's truck, loaded down with wood. "You going to be okay driving out there by yourself?" he asks undressing Cecelia with his eyes. "It's a large load, might be too much for a woman to handle."

I feel my temper welling in my chest and step forward. Cecelia touches my shoulder, stopping me. "We'll be fine, Eric, but thanks for asking," she says.

We leave the lumberyard and get into her truck.

"How do you let him treat you like that and not get mad?" I say.

"If I allowed his actions to bother me, then he would win. It's taken me many years to learn the minute that type of man feels threatened, that's when he becomes dangerous."

Chapter 10

By the time I get home, the sun is getting low. It's past supper time, and I hear my stomach growling as I lug the cooler filled with groceries inside. I wrestle the jugs of water out of the trunk and drag them into the kitchen, set out the mouse traps, blow up my air mattress, then plug in the space heater and lamps I brought with me.

I'm standing in the kitchen, eating a peanut butter and jam sandwich, marvelling over how good this jam is while trying to decide if I should start cleaning or have a glass of wine, when one of the bags I brought, stuffed with things I thought I might need, falls off the counter. A flashlight rolls across the kitchen floor. I look behind me hoping I don't see Cecelia's ghost, and chiding myself for letting that thought cross my mind, then turn on the outside light and step into the backyard.

It's so quiet I can almost hear my own heart beating. There's no traffic noise, no voices, no airplanes overhead, and no sirens to disturb the stillness. No dogs barking, no children screaming, no lawnmowers, and no music blaring from a neighbour's backyard. All I hear is the breeze rustling the leaves, ducks quacking on the lake, and a squirrel scolding me from the treetops.

Many times, in the past few months when my house wasn't selling, and I thought about all the work I had to do when it did sell, I came close calling it quits. The thought of packing up everything from the past thirty-five years, hiring a moving company and a contractor and dealing with the headaches that renovations can bring, not to mention doing all of that without a husband by my side, made me so anxious I could barely think straight. But the idea of living in a cabin at a lake—in particular, this cabin at this lake—kept pulling me back. Now, standing here, in the backyard, with nothing around me but wilderness, I know I made the right decision. This is where I'm supposed to be. In all my life I can't remember ever having as strong a feeling as this, not even on my wedding day when I had second thoughts practically as soon as I said the words *I do*. With the birth of my children, the world seemed to straighten out and I was happy for a few years, until the nagging feeling that this was not my life's calling began to surface again. I felt at loose ends, unfinished; like a meal half made, a lawn half mowed, or a house painted only as high as one could reach from the ground. The minute Chip and I walked inside this cabin last fall, even through all the mould and rot, it's almost as if it told me I was home; that after all my years of feeling lost, of not knowing where I belonged, I'd finally found my purpose.

I stand in front of the shed, then look across the grounds towards the cabin I'll be living in, and wonder which one I should tackle first, the shed or the Honeymoon Suite. Deciding that it's going to be dark soon, and daylight might be a better time to be so far from electricity, I pull open the doors to shine my flashlight into the depths of the shed. Cecelia certainly seemed to be prepared for anything. I see garden hoses and wheelbarrows, packages of shingles, a pile of doors, their knobs removed and placed in a box on top of the pile. Stacks of lumber have been balanced between cinder blocks so the wood isn't touching the ground, and lawn chairs, croquet games, and fishing poles are piled on top of the lumber. One corner is stacked with boxes marked *Christmas Decorations* on the outside, while another box sitting beside it, says, *Beach Toys*. Boxes of rusty pots and pans, dishes, cutlery, and jugs. Lamps without their sockets, tatty carpets, silvered mirrors; the amount of junk is endless. There's a dining room table in the far corner, and a row of at least twenty wooden chairs hanging from hooks that begin at the shed doors and disappear into the recesses of the building.

Bedframes lean against one side of the back wall, and a stack of end tables are balanced precariously in front of them making me think that when anyone was buying new furniture, they gave their used stuff to Cecelia.

On another wall there's a long shelf organized with hammers, screwdrivers, wrenches, and tools. Cans and boxes also line the shelves and I peer inside to see nails and screws so thick with rust and cobwebs after fifty years of disuse, they're almost unrecognizable. Shovels, rakes, hoes, saws, scythes, and axes of all sizes hang from hooks on the opposite wall. A lone canoe, the only thing that doesn't seem to have a duplicate, is resting in the rafters, draped in cobwebs like a lacy shawl. I begin pulling boxes out, at first looking inside each one, then, not finding much of value, start stacking them on the ground outside, to be thrown into the dumpster tomorrow.

An hour later and the sun about to set, I've cleared a path to the back of the shed and am standing in the dark, shining my flashlight on multiples of picnic tables, each tipped on its side and leaning against the wall. They're the old-fashioned kind with two-by-fours nailed onto crisscrossed legs and attached benches of the same size wood, once stained a lustrous dark brown, but now peeling to the point there is more bare wood than stain left. Hanging above the tables are four Adirondack chairs, at one time painted red, but now, like the tables, much of the paint is chipped or worn away. I tip one of the tables to its legs, drag it down the path I've cleared, then outside to get a better look at it in the fading light. I give it a wiggle. It seems sturdy enough, isn't missing any planks, and I decide that with a bit of sanding and painting, tightening a couple of screws, this is something I could use. I haul the table to the front yard, working up a sweat even in the cold air as I tug it over tree roots and saplings, then slide it into place where I'll have the best view of the lake where no trees blocking my line of sight. I go back to the shed and drag a chair to the front yard, then get the broom from the back porch. I pour myself a glass of wine, leaving the lights on when I return to the front yard, reminding myself to tell Wilson I want an outside light and a socket installed out here.

After sweeping the cobwebs off the furniture, I slide into the chair and look up. The sun has set and the sky is turning black. A shooting star passes over the yard. I make a wish. "Please let me do this without making a fool of myself," I whisper to the night. I turn towards Missy's cabin, hoping to invite her over to join me for a glass of wine, but I see no lights through the bushes; perhaps she's an early to bed, early to rise kind of person. I finish my drink, then with exhaustion overcoming me, I decide it's time for me to go to bed as well. I climb the worn-out front step, put on my pyjamas, then lie down on my air mattress in the same room Cecelia likely slept, surprisingly content lying in this tumble-down cabin, and close my eyes.

—

I fall asleep immediately, the complete darkness and the lack of noise allowing me to sleep more soundly than I've slept in years. I don't wake up until four in the morning, then lie here for half an hour, my brain churning with thoughts of all the chores I have to do today. Finally, unable to fall back asleep, I get up to look out the living room window. The sky is clear and I wish I could see the lake, but there are too many trees and shrubs blocking the view. Without a second thought as to whether I should or shouldn't, I enter the porch, pull on my winter coat, step into my new work boots, pick up my flashlight and climb the stairs. I slide the plywood away, then walk down the narrow hall towards the front bedroom. I step as close as I dare to the edge to look at the lake from the second floor.

It's clear and cold, though calmer than it was during the day, with not a leaf bending to the wind. In the dark, the shoreline is a sculpture of broken ice, and the water, with patches of ice still floating on its surface, is reflecting multiple jagged patterns of the stars and moon. I switch off my flashlight so I can see better. As I watch, a deer emerges from the side of the cabin and steps into view. Instinctively, I stand still, afraid any movement will scare it away. The animal sniffs the air, before lifting its head in my direction. I try not to breathe, but it must sense my presence, and runs into the bush towards the beach.

I wait by the would-be window, holding my coat tight under my chin, hoping to see another deer, when to my surprise, not an animal, but a human figure emerges from the bushes. She steps up to the picnic table and rubs a hand over the surface. My breath catches in my throat when I think it's the ghost of Cecelia come to look at the table that must have been hers, until I see a braid, poking out from under her sunhat, the gray glinting in the moonlight like silver strands of a necklace hanging down her back, and realize it's not a ghost, but Missy. I don't call out for fear of scaring her, but instead watch as she sits in the chair, rubbing her hands down the wooden arms, then as she's done before, disappear into the bushes, taking the same path the deer took. I'm surprised at her boldness for coming into my yard, but if she's lived out here alone for all these years, she'd be used to having the run of the place. A moment later, she's reappeared on the beach in front of the Vereschuk's cabin. She's looking across the ice when the deer walks by, seemingly not worried by her presence. I watch a few moments longer, then feeling guilty for intruding on her privacy, I descend the stairs, slide the plywood over the hole and go back to bed with the intention of getting up in an hour.

Chapter 11

The next time I wake up, it's to the sound of someone pounding on my back door. With stiff muscles, I climb to my feet, throw on my housecoat, then look at my bedside clock; 7:30.

"Her car's here," I hear someone say through the thin wood. "Maybe she's gone for a walk, or to the beach."

"We could start with the shower," someone else says. "That'll eat up some time until she gets back."

I yank open the door to see the faces of three men. Two of them appear to be in their late twenties to early thirties, while one looks like he's barely twenty, though telling people's ages is getting harder and harder the older I become. I pull my hands through the tangled mess of my hair attempting to look more presentable.

"Morning," I say. "Sorry, I must have slept in."

The two older men are grinning as they look me in the eye, the third is looking in the other direction, uncomfortable in the presence of someone old enough to be his grandmother, dressed in her pyjamas and housecoat, yesterday's mascara smeared down to her chin.

"That's okay, Ma'am," one of the older men says.

The first time someone called me Ma'am, I had just turned forty. It was a check-out boy at the grocery store and he asked, *Do you want paper or plastic, Ma'am?* At first it shocked me to hear him use that word, as I didn't feel old enough to be called Ma'am, until I realized people saw me differently than I saw myself.

He places his hand on his chest. "Name's Blair. This is Jim," he points to the guy standing to the right of him. Jim puts two fingers to his forehead and salutes me; I notice a wedding ring. "And this shy guy," Blair pats the shoulder of his younger companion, "is Darren." Darren looks at his boots. "You want us to wait in the truck while you, uh, get cleaned up?" His eyes twinkle and I think he likely has girls at his beck and call.

"No, no," I say, self-conscious under the stare of this man who's younger than my son. "You can start taking furniture out while I get dressed. Won't take more than a few minutes."

"Wilson sent us out with a shower," he says. "We'd like to get that set up first if you don't mind."

"A shower?" I ask.

He walks to the bed of his truck which is loaded down with equipment. "It's called a gravity shower," he says over his shoulder. "People use 'em when they're camping, that kind of thing." He lifts a plastic bag out of the back, then returns to the porch and hands it to me. "You just fill that bag with lake water and let the sun heat it up. Or you can fill it with the water you bought at Carnation's," he points to the jugs by the cookstove. "Though that's kind of an expensive way to shower. Lake water is free."

"Will it heat up in this weather?"

"For sure." He taps the bag in my hand. "As long as the bag is in the sun, it'll get warm. Then you hang it from the hook and voila, your own shower. Bought you the deluxe model. There's a valve so you can turn it on and off." He demonstrates how to use the valve. "Wilson said the plumbing in the bathroom won't be in good enough shape to hang this inside; said the septic is likely cracked. We brought out some wood to build a shelter for it, you know, so you'd have some privacy?" Again, he steps out of the porch and into the yard. "Which cabin are you staying in?" He scans the cabins, each one looking worse than the one before. "We'll build it close to where you're going to live."

"Over there," I say, pointing to the last cabin in the row.

"We'll get that septic tank unhooked and the pipe capped today so the cabin won't smell. Just keep the doors and windows open for a while, should air it out, if that's okay with you?"

"That's okay with me," I say. "And thank you."

"No problem. The three of us will put together the shower, shouldn't take too long, then we'll get started on taking out the furniture. Sound good?"

"Sounds good," I say.

He gives me the thumbs up, then they begin taking wood out of the back of the truck and hauling it across the yard towards the Honeymoon Suite.

Feeling my back ache from sleeping on the air mattress, I close the door on their youthful enthusiasm, then fill a basin with water to wash my face and brush my teeth. I pull on the same clothes I wore yesterday, walk to the beach with the shower bag in hand, break the thin ice at the shore, and fill the bag as Blair instructed. I lay it on the picnic table to get warm, hopeful that by this evening, after everyone has left, I can take a shower.

I'm in the kitchen making a pot of coffee to the sounds of saws and hammers, when I hear a voice. "Ruby, are you in here?"

I open the door and see my real-estate agent standing on the back step. "Chip," I say, happy to see a familiar face. "What are you doing here? Did you forget to tell me something yesterday?"

"No, no," he says. "Bought you a new mattress for that old bed frame, and I had a mini fridge and hot plate kicking around the house. Thought I'd bring them out, then stay to help you clean up the Honeymoon Suite."

"You brought me a mattress and a fridge?" I say. "You didn't have to do that. I'm sure that's far more than you do for your other clients."

"Other clients didn't inherit a hundred acres of land at a northern lake. Besides, I think I like it out here." He takes a deep breath then coughs and pounds his chest. "Fresh air will do me good." He folds a piece of gum into his mouth as he turns to look at the men laughing and shouting at each other. "What are they doing?" he says over the noise of the saws and hammers.

"Building me a shelter for my gravity shower," I say. "Wilson's idea apparently, since I won't have a bathroom for a number of weeks."

"Really. That's surprising. Guess you shouldn't judge a book by it's cover. Now, if you can put on that coffee," he nods towards the kitchen, "I've worn my work boots." I look at his feet; the expensive shoes are gone and expensive work boots take their place.

While I fill a tray with coffee cups and cream and sugar, Chip strings the extension cords I bought at Carnation's, across the yard, and moves the space heater, the bar fridge, and my floor lamp to the Honeymoon Suite.

By the time the guys have the shower stall built, the septic tank disconnected, and the cabin emptied of furniture, Chip and I have my little cabin disinfected and scrubbed, the old icebox removed and the fridge put in its place, and the mattress on the bedframe. The shed has been emptied and we've made two piles in the back-yard: one to keep, and one to throw away. I'm rifling through a box to see if it's for the keep or throw away pile, when a large piece of paper blows out, twists through the air, then wraps itself around a tree, its edges flapping in the breeze. Chip untangles it from the trunk and holds it in front of his face.

"Whoa," he says, passing it to me. "This might be something you want to keep. Maybe it's a map to some hidden treasure."

I take the paper from him, holding it in front of my face. "This looks like floorplans to this cabin."

"You know how to read floorplans?"

"I do," I say, "Well, kind of. My dad was an architect."

When I was young, to keep myself involved in Dad's life, I would sneak into his office when he was out of town, and study whatever he happened to have clipped to his drawing board. It was always something different; a shopping mall, an office building, houses, libraries, museums. I was good at math, and easily learnt how to draw windows, doors, and stairs, calculating proportion and scale. I'd look through his architecture books, teaching myself about load bearing walls, circulation, balustrades, headers, roof lines and bay windows. Then I'd go back to my room and practice drawing the floorplans of houses I'd like to live in, hoping one day I could be an architect too. I even left a drawing clipped to Dad's easel, hoping he'd notice and give me some encouragement, or praise. But he never mentioned it to me, either to criticize or commend, and I never saw that floorplan again.

I look up from the drawing; Chip, Darren, Blair, and Jim, are tossing the items from the throw away pile, onto the truck, joking with each other, having contests about who can throw the furthest or the highest. Figuring I'd only get in the way if I tried to help, I take the floorplans to the front yard and spread the paper out on the picnic table, pinning the edges down with rocks. I bend over the page thinking about how Cecelia, even through all the adversity she faced: having had to give up her baby, the depression, and the chauvinistic attitude of men, made her dream come true. If she could accomplish all she did, with all she had going against her, surely, I can handle living in a musty cabin for a few weeks while others renovate this cabin for me.

On the back of the floor plan is a drawing of the grounds and cabins. The colours are still vibrant, likely not having seen daylight for the past eighty-six years.

I scour the page looking for a signature or a date. Architects always date their sketches, sometimes more than once as they go through the process of designing. In the bottom right-hand corner, to my surprise, I find the initials C. J., with the date, 06/04/31. Cecelia drew this herself, and, according to the date, she'd planned the resort before she even broke ground for this cabin, before she even hired Gerry. From the very beginning, she knew that the resort was going to be her way of making a living.

—

By three in the afternoon, the guys have all the things I don't want, thrown into the dumpster, and the things I want to keep, stowed in the shed. Wilson pulls into the yard with a porta potty on the back of his truck, and places it next to Cecelia's cabin. He disappears inside the cabin to measure the top floor, then returns outside to measure the space beside the kitchen where the addition will be built, writing all his calculations down in his pad. When he's done, he talks to his crew, then leaves without talking to me. Blair approaches.

"Boss said it's quitting time. Be back tomorrow at seven-thirty in the AM if that's ok with you?" he says, teasing me about being in bed when they arrived this morning.

"I'll be up," I say.

"Think I'll head out as well," Chip says. "You going to be okay finishing this up yourself?"

"I'll be fine. You go. All I have left to do is put my dishes in the cupboards and make my bed. If my plan is to live out here year-round, I need to get used to being here alone. Thanks for everything, you've done more than you needed to do. I owe you a beer."

"It's a deal," he says.

I watch the four of them drive away with a feeling of loneliness. They may be loud and sometimes crass, but it sounded nice to have people out here enjoying what Cecelia built; something that hasn't happened for five decades.

For the next hour, I stack two plates, bowls, glasses, wine glasses, and coffee mugs, the only thing I brought more than two of, into the cupboards Chip and I scrubbed this afternoon. Cutlery is nestled in the only drawer and a coffee pot and toaster are crammed together on the counter top. The hot plate sits on top of the broken stove with two pots crowded on the crooked burners, and every time I walk, they clank together. Towels are squished on one towel rack in the bathroom, and all three water bottles I bought at Carnation's, fit snugly in the shower that won't be used. My cooler is on the tiny table, and my sleeping bag is unrolled on the new mattress, my clothes hanging in the tiny closet, and stuffed into the three-drawer dresser that somehow escaped the wrath of the teenagers. There is still the scent of sewer, but not as strong as it was yesterday. Hopefully, after I air the place out, it will disappear altogether.

When I'm done, I stand on the front step and look inside, glad I'm not a claustrophobic person, hopeful I don't have to live here for too long. A gust of wind blows behind me and I think I hear someone speaking softly in my ear. I turn, thinking Chip or one of the guys has returned to play a joke on me, but no one's there. Shaking my head at my overactive imagination, I switch on my space heater, take a shower, have a sandwich, then shivering, crawl into bed at nine o'clock and don't get up until seven.

1932

Cecelia and I stand at the waters edge, our backs to the lake admiring the finished cabin. "It's beautiful, Gerry," she says, "more than I could have imagined."

"It is," I say even though I have my eyes closed as I breathe in her sweet smell.

"My next project is refurbishing the Vereschuk cabin," Cecelia says. "Do you think a family would want to rent it for the summer?"

"Maybe," I say.

She looks at me and I can see the hopefulness in her eyes.

"Of course they would," I say. "Who wouldn't want to spend a holiday here. I mean, look at this place, it's beautiful."

"When I bought this land," Cecelia says, "my plan was to fill it with cabins and rent them out so I don't have to be indebted to my father anymore. I want to make my own way in the world. Refurbishing the Vereschuk cabin is just the beginning, Gerry, just you wait and see!"

Chapter 12

At seven-thirty, I'm standing at the porch window Chip and I cleaned yesterday, watching as Wilson arrives behind the wheel of his half-ton truck, the truck-bed loaded with tools. Jim is behind him driving a flatbed with a backhoe and bobcat on the back, and Blair follows driving a dump truck. At the back of the trio is a flatbed truck with the logo, *The Garbage Guys,* painted on their door, the back loaded with two dumpsters which they squeeze between the trees in the backyard as close to the cabin as they can. Darren arrives last driving his own vehicle and parks in the backyard of the Vereschuk's cabin, as far away from the other vehicles as he's able. Wilson climbs out of his truck and crosses the yard to the Honeymoon Suite. He enters without knocking.

"Mrs. Phillips," he says. "I see you've got the cabin cleaned up. That's good because we're knocking down that second storey today. Not safe inside." He whips a piece of paper from his coat pocket. "Here's a list of what I'm going to do and the total cost of the renos." I take the paper. At the bottom of the page, circled in red is the number, $190,000. "Ordered the wood for the addition and the second floor yesterday," he says. "They're delivering next week. I've hired a man to take out some trees. I need a place to stack the lumber and bring machinery into the yard. As it is, we couldn't get those things," he points at the dumpsters, "as close as we wanted." He passes me a stack of binders. "Samples of hardwood, linoleum, tile, countertops, and cupboards."

"You want me to pick these out?"

"Your cabin, Miss. I don't know your taste, and I'm too busy. Don't need to know yet, but I figure women take a long time picking out such things so thought I'd get them to you early. Next couple of weeks should do. They could take a month to come in." He taps the flooring book. "You'll want to stay away from wood for the bathroom floor. Ceramic tile, laminate, or linoleum only. Other than that, anything in any of these books will work." He steps outside then points at my car parked beside the shed. "And move your car. It's in the way."

"How long do you think I'll be living here, in this cabin?" I call to his retreating back.

"Until I tell you we're done," he says over his shoulder. Then with a sigh, he turns. "Three months at the very least, likely longer, depending on what we come up against. Just make sure you stay out of the way, wouldn't want you to get hurt."

Darren walks past with a tray of coffees and a box of donuts.

"You might have time for coffee and donuts," Wilson says without taking anything, "but I've got work to do," and I wonder why he's being so rude.

I take a coffee and a donut, tell Darren thank you, then head to the shed to look for a spade, with the intent of tackling the bushes in the front yard. I'm closing the double doors of the shed, when I pass Wilson, Blair, and Jim, heading towards the cabin. Wilson grunts as we pass, Blair winks and says *Hi beautiful*, and Jim, once again, gives me a two-finger salute. I've no idea where Darren has gone.

I'm in the front yard, trying to push the shovel into the root filled ground beneath a dead rose bush, when studs, plastic, and old pieces of plywood begin to sail off the roof and land in one of the dumpsters, whose lid yawns open like a gateway to hell. The noise is loud enough to wake the dead and I look towards Missy's cabin, hoping we aren't disturbing her. As if on cue, I see her through the bushes, watching the men work.

"Missy," I call. "Come and see."

She shakes her head.

"It's okay." I wave my hand, urging her forward, but she stays where she is.

"Mrs. Phillips," Wilson calls from the roof. "What do you want done with the toilet, sink, and tub? They've never been used."

"I think I'd like to buy new; teal isn't the colour scheme I'm looking for. Unless you'd like them?" I ask Missy.

"No," Wilson says. "I don't need them."

"I wasn't talking to you," I say. "I was asking Missy." I turn to talk to her, but the woman has once again left without saying a word.

Wilson looks in my direction for a moment longer, then pulls his head back and disappears into the maze of old wood and plastic.

Over the next two hours, the top floor is disassembled, while I manage to dig out exactly two rose bushes.

"You want some help?" a voice says behind me.

I turn to see Darren.

"If you like, I could grab the bobcat and dig up the scrub. Can't do the trees, of course, leave that up to the tree guy, but all of this," he points at the straggly rose bushes, poplars, and evergreen saplings blocking my view, "I can get rid of in no time. I've finished my jobs, and the bobcat won't be needed until Jim breaks ground with the backhoe for the trench."

"Wilson must be glad to have someone working for him who's so industrious."

"Mostly I get the grunt work," he says. "Raking up the ground where we were building your shower, unloading the truck, setting mouse traps, sweeping up the mouse droppings. Not the most glamorous jobs but Wilson doesn't trust me to put the jacks under the cabin, or dig the trench. Surprised he let me build the shower."

"Won't you get into trouble helping me?"

"Been in trouble before, one more time won't hurt me. I'll dig 'em up, then all you have to do is load them into one of those wheelbarrows you have in the shed and toss them into the dumpster. I'll clear in front of the cabin you're staying in too. May as well enjoy the view if you're going to be living there for a few months."

While I grab a wheelbarrow, Darren jumps onto the bobcat and forty-five minutes later he has the brush, suckling trees, shrubs and roots dug up and pushed into a pile in front of both cabins. I stand amid the mess and admire the view of the lake, albeit, still covered in ice.

"Pretty, isn't it?" Darren says. "Surprised more people haven't bought property around this lake."

"I think most people think I'm a crazy old woman for doing this."

"Well," he says, "in my opinion you'd have to be crazy *not* to want to live out here." He loads his arms with the dead bushes and presses them into the wheelbarrow. "Sorry Wilson is so gruff," he says quietly. "His dad was an angry man, volatile, if you know what I mean. Could explode at the drop of a hat. Didn't set a good example for his kid."

"I suppose every family has its troubles."

"You going to stand there all day and flap your jaws, doing things that aren't on our schedule?" Wilson is standing on the front step, his hands on his hips. "This job is going to take long enough without you stopping for coffee breaks all the damn time." Darren's face turns red, as does mine.

—

By four in the afternoon, the top floor has been demolished, and the kitchen gutted. The old swimming pool, water and septic tanks have been removed, and the spot where the addition is going to be built, has been cleared and staked out. There's a four-foot-deep trench around the perimeter of the cabin, and steel posts lie at the bottom.

I'm sitting in the backyard of the Honeymoon Suite, amazed at all the work that got done in one day, waving goodbye to Blair, Jim, and Darren, when Wilson approaches. "We're done for the day." He looks at his watch. "Likely be done this time every day unless something happens to interrupt the schedule. That's an eight-hour work day with a half-hour lunch break, Monday through Friday.

That okay with you?"

"That's fine. Can I give you a progress payment?" I ask.

He looks surprised.

"My dad was an architect," I explain. "I heard contractors talking in our house all the time. What would you like? Forty, fifty?"

"Let's not get ahead of ourselves," he says. "Twenty will do."

I write him a cheque for twenty-thousand; he takes it without saying thank you. "If you go inside, which I figure you're going to do as soon as you see our taillights in the dust, don't touch anything, and don't go up those stairs; they might be stable, but the top floor certainly isn't. There's nothing up there to look at anyhow." He pulls a notebook out of his pocket and reads his list to me. "Tree man will be here in the morning. Tomorrow, Wednesday, and Thursday, we'll be taking out the fireplace, and jacking up the cabin then cementing in the posts. On Friday we'll level the ground under the cabin with back fill. Monday we'll lower the cabin onto the posts, fill in the trench and frame the floor for the addition. We'll pour the cement floor on Tuesday." He shoves his list back in his pocket.

"Sounds like a plan," I say, finishing my glass of wine and smiling up at his stern face.

He eyes my empty glass. "I've got a couple of two by eights strung across the trench. Be careful you don't fall over the edge when you go inside. Ladders been pulled up for the night. Fall in, you're there until morning."

"I'll try," I say, my sarcasm lost on him.

He turns, and without saying goodbye, gets behind the wheel of his truck and drives away.

The moment they're out of sight, I stand and make my way across the two-by-eights without falling in, and enter the cabin. With the little bit of light filtering through the dirty windows, and dust motes thick in the air from ripping out cupboards and the demolition of the second floor, the place is as dim as if I were looking through a dense fog. The kitchen has been emptied and I wonder where they put the cookstove until I remember, just before quitting time, I saw Darren and Wilson lugging it to the shed, Wilson berating Darren with every step. On the wall behind where the upper cupboards hung, I see the original green colour, as bright as if it were painted yesterday, and on the floor beneath where the lower cupboards sat, the wood has retained its dark brown stain; still glossy after all this time.

I'm in the living room, facing the old fireplace, imagining sitting in front of my new fireplace enjoying a glass of wine, when out of the corner of my eye, I see something flutter on the kitchen floor. I turn, praying it isn't a mouse or a snake, and squint through the dust towards where the cookstove sat for eighty years. I see something, but at this distance I can't discern what it is and take a few hesitant steps forward. After deciding it likely isn't an animal, I enter the kitchen then bend forward to take a closer look. It's money, but different than the money we use today. I pick it up and see that it's a one-hundred-dollar bill. An old one-hundred-dollar bill, the paper kind I remember from when I was a girl, or perhaps even older. I flip it over, not understanding how money as old as this, and in such a large denomination could have gotten here. Perhaps Jim, Blair, or Darren is a collector and it fell out of their pocket? But you wouldn't think they would bring something this valuable here, to a worksite, where it could be easily lost. I shove it in my pocket with the intention of asking the guys about it tomorrow, then leave the cabin thinking I'll walk to Missy's and ask her back for a glass of wine. But when I look through the bushes, her lights are out once again.

1933

"What are you doing?" I ask Cecelia when I enter her cabin and see her stuffing something in the warming drawer of the cookstove. "It's ninety degrees out there. We don't need a fire."

"Not building a fire," is all she says.

"Are you hiding money again?" I ask. "You know you should put it in the bank."

"My father said the bank he's dealt with all these years has closed, taking most of his fortune with it," Cecelia says. "He can't afford to send me money anymore. Been thinking about turning my money into something other than cash; something that increases in value. I'm thinking of investing in gold. What do you think, Gerry? Do you think it's a good idea?"

Chapter 13

In the morning, I'm awakened by the sound of saws, hammers, and the voices of men kibitzing with each other, as men seem to be able to do with no hard feelings.

I would like to go and see what they're doing, but remembering Wilson's advice of staying out of the way, I decide to make my breakfast instead. I'm scrambling an egg on the hotplate Chip has lent me, when there's a knock at the door.

"Come in," I say. Darren sticks his head inside.

"Morning, Mrs. Phillips," he says.

"Please, Darren, call me Ruby. Mrs. Phillips makes me feel old. Did you lose something yesterday?" I ask.

"Lose something?" he says.

"I found some money in the cabin last night."

"No, Ma'am, not me. The crew on Wilson's team never carry cash with them; one of Wilson's rules." He points at the man with him. "This is the tree guy. Wilson said you're to show him around the property so he can decide what trees need to come down. I'd better get back before Wilson gives me heck." I look towards the men standing beside the trench and see Wilson laughing with Jim and Blair.

"Hello," I say after Darren has gone. "Ruby Phillips." I shake the man's hand.

"Ernie Stabler," he says.

Ernie Stabler is tall and lanky, his hands hanging to his knees, and his hips higher than my waist. If ever there was someone perfectly suited to their job, it would be Ernie. I can just imagine him climbing a tree like a monkey. For all his lankiness, he moves with grace, arms swinging slightly by his sides, feet touching the ground with the lightness of a dancer.

As efficient as Ernie is in movement, he's also a man of few words. By the time I'm done touring him around the yard, he's marked six trees with the numbers one through six, all while barely uttering a sentence. The first tree is near the staked-out land where the new addition is going to be built, and marked with the number 1. Two are on the south side of the yard between the Vereschuk's cabin and mine, each sporting the numbers 2/3. Another one is next to the trench, again on the south side and marked with a 4, and the last two are in the backyard, each marked with a 5/6.

"Why the different numbers?" I finally ask, breaking the silence between us.

"Order they come down. One," he says, pointing to the tree growing between the staked-out addition and the lake. "Two and three." He points to the two trees growing on the south side between my place and the Vereschuk's. "Four," he swivels to the tree nearest the trench, also on the south side. "That one will be the easiest, fell it directly towards the water." Then lastly, he points to the trees in the backyard, "five and six."

"Why did you mark those two with two and three and those two with five and six?"

"Depends on the widow-makers."

"Widow-makers?"

"Detached branches that are tangled with non-detached branches. You cut in the wrong place and that loose branch will come out of the blue and kill you before you know what's happened. I've seen some gruesome accidents in my day." He cranes his neck back and looks up the trunk. "I won't know which one to take down first until I climb up and look. First four should take me most of tomorrow. I'll be here at sunrise, done around suppertime. Finish up the two in the backyard by Friday at noon. That'll get me out of the way before the lumber arrives next week. The rest of the property I'll do this summer. Some of the bigger trees need to come down before they fall on their own."

———

The next morning, I'm up at the crack of dawn with my coffee, waiting for Ernie to arrive. Wilson said he and the boys wouldn't start until ten today to give Ernie time to get the first tree nearest the worksite down, but they'd stay until six without a lunch break to get in their eight hours of work.

I'm enjoying the view of the lake, warming my hands around my cup, when I turn at the sound of a truck driving up. A moment later Ernie's long legs stride around the side of the cabin.

He's wearing an orange jumpsuit and his arms are loaded down with ropes, cables, belts, and harnesses. He has on a helmet with the visor pushed back, and noise cancelling head phones on the helmet. The man accompanying him is carrying a chainsaw.

"Morning, Ernie," I say. "You need a lot of equipment."

"Can't be too careful," he says. He points his chin towards his companion. "This is Byron."

Byron nods at me as his eyes dart around the property.

"You're welcome to watch," Ernie continues, "but I need you out of the way."

I position my lawn chair in the front yard of the Honeymoon Suite, far enough away to prevent a tree falling on me, but close enough so I can still see. Because of the curve of the shoreline, from here I have a clear view all the way to the Vereschuk's cabin.

Byron has placed the equipment at the base of the first tree to be taken down, and is busy dragging the picnic table and Adirondack chair out of the way.

Ernie stands beneath the tree and picks up a branch and draws a large half circle around the roots on the side facing the lake. "Drop zone," he says to Byron. He attaches a weight to the end of a long coil of rope, and standing back, tosses that rope over a branch about twenty feet up the trunk, attaching a carabiner hook at the end. He puts on the harness, then attaches the rope to his harness, steps into his spurs, pulls down the visor on his helmet, then puts on ear protection. He takes the chainsaw Byron is handing him and attaches it to his harness. He looks up the trunk.

"It's free and clear; no widow-makers. I'll limb it from bottom to top."

Byron nods and Ernie digs his spurs into the tree. He stops on a branch just above the first branch. The sound of the saw breaks the silence as he bends forward and cuts off the lower bough, then climbs to the next, and the next, each time, felling the lower limb and dropping it into the circle he drew on the ground. Whenever the saw stops and a branch drops, Byron moves in to pick up the felled bough and drag it to the woodchipper in the backyard. The din of the machinery reverberates through the forest and I look at my watch; 6:30. Good thing Missy is an early riser.

Two hours later, Ernie's reached the apex of the first tree, and now the top is the only thing left spearing the sky. He looks below him to make sure all is clear, then makes a cut on the side of the trunk facing the lake. He gives the trunk a push, the top of the tree creaks, then it topples to the ground, directly into the drop zone.

Byron moves in and takes the trunk to the backyard, stacking it with the logs already piled near the outhouse.

"Firewood," he says to me.

Ernie rappels down the tree, cutting off the trunk piece by piece as he goes, then dropping the log to the ground. Byron retrieves each piece and stacks it next to the outhouse. I see him occasionally peer up the road into the forest, as if looking for something, then rushing back to the front yard to grab another log.

The two of them continue in this manner, Ernie taking the trunk down in pieces, while Byron stacks the wood, until Ernie's back on the ground with only a small portion of stump left poking out of the ground. I hear trucks arriving and look at my watch; ten in the morning.

"Good timing," Ernie says to Wilson. "Should I take out the

stump before I move on?"

"Nah," Wilson says. "Backhoe can cut through those roots." He points at Jim who slides behind the wheel of the backhoe, starts it up, and begins clawing at the roots.

Ernie and Byron coil up their ropes, then move their equipment to the south side of the cabin between the Vereschuk's and my place. Ernie points skyward through the tangle of branches. "That one is limb tied with that one," he says. "I'll climb this tree first," he says, tapping the trunk of the tree closest to him, "find out where the widow-makers are. Drop zone is here." He draws out a circle around the two trees. Then as he did with the first tree, he rigs up one of the trunks, digs in his spurs, and starts his ascent, limbing the free branches as he makes his way to where the branches of the two trees are tangled with each other.

While Jim continues to dig out roots, Wilson, Blair, and Darren move to the back of the cabin, where Wilson directs Blair to descend into the trench, then follows him down the ladder, leaving Darren standing at the top by himself. Over the noise of the chainsaw, backhoe, and woodchipper, I hear Wilson yell at Darren to quit standing around with his hands in his pockets and make himself useful by grabbing a rake and helping Byron.

The work continues, the noise of the machines splitting the silence as Ernie cuts off branches, while Byron uses the woodchipper and Jim operates the backhoe. I decide I've had enough of watching, and get the sample books of flooring, countertops, and cupboards from the Honeymoon Suite, then sit at my picnic table, trying to tune out the noise.

I have my nose buried in the countertops book when I hear Ernie yelling, "Watch out!" from the treetops.

I look up. Byron is pushing Darren to the ground, as a loose branch sails from the tree tops, then careens sideways, piercing into the soil by Byron's feet outside the drop zone.

Ernie rappels down the tree. "You ok, kid?" he asks. "Didn't see that widow-maker until it was already falling."

Darren stands. "I'm fine," he says, brushing dirt off his pants.

"What the hell do you think you're doing?" Wilson has climbed out of the trench and is yelling at Darren. "You just about got some-one killed, for God's sake."

"Take it easy, Wilson. He wasn't in the drop zone," Ernie says. "My fault, not his. I'm usually pretty good at knowing where the tangled branches are going to go, but she decided to misbehave. That's why they call them widow-makers. They like to hide, then jump out and finish you off before you even know that they're there."

"Quit defending him, Ernie," Wilson says. "Kid doesn't know his ass from his elbow."

"It was an accident, Will. These things happen," Ernie says. "Could have just as easily happened to anyone."

"Not on my crew," Wilson says.

Ernie looks up the trunk he just descended, musing on the tree as if it purposely tried to kill someone. "Unforgiving ladies, these old trees," he says. "Had a wife like that once; got joy out of pounc-ing."

Wilson steps close to Darren, talking quietly. When he's fin-ished, he points at Darren's car. "I want you gone; you hear me? Off this worksite. You're done for the day."

Darren doesn't argue.

"Blair will help clear branches," Wilson says to Ernie. "Posts will have to wait until tomorrow."

The tree that stands beside the trench is felled without incident, making an unmistakable sound as it falls directly west, just as Ernie predicted.

—

The next day neither Darren nor Byron shows up to work. "Perhaps one of your crew could clear the logs and operate the chipper for the last two trees?" Ernie asks Wilson. "Byron won't be back and I couldn't find anyone else on such short notice."

1936

"Don't you think you have enough?" I ask when Cecelia tells me she's planning on clearing more land north of the original cabin.

In the past five years, Cecelia and I have become comfortable enough in each other's company that we feel we can talk freely to one another. For example, two years ago, I told her she should consider wearing dresses occasionally, that she might land a man if she prettied herself up, and she told me to go to university and get my degree in business. I graduate next year; I don't think she even owns a dress.

Since we finished her cabin, we've renovated the Vereschuk's and built another one on the other side of hers. They've both been a moderate success, renting out for most of the summer and garnering her a modest living, spurring her on to build more.

She spreads her arms. "I'll call it Sunset Lake Resort. I know, I know," she says, "you think it's a bad idea."

"No," I say. "That's not what I was thinking. Not at all."

"Then what do you think?"

"I think you are the most courageous woman I've ever known. You're never afraid to try something new. And you always jump in with both feet. I just don't want you to bite off more than you can chew. But if I know you, you'll do what you want no matter what I say."

"If it doesn't work, I'll be in the poorhouse."

"If it doesn't work, I say, "I'm quite sure you'll figure something else out. But it will work. This depression isn't going to last forever; we just need to be patient."

"Right?" she says, her voice hopeful. "And when its over, people are going to be itching to spend, itching to take their families on holidays, itching to get away from their daily grind and try something new. And this is where they'll come, just you wait and see."

Chapter 14

Darren doesn't return until Friday. Since the renovations began, at the end of each workday, the guys have tidied up the yard by putting the tools and whatever else they can fit into the shed, the remainder piled on a pallet with a tarp cinched over top. Without Darren to help this past week, the work took them right until quitting time today, so the yard hasn't been cleaned up. Jim and Blair are driving away when Wilson walks up to Darren.

"We're going out for a beer. You're staying to clean this up. If you don't," he says when Darren starts to protest, "you'll get docked another day's pay. And since you've already lost three days, you're lucky I'm even letting you back on the worksite." He points around him. "I want this yard spic and span." He heads to his own truck then follows Blair and Jim down the road, shooting gravel in all directions. Darren slouches across the yard and begins carrying equipment to the shed.

"Hi," I say. "You okay?"

"I'm alright," he says.

"You weren't invited out with the others?"

"Probably wouldn't have gone anyhow. Don't really fit in with those guys."

"Do you need help?" I ask.

"I'd better do it myself," he says. "Wouldn't want to get you into trouble."

"No one's here to see and I won't tell. Come on, I've been sitting on my butt all week. I need some exercise."

"Thanks," he says as he hands me a box of nails and a couple hammers.

"Missed you the past few days," I say, when I get back from the shed.

"You're the only one," he says.

"You weren't scheduled to work?"

"I was."

"Oh," I say.

"Look," he says. "You saw what happened, you heard what Wilson said. I'm a loser and have been one all my life. I guess I'm lucky he kept me on. If I wasn't his son, I imagine I'd have been canned."

"You're Wilson's son?" I say.

"I am."

"Well, that explains a lot."

"Does, doesn't it?" he snorts.

"You don't call him Dad."

"He told me not to. Said on the job he's Wilson. The first time I call him Dad he won't answer. Second time, he'll fire me."

I'm quiet for a few moments. "Have you worked for your dad before?"

"I usually get on with other crews for the summer, and truthfully, he usually doesn't ask me to work for him. But he couldn't get enough guys to come out here, so he asked me. Most are afraid because the place is supposed to be haunted. Been a few accidents out here over the years. People tripping over logs and breaking their arms, near drownings, there was even someone who fell into one of the old outhouses. Friends rescued him, thank God. When Dad asked me if I'd work for him this summer, I hadn't got on with anyone else yet, so," he picks up an armload of unused lumber and stacks it on the pallet, "I sais yes."

"You're not afraid of ghosts?"

"Only ghosts out here are the memories of my dysfunctional relatives."

"Hopefully parenting gets better as generations pass," I say.

He laughs to himself. "If I didn't need the money, I wouldn't be working for my father, I can tell you that."

"What are you saving up for? A new car?"

"University. Third year."

"Oh!" I say, surprised at the answer. "What are you taking?"

"Nursing."

"Wow. Good for you. That's a job with a calling if ever there was one."

"If I don't make some money this summer, I won't be able to finish. I worked all through high school and saved up enough for the first two years, but I still have two years left, and Dad won't lend me the money. If I was taking something like law, or agriculture, something that he considers as a job for men, he'd dole out the money. But for nursing, he won't give me a dime."

"That's just silly," I say. "Men can be nurses. Just like women can be doctors."

"Tell Dad that. No, on second thought, don't. He'll criticize me for crying on your shoulder. Says real men don't complain, or bare their souls. Especially to women."

"I'm sorry," I say. "What about a student loan? Do governments still do that?"

"They do, but because I live at home, I can't get a loan; government says my dad makes too much money. And I can't move out because I can't afford it."

"Maybe it's none of my business," I say, "but what did Wilson say to you that made you so angry you didn't come into work all week?"

"You don't wanna know," he says.

"I wouldn't have asked if I didn't want to know," I say.

"He told me I was an embarrassment, and if I want to keep working for him, I'd better grow up and start acting like a man. Nothing I've not heard before."

"But it wasn't your fault. You heard Ernie; it was a freak accident, could have happened to anyone."

"But it happened to me, not to anyone else, me. Trouble is, I'm always making mistakes, and he always notices. It's as if he's waiting to pounce."

"Why?"

"Because…."

"Because why?"

"Because my mom died when I was born, okay? Because of me, he doesn't have a wife. He's never forgiven me."

"I'm so sorry, Darren, I didn't know."

"I've been a loser since the day I was born. Twenty years of not doing anything right."

"He didn't just lose a wife," I say. "You lost your mother."

He shrugs. "Didn't know her; don't know what I lost."

"What does your dad want?" I ask. "For you to be grown up by the time you're twenty? I'm in my sixties and still growing up. I think it never stops until the day we die. And you're going to university! You've got your future planned."

"He has no respect for what I've chosen as my life's work. By the time Dad was twenty-one, he was partner in a construction company. He didn't get married until he was forty, didn't have me until his mid-forties; too busy making money."

"I suppose everyone's idea of success is different," I say. "My husband liked money too."

"He's dead?"

"We're separated. He left shortly after we read my dad's will. Steve thought I'd inherit a fortune, but all my dad left me was this place. Left his young wife of three years, ten million."

"You inherited all one-hundred acres?" Darren says.

"I did."

"Well," he says. "You got the good end of that deal. I'd love to inherit a place like this. That's my dream. To buy some land in the country. Do you have kids," he asks. "Or grandkids? They might like coming up here."

"I do. My son Robert, he's my oldest, is married with twin boys, Bruce, and Michael. His wife's name is Sheryl. She's a stay-at-home mom. Lovely woman, though I don't know how she puts up with my son. He's a banker. Always giving me advice about investing and interest rates; everything I know nothing about. Then there's Jessica, my middle child. She's a librarian. And Debby, my youngest is pursuing a career in the tech industry. She's in IT, whatever that is, and works for the government. I don't ask what it all involves because I wouldn't understand her if she told me."

"You're going to live out here by yourself?"

"All during my marriage, whenever I was asked what I wanted for my birthday, I always said I wanted a cabin at a lake. My husband always said we couldn't afford it."

"So, now you have your own cabin at the lake," Darren says.

"So, now I do," I say.

Chapter 15

I open the fridge and bump Robert's elbow with the door. He frowns but says nothing. Then I reach over Debby's head to take the wine glasses and mugs out of the cupboard. She ducks without taking her eyes off her phone.

"No matter how much you fiddle with that thing," I say, "there's no cell service here."

My youngest tucks her phone into her pocket and sighs. "I don't know how you stand it, it's like the Dark Ages up here."

Half an hour ago I was by the water's edge, marvelling at all the ice that had melted in the last couple of weeks as the lake continued its spring thaw, when it began to snow. I had just returned to my cabin, switched on the heater then curled up on my bed with a book, when I heard a car pull up. Since this is Saturday, I knew it couldn't be Wilson or one of the contract workers he hired—unless he has to, Wilson isn't one to stray from the rules, and workmen don't come out unless he's here to direct them. I looked out the porch window, and was surprised to see my children climbing out of Jessie's car. All four of us are now crammed into a cabin meant for two.

I line up the glasses and mugs on the table. "Sorry, I wasn't expecting company until I got my things out of storage. All I brought in multiples were the mugs in case the crew wanted a cup of coffee. Everything else, I only have two."

"That's okay, Mom," Jessie says. "I can use a mug."

"I'll take a glass. Don't think I could, in all good consciousness, drink wine from a coffee mug," Robert says.

Robert is seated across the kitchen table from Debby and I pour him a glass of wine. He picks it up and has it half guzzled before I've finished filling the other glass for Debby, which makes me think that his sisters dragged him out here under protest.

"So," Robert says, drumming his fingers on the base of his wine glass, "this is where you're living now." He looks around. "Very homey. So much nicer than the house in the city where you had all the amenities and comforts you could ask for. A house that was totally paid for, I might add. Choosing to live," he pauses, "here. Very nice, Mom."

"I think it's kind of cozy," Jessica says, knowing full well her brother was being sarcastic.

"Of course, you're going to say that," Robert says. "Eager to please Jessica."

Jess blushes.

"I'm hoping by next month I'll be living in the house." That's an exaggeration, but I don't want to tell them I'll likely be here until August at the earliest. "And count your blessings, Robert. If it wasn't for these other cabins already being here, I'd have been living with you and driving back and forth."

"I really do like it, Mom," Jess says. "All by yourself, no one to bug you, no obligations. It's small, but it's not like you're hosting Christmas or something."

"When the cabin's finished, I will most certainly host Christmas."

"I can't wait," she says.

Robert sighs and looks out the window, shaking his head at the naivety of his sister and the stupidity of his mother.

"Most of the work to date has gone into levelling the cabin and building the addition."

"The cabin was crooked?" Debby asks.

"It was leaning," I say. "The soil is mostly sand, and the cabin is close to one hundred years old. Next week, Wilson will begin the renovations on the original part of cabin. Either that or start the second storey; depends on the weather."

"You're building a second floor?" Robert says, and his tone implies he thinks I'm spending too much on something that's is a waste of money.

"When these cabins were originally built, outhouses were legal, but in 1960 they were made illegal, so I need a proper bathroom built. I'm putting one as well as two bedrooms on the top floor so when you come to visit, you'll have a place to sleep. Cecelia had started the second floor, but never got it finished."

Robert looks away and I sense visiting me is not at the top of his to-do list.

"Why was the second floor never finished?" Debby asks.

I open my mouth to tell them, but before I can utter a word, Jessie says quietly, "She died."

"Pardon?" Debby says. "Who died?"

"The owner," Jessie says. "She died so never finished the project. Isn't that right, Mom?"

"It is," I say. "How did you know?"

She holds out her fingers, counting them off. "She either ran out of money, got gravely ill, or died. You said she loved this place; I doubt she would abandon her dream unless something horrific happened."

"I've always thought of you as spooky," her sister says. "But that certainly seals the deal."

"Can we look inside?" Jessie asks.

"No sense driving all the way out here without getting the grand tour," I say.

Robert grunts.

"Come on," I stand, wine mug in hand, and gently punch my son in his shoulder. "I'd like to show you what I've planned. You'll love it when it's done."

Robert refills his glass, finishing the bottle, and the four of us step out of the tiny cottage into the snow that's still falling.

The air is mild, and I hold my face to the sky, letting the flakes melt on my cheeks. Jessie puts her arm around my waist. "You seem happy, Mom," she says.

"I am," I say. "Happier than I've been in years." We cross the large yard our arms linked. I open the backdoor of my cabin, flip the switch, turning on Wilson's portable lights, then stop in the kitchen to watch my kids walk through the main floor; their arms wrapped around their waists for warmth as their breath creates clouds of mist in front of their faces.

Suddenly, I'm taken back to the top of a toboggan hill many years ago. It was one of the few times Steve had accompanied us on a family outing and he, Robert, and Jess, had already sailed to the bottom. Then with Debby on my lap, the three of them turned to watch me do the same thing. I was wary, worried about falling off and hurting my child. Steve stood there, his hands on his hips waiting for me to follow them down. I remember seven-year-old Robert intently watching his father, mimicking him with his hands on his hips, and I wanted to tell Steve to quit setting a poor example for his son, but I didn't want to start an argument on what was supposed to be a fun day in the park. Jess, who was five at the time had also noticed her dad and began calling words of encouragement, telling me it was fun, and that if she could do it, so could I, cheering me and her baby sister on. The line behind me had gotten long, so I had to either do this, or embarrass myself, and likely my husband, by leaving the queue. Screwing up my courage, I wrapped my arms around my youngest, counted to ten and closed my eyes before tipping us over the edge. All the way to the bottom, Debby's sweet two-year-old breath created clouds of mist with each giggle and I remember, in that moment, being very happy and proud of myself. Until we arrived at the bottom and Steve commented that perhaps I should go and wait in the car if this was too much for my delicate nature.

"Mom," Jessica says snapping her fingers in front of my face. "Mom, are you with us?"

I shake my head. "What? Sorry. Did you say something?" I ask.

"I asked if there was furniture," Jess says. "In the cabin?"

"There was," I say. "And dishes in the cupboards and bedding on the bed; but nothing worth keeping. It's amazing the damage time can do to things. I did save the cookstove. It's in the shed waiting to be moved back in when everything's finished."

"What all are you doing?" Jessica asks.

I run down the list of renovations, finishing with, "I'm having a balcony constructed outside my room upstairs so I can watch the sunset."

Robert is looking like he has something to say. "I don't get it," he says. "You never got this involved with the house in the city; the house you raised the three of us in, the house you cooked and cleaned and the yard you gardened in for thirty-five years. You said you wanted out because that house was too much work and too much money to make it liveable. Now you're doing all of this?" He crosses his arms over his belly. "I don't understand."

"I suppose I don't, either," I say. "It was a feeling, that's all. I knew the first time I walked in that I wanted to live here. Believe me, I tried to talk myself out of it, wondered if I was making a mistake, thought about simply selling the place. I mean," I look around at all the work left to be done, "who wouldn't? But that first day, even with the mess it was in, I kept on looking, kept on dreaming of living out here. And you guys know that the house in the city was never really mine. I may have been the one to cook and clean and garden there, raise you three, but your dad's the one who bought it, paid all the bills, decided what needed fixing and what we could do without. Here, I'm involved in every aspect of rebuilding. I feel like this house belongs to me."

Robert is moving towards the staircase. He steps on the bottom step and pumps his weight up and down. "Creaks," he says.

"I know. Wilson said he can fix that." Robert takes the stairs two at a time. "You can't go up there," I call. "The floor isn't stable."

"Calm down, Mom," he says. "I'm just going to look." He removes the plywood at the top and sticks his head out before coming back down.

"Come on," I say. "Let's go outside. The ice is just about all gone."

The four of us stand near the shore. No matter what Robert thinks of the cabin, I'm hoping that he can be awed by Mother Nature.

"How did the owner die?" Debby asks. "Or maybe my spooky sister knows the answer."

Jess sticks her tongue out at her sister.

"Actually," I say, "there's two sides to that story. Some say she was working on the second floor in a blizzard, and fell over the edge, bumped her head and died."

"Oh my!" Debby says.

"Then there are those who think she was murdered. She'd already lived up here for over thirty years and she would have known better than to climb up there while it was snowing. Apparently, she was quite the outdoorswoman. They say her ghost still haunts this place."

"That's scary," Jessie says.

"It happened in 1965, and no one's been murdered since. I don't think I'm in any danger now," I say.

"You should do that too, Mom," Jessie says.

"What?" Debby says. "Commit murder? Become a ghost? What?"

Jessie rolls her eyes at her sister. "No, renovate all the cabins, re-open the resort. Haven't you always said you wanted to do something more than be a housewife and mother, haven't you always said you felt unfulfilled? Maybe that's why you felt the need to buy the cabin; to start your own business; it was calling you."

"Oh, come on, Jessica," Robert says. "Even for you that's a bit much."

"I wouldn't have a clue how to do that, sweetie," I say.

"Or the finances to do it," Robert says.

"Robert," Debby says, "you of all people know that Mom could always get money. All she has to do is go to the bank and tell them her plans." She turns to me. "I'm sure they'd give you a loan for something like that, Mom. Better yet, I'll bet there'd even be government grants you could apply for. Beautifying our province or some such thing. Government's always handing out money to entrepreneurs, especially when it can benefit them or benefit the province.

You already have a contractor who lives close by who would likely appreciate more work, and nowadays, learning how to do things is easy. Just google it. I'm sure there's all kinds of information on the web about who to contact if you want to open a resort." She pats her back pocket holding her useless phone. "I'd look it up if there were cell service here."

Robert glares at his sister. "Quit encouraging her," he says.

"Don't worry, Robert," I say. "I have no intention of opening a resort. I moved here for peace and quiet, not to surround myself with more people and more work."

"Does anyone else live up here?" Jess asks.

"Maybe some fishermen or a hunter or two on the other side of the lake, but they're not there all the time, and the cabins are more like shacks. Then there's Missy."

"Missy?"

"I met her a couple of times. Rather, I met her once and have seen her a couple other times. Told me she lives over there," I point towards the beach. "But I don't know if she meant in that old cabin, or across the lake. She's never really been specific. And I've never been to her place, she's only been here."

"You mean she's a squatter?" Robert says.

"If she's in the original cabin, yes, she is living here illegally," I say.

"Kick her out," Robert says. "No one gets a free ride in this world, why should she?"

"I don't want her to leave. It's nice having someone else out here besides me."

"We should walk over and introduce ourselves," Debby says.

I crane my head towards Missy's cabin. "Doesn't look like she's home."

"You can't tell from here," she says. "I'm going." Without waiting to see if anyone is following, she heads across the property. I follow while Jessie and Robert lag back, though I think, each for different reasons.

"I don't think she lives here, Mom," Jessie calls from behind me when we reach the cabin.

"Why?" I say.

She shrugs. "Looks kind of abandoned? No firewood stacked up like there is at your place, no trails in the dirt leading to the cabin. Nothing that would indicate a person lives here or has lived here for a very long time. Not even a car in the yard or tire tracks where she would usually park. Everything's just too, I don't know, neglected to have someone living here."

"I don't think she owns a car," I say. "I've never seen her drive by on her way to town."

"How does she get provisions?" Robert asks.

"You know," I say, "I've never asked. I suppose she must walk. She seems in good shape for someone her age. And the town isn't too far, just a couple of kilometers. I'm sure she could easily walk that distance."

"Have you seen her walk by your place on her way to town?" Robert asks.

"I haven't," I admit. "But I could have been sitting out front and I didn't notice. Or in the bathroom, or having a shower."

"Well," Debby says, "I'm not going to stand here talking about it. I'm going to see if anyone's home." She marches up to the back step and before I can object, has pounded on the door. The noise sounds hollow, as if her knocks are echoing off empty walls. When no one answers, Debby rattles the knob; it's locked. She leans forward to peer through a dirt covered window, then jumps off the step. "Curtains are closed. I'm going to the front, see what I can see from there."

"I don't think this is a good idea," I say, trying to stop her. "We should go."

"Don't be silly, Mom," she says. "All this time and she hasn't asked you to her place. Don't you think that's weird? I mean, you and her are the only ones living out here. You'd think she'd be your best bud by now. Has she ever knocked on your door to ask for a cup of sugar, coffee, anything?"

"Never," I say. "But I think she's pretty self-sufficient having lived here alone for a few years."

"Whether you want to admit it or not, something's fishy and I'm going to find out what," Debby says. She disappears around the corner of the cabin.

Robert stays where he is, glancing at the sky, then at Jess's car behind him as if he's anxious to leave. Jessie takes a couple more steps into the yard then pauses, as if unsure what to do, while I remain between Jessie and the cabin, thinking we shouldn't be here. A moment later my daughter returns.

"Have you never looked inside, Mom?" she asks me.

"I haven't," I say.

"There's no one living here. Front door wasn't locked. I stuck my head in and called her name. Dirt everywhere, moth eaten furniture. No evidence whatsoever that this place is inhabited. Didn't want to go in too far; gave me the heebie-jeebies."

"Maybe she meant she lived in a cabin across the lake," I say. "I was just positive this was the place she pointed to."

"Well, if she does live at this cabin, she's not here now," Debby says. "And having seen inside, I'm pretty sure this isn't the cabin she was talking about. I doubt even a ghost would want to live here."

"I don't know about the rest of you," Robert calls, pointing to the clouds, "but I think we should get going. Looks like more snow is coming and I don't feel like being stuck out here in that tiny cabin with the three of you for the next forty-eight hours."

"He's right, Debby," Jessie says, looking towards the gray sky. "It's time to leave."

We head back to the Honeymoon Suite, with Debby and Robert not giving a backward glance. I turn, and for a fleeting second, see a figure disappear into the bush beside the Vereschuk's cabin.

"What is it, Mom?" Jessie asks. "Did you see something?"

"No," I say. "Did you?"

"I didn't," she says, but her face tells me she did.

1939

"From the frying pan to the fire," Cecelia says.

"What?" I say as I stand on a ladder to change a light bulb in cabin number three.

"First the depression, now the war. All I hear the government saying is to buy war bonds and not spend our disposable income on ourselves. We need customers if we're going to stay in business. How are we supposed to survive?"

"More people have jobs now," I say. "They'll start spending again soon. It'll just take a little while."

"I need to advertise, Gerry, and not only locally, but across the country. More and more families have motorcars. Now that the depression is over, we need to entice them to come here, to try something new. We can't rely on people from around here renting out my cabins all summer long, we need to get people from other parts of the country, hell, from other countries."

"You'll have to get along without me for a few months," I say. "Got my conscription letter yesterday. I ship out next week for Germany."

"Have you told Lila yet?"

"Told Mom last night and she was still bawling this morning. Don't know how to tell my girlfriend."

Cecelia glares at me.

"But I will. Tonight. I promise. I'll tell her tonight."

Chapter 16

The workmen have left for another day and I'm standing in my front yard, looking up at the newly constructed second storey. The inside is far from being finished, but the outside is closed in, the balcony hung and supported on posts, the shingles laid, and the siding finished.

Today, they enclosed the bathroom while Wilson hung the French doors leading to the balcony. And though the plumber has plumbed the entire house, I can't use the bathroom as the fixtures have yet to be installed.

But the outside is done and standing out here, staring up, I can almost imagine myself sitting on the balcony, enjoying the view of the lake. I'm thinking about Missy, when I see her in my peripheral vision, standing in the bushes to my right. "Missy," I say. "Haven't seen you for a long time."

She's quiet as she brushes her weathered hand over a face that shimmers in the dim light of dusk.

"My kids and I walked over for a visit a while back; I wanted to introduce you, but you weren't home. That is where you live? In the original cabin? That's what you told me?"

Still, she says nothing.

"You know," I say, "if you ever need help with anything; yard work, housework, picking up supplies at Carnation's, anything at all, don't hesitate to ask. I could bring them by, if you'll tell me where to drop them off?"

"I don't need any help," she says then turns and walks back towards the Vereschuk's cabin without uttering another word.

"Well," I say to myself, "nice talking to you."

Chapter 17

I used the porta potty just a couple short hours ago, but of course, I have to pee again. That's one of the many troubles about growing older: aching back and knees, stiff hips, and forgetting why I entered a room, to name a few. Hopefully I get a good fifteen years of living out here before my kids insist I move back to the city. I lie here for a few more minutes, wishing the bathroom in the cabin was done, hoping to fall back to sleep and forget about having to pee until morning, but it's no use, my brain won't let go of that thought. Plus, I read somewhere that holding it can weaken the bladder. And with incontinence being a problem among senior women, something that's staring me in the face, I decide I'd better use the facilities before I have to start wearing adult diapers. At least the weather has improved. Getting up at two in the morning to go outside when the air was still cold, was in itself, enough to make me pee, and there were nights I barely made it to the porta potty in time. Tonight, the thermometer hanging outside the kitchen window—that has been there since God knows when—read 50 degrees Fahrenheit at bedtime, much warmer than the ten degrees it was a month ago.

With my eyes closed, I sit up, then drop my feet to the floor. I feel with my toes for my slippers, and stand. Only then do I open my eyes.

It's two-thirty in the morning and, with the cabin being so small, it's easy to see directly from my bed to the black waters of the lake out the living room window. With no other cabins, or street lights, there is no ambient light to make out shapes, and everything looks foreign in the darkness. I slip on my housecoat, fumble for my flashlight on top of the dresser, walk through the tiny kitchen, then open the back door; the sound of the night rushes in.

I've always liked nighttime better than the day. Growing up in a house where my dad also had his office, was restrictive, and much of my day I spent in my room avoiding the business people in the house, the hours ticking so slowly by, I felt as if I were being dragged along with them. But at night, when there was no one around, and I could sneak outside to lie in a lounge chair and imagine what my life would be like if I could exchange Dad's wealth for my freedom, the hours raced by when all I wanted them to do was slow down.

Tonight, I step outside then stand with my eyes closed, breathing in the sweet night scents, before turning on my flashlight to begin my trek across the yard.

The porta potty has been placed closest to the cabin the men are renovating, which I'm grateful for. Sharing a bathroom with four men has not been the highlight of my time at the lake. Even though one of Darren's tasks is to add chemicals to the toilet everyday, the smell that emanates from that thing has been, at times, enough to send me into town with the excuse of doing errands, then have a beer at The Kernel and use that bathroom.

I sweep the flashlight back and forth as I walk, watching for tripping hazards. A few steps from the Honeymoon Suite, I remember that I forgot my bear bell. I don't use it during the day as there's always so much noise and commotion in the yard, no bear would dare come near the place. But Wilson has emphasized that when I'm here alone, especially if I'm outside at dusk or dawn, I should always have it with me.

Since I need to make it to the bathroom before I pee my pants, instead of going back to collect the bell, I forge ahead. I'm halfway there when I hear a rustling behind me and turn, swinging the flashlight in the direction of the sound. My breath catches in my throat when I see the light bounce off two red glowing embers in the dark; what old wives, and hunters call eyeshine. A large hulk is standing between me and my tiny temporary home, and my legs become weak when I realize it's a bear. Likely having smelled me before I saw or heard him, he keeps me in his sights, while he paws at something on the ground. I weigh my options. In order to get to the Honeymoon Suite, I'd have to pass by the bear, so that's out. My eyes fall on the shower that stands the closest to me, but which I doubt is strong enough to protect me from a charging bear. In the other direction, I see the porta potty, and beyond that, the cabin which would give me the best protection, but is likely too far. Wondering what Wilson would do if he were in this situation, which, he would remind me, he would never be, I decide on the porta potty, and begin to slowly walk backwards, keeping my eyes on the bear. When I'm close enough that I think I might be able to make it there before he catches up, I turn and run, bang open the blue plastic door and jump inside, pulling the door closed and latching the hook and eye; as if that's going to be enough to keep a bear out. I hear huffing and snorting as the animal thunders across the yard, and brace myself as best as one can in a smooth plastic box, waiting for impact. I feel my teeth rattle when it thumps its body against the door. The two-by-two cubicle shakes but doesn't tip. There's a splashing sound beneath my feet. He walks around the box, and again, thumps against the wall, and I wonder if this is where I'm going to die; in a chemical toilet in the middle of the woods, covered in excrement.

Suddenly, my world tilts and rocks as the bear begins to push on the outhouse. Back and forth I go, the cubicle rocking further and further with each shove. The bear is pushing on the side without the door, and I'm tempted to make a run for the cabin; it's only about seven feet to the left, just a few long strides, but before I make up my mind if I want to take that chance, the bear gives one final push, and the outhouse, with me inside, tips over. I hit the ground with a thud and feel my legs become wet as the holding tank beneath the toilet seat, spills. I don't move, hopeful that pushing me over has scared the bear into retreating, but it seems he isn't done with me yet. I hear the walls squeal under its paws as he does a few thumps with both feet and I'm sure I'm a goner, but the plastic holds tight.

His paws scratch against the side wall, then suddenly I roll over, hitting my head on the toilet as the bear pushes his weight against the porta potty. He gives another push and I flop again, then again and again, until we come to a stop and I realize he's wedged me and my foul-smelling prison against the back step. I count my blessings this didn't happen when the trench was open. I hear him out there, huffing and puffing, occasionally swatting the toilet with a paw as he can likely smell the excrement, until eventually, after numerous tries to break through the wall, it becomes quiet. Unable to see what's happening, I can only hope he's left. Using all my willpower not to bolt out of here screaming in disgust, I lie still for quite a while, not wanting to draw his attention back to me. What seems like an eternity later, I decide he must have left and begin feeling for the hook and eye.

Because I was rolled, I can't tell where the door is, and from a prone position, I fumble for the flashlight I dropped when I hit the ground. I find it by my foot and switch it on to look for the handle but the porta potty appears to have stopped rolling with the door against the ground. I scream so loud I'm sure every bear around the lake must hear me. I thump and push my body against the sides, trying to roll the thing as the bear did, but it's stuck under the edge of the step and won't budge. I lie my head down and wait for morning.

—

"Ruby," Darren calls. "Ruby, are you in there?" He knocks on the plastic.

I open my eyes, not believing I must have dozed off. "Get me out of here," I yell.

"The door is against the ground," he says.

"Do you think I'd still be in here if I could get out?" I say, not hiding my sarcasm. "Of course I know I've stopped on the door. Just get me the hell out of here!"

"Just a sec," he says. "We have to turn you. Is there something for you to hang on to?"

I grip the edge of the slimy toilet, and the guys push the porta potty. The moment the door clears the ground, I kick it open and roll outside. Jim and Blair step back, their hands to their noses, but Darren steps forward to help me up.

"What happened?" he asks.

"Bear," I say. "Outside. Chased me. I ran into the outhouse, but he pushed it over then rolled me across the yard. Couldn't get out."

"What time was that?" Jim asks, his eyes watering.

"Two-thirty this morning."

"You've been stuck in there for five hours?"

I nod.

"Good thing it wasn't Friday," Blair says. "You'd be stuck in there for three days."

"You forgot to take your garbage to the dump," Wilson says, pointing to the garbage strewn across the yard. "That's why you had a bear."

Darren says, "It wasn't her fault. I'm the one who forgot the garbage. Ruby asked me to do it and I forgot."

Wilson shakes his head. "Should have expected that from you," he says.

"Darren," I say. "Quit covering for me." I turn towards Wilson. "I tossed it out the door yesterday afternoon with the intention of putting it in the trunk of my car. I did not ask Darren to do it for me."

Wilson looks at Darren, a puzzled look on his face, then stomps towards the cabin. "Pick that thing up," he yells, pointing to the overturned porta potty. "Then pour some bleach where the garbage spilled. Might be enough to stop him from coming back."

"I'm sorry," I yell. "I made a mistake."

Wilson turns. "Mistake like that could have cost you your life."

"You think I don't know that?" I say, realizing that standing here covered in slime, it doesn't look like I know anything. "I'm sure you've never made a mistake in your entire life."

He looks at me as if I've just accused him of urinating in public. "Hard to be human and not make at least one mistake," he says.

"What?" I say, my slimy arms crossed over my slimy chest.

"What mistake could the perfect Wilson ever have made?"

He stares at me with that stern look that keeps everyone at a distance, and I think perhaps he's going to tell me, but he leaves without uttering a word.

"Just so you know," I yell at the man's back. "When I was trying to decide what to do, I thought, what would Wilson do if he were in this predicament. So, thank you." I turn towards Darren. "Why did you say that? It wasn't your fault, it was mine."

Darren shrugs. "He doesn't like me anyhow, what's one more reason to despise me."

Not caring if the guys are here or not, I get a change of clothes and take a shower until the bag is empty.

1946

"There sure are some ignorant men in this world, Gerry. Glad your parents raised you right."

"What happened?" I ask, reaching into the truck bed. I take two bags of groceries out while Cecelia grabs the other one.

The war ended last year and this summer all of the cabins are booked solid. I either bring groceries out every day, or Cecelia picks them up when she has other errands in town. Today she had something to pick up at Garret's Hardware, so she stopped for groceries on her way home, then I followed her back here to help with the wiener roast tonight.

"Just Eric trying to prove how tough he is. After all these years, you'd think he'd have grown up. He and his buddies followed me around town in that old truck of his, yelling obscenities. Makes me sad to see grown men acting like juveniles."

I feel my temper rise, knowing the kinds of offensive words he would yell at her. Homosexual, dyke, lesbian. "If I'd been there, I'd have punched that moron in the nose," I say.

"Gerry, you remember what I told you; antagonizing a man like that just makes things escalate. He's threatened by my success. That's his problem, not mine. Better to turn the other cheek and let him think what he wants to think. Besides," she says as we enter the dining hall, "you know you're a lover not a fighter. Speaking of which, how much longer before that baby is born?"

"Her due date is next week."

"You've got to promise me that if this baby turns out to be a boy, you'll make sure he grows up respecting women. And if it's a girl, she has to learn to respect herself and not allow men to walk all over her."

"Of course," I say. "You already know I will; Mom would kill me if I didn't." We set the grocery bags on the counter and start emptying them. "You know what you need to do? You need to learn how to shoot a gun."

"Why? So I can shoot every man who tries to belittle me? Half the men in town would be dead if I did that." She shakes her head. "Eric isn't going to come out here with all these people around." She looks out the windows towards the beach crowded with adults lying in the sun, and kids splashing in the water.

"Nothing stopping him from accosting you during shoulder season."

"The man is all talk, you know that. That's why he harasses me when his buddies are around. We both know he only calls me names because I insulted his manhood by not succumbing to his so-called charm. So," she shrugs, "he tells his friends I don't like men. Why would I care? Some men think that when women don't fall at their feet, it's the woman's fault. It makes them angry."

I cock an eyebrow and meet her gaze.

"He's not going to hurt me, Gerry." Still, I look at her. "I've lived out here all these years without knowing how to shoot." I don't avert my gaze. "You really think I need to learn how to use a gun?" she asks.

"Have I ever told you that I can knock a can off the fence at a hundred paces. As soon as it's shoulder season, we can practice on the beach."

Chapter 18

It's the middle of July but I'm finally in my new cabin, a month earlier than I anticipated. I think after my near miss with the bear, Wilson put a rush on the bathroom. I have no appliances, and the entire main floor has yet to be painted and baseboards attached, as well as ceiling lights installed and cupboard doors hung. My furniture is still in storage, I'm sleeping on a mattress on the floor, and I'm still using the bar fridge and hot plate that Chip lent me, but I'll gladly put up with these minor inconveniences, to have the luxury of indoor plumbing.

I'm sitting in the front yard in my Adirondack chair which I've painted red, eating a sandwich, and drinking a glass of wine, when I realize that it's become awfully quiet. There isn't a breeze, not even a hint of a breeze. No squirrels are chattering back and forth or running across the yard. No ducks are swimming past like they do each evening, and I don't hear the knocking that echoes through the forest when woodpeckers search for bugs. I stand, and with my glass of wine in hand, wander to the backyard.

There are more deciduous trees here than in the front yard, and I crane my head back to look up through the branches. I have my eyes trained skyward when a drop of water hits me smack in the middle of my forehead and I wonder how one drop of rain could fall out of a completely blue sky. A gust of wind stirs the hair around my face and I look down the road to see a small dust eddy swirling towards me, followed by a larger one. They turn into the Vereschuk's yard and onto the beach, then dissipate, the dust falling to the sand without the wind to keep it aloft.

At the horizon, where the road meets the sky, gray clouds are forming, pushing their way over the tops of the trees. I take a deep breath and smell rain. A crack of thunder rumbles in the distance while a flock of geese flies overhead; their honks piercing the silence and Wilson's warning that, because we're surrounded by trees, a storm can sneak up on you without you even aware that it's near, comes to mind. I decide I'd better get inside. I run to the back of the cabin, jump across the threshold and slam the door just as large drops of rain begin to hit the wood. I look out the porch window. The storm has come up so fast, that I can't see the road through the deluge. It's as if someone is throwing pail after pail of water at the window. A bolt of lightning flashes, followed by a crack of thunder, and I flick the light switch; the power is out.

The wind howls as the trees bend and I run through the kitchen and into the addition, grateful to Wilson for insisting on cinderblock walls. Rain, sounding like bullets, pelts off the roof, and I hope my little cabin survives the storm. Every couple of seconds, the room lights up with lightning, followed by a boom so loud, I can feel the vibrations in my feet, even in this concrete room.

I peek out the window facing the lake. The wind is blowing the rain sideways and the trees are bending low. The lake is churning and boiling, not at all resembling the small prairie body of water it is, but instead, looking like the middle of the ocean. On more than one occasion, I hear a sound like trees being felled.

An hour later the rain stops as quickly as it began, and I cautiously leave my shelter to inspect the damage. After listening to the intensity of the storm for the past hour, it's eerily quiet, the acrid scent of lightning, overpowering the earthy smell of wet ground.

I crane my neck back, expecting the roof of my cabin to be torn to shreds. The backyard, the roof of the shed, and the roof of the cabin are littered with fallen branches, though from this angle, I see no damage to either the shed or the cabin. I look across the yard.

Four of the cabins remain standing. The one casualty: the Honeymoon Suite has been flattened by a falling tree.

Along the perimeter of the cleared land, trees that Ernie was going to take out this summer are gone, some broken off, some uprooted. The tree that took out the Honeymoon Suite, is lying across the road, blocking access both to and from my cabin.

I hear tires crunching on broken branches, and turn to see Wilson's truck, him at the wheel, and Darren in the passenger seat. They stop behind the fallen tree and Darren jumps out.

"Are you okay?"

"I stayed in the addition," I say. "Figured it was the safest place to be."

"Good idea," Darren says. Wilson says nothing.

"Could it have been a tornado?" I ask.

"More'n likely a plough wind," Wilson says. "Not as common this far north, but not unheard of. You can tell by the way the cabin is levelled. Not twisted; lying flat. Everything pushed in one direction. Wind came from the south," he points towards his grandfather's place, "blew across the land, then straight north, taking out that tree which took out the cabin." He points to the Honeymoon Suite with the tree cutting it down the middle. "Helluva strong wind to do this much damage." Pushing his way through the broken branches, he wades towards the front yard. Darren and I follow.

Another downed tree is lying across the picnic table. The table is broken in two, but it's missed hitting my cabin by mere inches. My Adirondack chair is in the lake, half submerged with only a portion of the back poking out of the water. The sand lining the shore looks like most of it has been washed into the lake. A few fish lie flopping on the mud.

I face the direction Wilson said the wind came from, but no dilapidated roof breaks up the skyline. "Missy," I whisper, then crunch my way through the debris to see that the Vereschuk cabin has also been levelled by the force of the wind.

Lamp shades, clothing, dishes, a broom here, a pair of boots there, and a dresser, which used to be inside the cabin, are now lying outside, the rain hitting the ground with such force, it's coated everything in its wake with sludge. Rivers of muddy water are receding from under the rubble and back to the lake. I pull a few boards away, saddened at the loss of the hundred-year-old cabin, but hopeful that Missy is safe and sound someplace else.

"That's too bad," Darren says, coming up behind me.

"I'll contact Ernie. Let him know he has a job," Wilson says, staring at his grandfather's place. "You need to invest in a generator in case the power goes out again. I'll hook it up for you. Darren, we're leaving," he says to his son, turning to go, then stops and says over his shoulder, "Good thinking staying in the addition."

Darren gives me a hug and tells me he's glad I'm okay, adding that's probably the nicest thing he's ever heard his dad say, then he and Wilson leave. For the next week and a half, the forest buzzes with the sound of chainsaws as Ernie and his crew cut up broken and uprooted trees. My stockpile of firewood is growing.

Chapter 19

While spring slowly made its appearance, melting the ice, leafing out the trees and blowing warm breezes across the lake, the cabin was jacked up and levelled, the addition built, the second floor and balcony built, and the exterior siding and shingles nailed down.

During the dog days of summer when the water lapped gently on the shore, the cabin was rewired, the wallboard on the main floor hung and painted the off-white colour I took weeks to decide on, the fireplace installed, the hardwood laid, the bathroom finished, the kitchen cupboards mounted, the countertops slid into place and the taps attached.

Then we were delayed a week while Ernie felled and cut up broken trees, and Wilson hauled away the remnants of the Honeymoon Suite and the Vereschuk's cabin that were levelled during the storm.

It's now the first week of September, and while the squirrels rain pinecones on our heads preparing for winter, the baseboards are attached, front and back doors are replaced, the light fixtures wired in, the appliances installed, a deck built on the front of the cabin, and my furniture brought out of storage. Four and a half months since the day I moved into the Honeymoon Suite, the cabin is finished.

Today is Gerry's one-hundred and second birthday, but he said he didn't want a party, just a little gathering with friends would be plenty. So, on this day, when the cookstove being brought back to life is the only job to be done, Chip, Louise, Wilson, Darren,

Gerry, and my family have come out for the day. I invited my aunts, but Bernice has a bit of a cold and they didn't want to take any chances on her getting pneumonia again. So, even though Bernice insisted she would be fine, and to quit making a fuss over her, they've opted out.

Robert has sent his family to the beach without him. I heard him say quietly to his wife that she could use the exercise and I can't understand how she can stand up to him on so many topics, but not about him harassing her about her weight.

It's the first time in decades Gerry has set foot on the property, and he's in his glory as he pushes his walker around the cabin, talking about how it used to look, or how they built this and how they struggled with that. I take him outside to the deck where he sits in an Adirondack chair.

"Are these Cecelia's?" he asks, rubbing his gnarled knuckles down the freshly painted arms.

"They are," I say. "And the picnic table as well. Found lots of treasures in the shed."

"I have so many memories of sitting side by side with her in these chairs, right here in the front yard. We'd talk about her business, about my family."

A few weeks ago, I had Cecelia's drawing of the cabin that we found in the shed, framed, and today I bring it out to show him. His eyes fill with tears.

"Oh my," he says. "This takes me back. I remember the day she brought me out here as if it were yesterday. We were so innocent, so naïve. Thought we could do anything; like all young people. Thought we were invincible."

"Happy birthday," I say.

"No," he says. "You mean you're giving this to me?"

"I am."

"You should hang it in the cabin, not give it to me."

"I want you to have it," I say. "Hang it in the store. You're the one who needs to enjoy looking at it, not me. You have the memories of this place; I have the real thing all around me."

"I'll take it if you promise me that when I die, it comes back here, to this cabin where it belongs."

"I think, Gerry," I say, "that you still have a few years left in you."

I'm spreading the table cloth on the picnic table I dragged out of the shed after the first one was lost in the storm, when I notice Chip and my son standing near the shore having a conversation, though it seems Robert is doing most of the talking.

"I told Mom this place wasn't worth renovating," my son says as the two men look at the cabin. "Tried to talk her out of it, as a matter of fact. But you know women when they set their minds to something." He takes a swig of his beer.

Chip smiles but says nothing. He sticks his hand in his pocket and I think he's going to pull out a package of Juicy Fruit, or perhaps even a cigarette, but he doesn't. I've noticed of late he seems to have dropped the habit, but not wanting to embarrass him, I haven't said anything.

"I suggested she move into a seniors home, but she balked at the idea. She's just going to have to move to one in a few years, she could have saved herself a lot of time and money moving to one now instead of doing," he waves at the cabin, "all of this."

"I think she's still young enough to continue living her life as she sees fit," Chip says, "instead of holing herself up in a seniors' home before she needs to. Life is too short to always be worrying about what's going to happen next. Until recently that's how I lived, but since I met your mom, I've begun to live in the moment."

My son turns towards the lake and lifts his face, which looks so much like his father's, towards the sun. "I suppose it would be a nice place to live if you're into the beach and walks in the woods," he says. "Me? I like the city life. Restaurants, stores, movies, bars. This is just too much—" he pauses, "—tree hugging for me."

"I like it," Chip says. "As a matter of fact, I've been looking at some property not too far from here."

"Have you?" Robert says. "Don't get me wrong, it's a beautiful place, beautiful scenery, and I'm sure the cabin has increased the value of the property, but she could have been pulling in a nice in-

terest with the money from the sale of the house in the city combined with the sale of this place. How much is it worth anyhow?
Two or three hundred? Probably sunk more money into it than it's
worth. Am I right?"

"Not really, no," Chip says. "Before the renos it was valued at one
and a half million. Now, with this gorgeous cabin, I can't imagine it
going for any less than two to two and a half."

"What?" Robert says, looking confused.

"A lot of the value is in the land. But like I said, now with this
brand-new cabin, it's higher than that. If the property were a few
kilometers further south, it would be worth more."

"The land? What land?"

"The resort," Chip says. "Your mom owns all one-hundred acres."

"Pardon?" Robert says. "Mom owns one-hundred acres of land?"

Chip glances at me, realizing he's spoken out of turn. "But of
course, there's not a lot of people wanting to buy this far north," he
says, backpedaling. "It might be valued at two and a half million,
but the right buyer would be hard to find. Lots of cabins to choose
from in this part of our province. Most at larger lakes, closer to
cities, more amenities, and not so secluded. I've found that people
who want to spend that kind of money, also want amenities. So,
even if it's valued high, this place might never find the right buyer."

"Oh yeah?" Robert says.

"Yes," Chip says. "Most times, when the property is as rundown
as this place was, and the client is inclined to sell, I'd advise them
to sell as is, as they might put more into it than it's worth; as you
already said. But with the property valued at one and one half million, and your mom having no intention to sell," he shrugs, "I think
she did the right thing."

"But," Roberts says, "you're saying if the right buyer did come
along, with the new cabin, it would sell for two and a half million?"

"But," Chip counters, "it makes no difference. Your mom is not
thinking of selling." He pats my son on his shoulder, then leaves
him staring at me while he approaches Jess to strike up a conversation with her.

Robert scurries across the yard and grabs me by the elbow, then leads me away from the others. "Why didn't you tell me you owned so much land?" he asks. "Why didn't you tell me what it's worth?"

"Didn't I?"

"You know darned well you didn't. You said you didn't ask because you had no intention of selling. This place is worth over two million dollars, Mom? What the heck?"

"If I'd told you, you would have harassed me into selling and I didn't want to sell. I want to live out here."

"Live out here, sure," Robert says. "But put it on the market while you're here. It might take a year to sell, and you'd be able to enjoy your new house in the interim."

"With me having to vacate the place every time Chip brought potential buyers out to look. People tramping all over my house. No, thank you. I've done enough of that for a while. I want this house to be my home."

"But," Roberts stammers, "you could live comfortably in the city until the day you die with the money you'd make from the sale of this place."

"I can live comfortably out here," I say. "I'm financially secure with the investments you've made for me. I don't need to sell just to have more money in the bank. To me, this," I wave at the scenery in front of us, "is worth more than money in the bank."

"I'm only thinking of you, Mom," Robert says. "I worry about you out here all by yourself."

"I'm not alone," I say, looking at my friends enjoying my front yard. "Now," I put my hand on his cheek, "I have to get a meal on the table." I can feel his eyes on my back as I walk away.

"Couldn't find a better house if you scoured the city," Wilson is saying when I walk up, looking pleased as he critiques his creation.

"It certainly is a feather in your cap," Gerry says.

I hand Wilson a cheque for the balance of the bill; sixty-seven-thousand dollars, and as he's done each time I've paid him, he puts it in his wallet without saying thank you.

"Thought you were crazy, you know," he says instead.

"You told me," I say.

"Still think you're crazy. Greenhorn like you living out here all by yourself. Just don't cut off your foot when your chopping wood this winter."

"Wilson," Gerry says. "Give her a bit of credit. Staying out here in that musty little cottage wasn't a bed of roses and you know it. That place was so small you couldn't swing a cat. And I'm sure the smell from that ancient septic was enough to choke a horse. She was here by herself during that storm and managed to survive, even fought off a bear, all while putting up with you and your ornery ways. In my opinion, if she can do all of that, she can do anything."

"A bear?" Debby says. "You fought off a bear, Mom?"

"Gerry makes it sound like hand-to-hand combat. More like I hid while it played chicken with me. My own fault. Left a bag of garbage outside. Learned that lesson the hard way."

"Everyone has to learn," Wilson says. "Just glad you didn't get hurt." Darren whips his head towards his dad then looks at me and raises his eyebrows.

"It's so peaceful," Louise says. She looks up at the second floor. "Buy yourself one of those deck heaters and even in the winter the balcony will be a nice place to sit."

I look at my balcony, the posts cemented six feet into the ground. Wilson said three feet was plenty, but I insisted on six. Jim said it would withstand an earthquake.

"It will be nice," I say, "sitting out there with a cup of coffee looking at the ice on the lake. But it's not living out here during the winter that has me worried, it's driving the winter roads that scares me the most."

"I have confidence in you, Mom," Jess says. "After a couple of times, you'll be a pro."

"She's right," Gerry says. "They spread sand and plow the road every month, more if there's a storm; not like the old days when they only plowed a couple times a winter. And the highway is always being plowed and salted. It's simply a matter of doing it and becoming comfortable. Come to town only on the good driving days, stock up with enough groceries to last you for a month or longer. If you play your cards right, living out here is very doable. And with that sat-ellite dish, I'm sure you'll get all kinds of weather stations. Cecelia lived here for thirty-five years with barely a radio. Drove into town only when she needed supplies and never once hit the ditch. She was always careful with everything she did. Knew that one lapse in concentration could cost her life. That's why I know she wasn't on that darned roof in a blizzard. She wouldn't have been so careless." His voice cracks. "But," he looks into his daughter's eyes, "there's nothing I can do to change history. Like your mother and you preached at me for all those years, I need to let bygones be bygones."

"And they're right," Wilson says. "Time to let it go; it's been fif-ty-two years for, God's sake. There're too many theories still being told by too many people who don't know anything about it." He counts off his fingers. "She was killed by gang members. Her fam-ily had her killed." He shakes his head. "I've even heard people say aliens pushed her off the roof."

"Do you have a theory?" I ask Wilson.

"I was pretty young when she died," he says. "But I tend to agree with Gerry. The few times I was out here I found her to be a careful woman, a meticulous woman. She wouldn't have been anywhere near the roof when it was snowing." He scratches his large nose. "Could have been someone from her life before she moved here, I suppose. Heard how successful she'd become, came out to get some money from her. And there were lots of men from town who didn't like her. Could have been one of them. Maybe an argument got out of hand, though it doesn't seem probable. Town's small; someone would have blabbed."

"So many times, I tried to come to her defense," Gerry says. "But she would never let me. Taught her to use a gun, thought it was the least I could do, even though she didn't want to learn. Got to be a better shot than me. Killed rabbits for stew every winter after that. Didn't have to come into town as much."

"Well," I say. "I certainly don't plan on learning how to use a gun and kill rabbits. But I do plan on making my own bread. That will save me some trips into town."

"You know what you should do?" Louise says. "Go berry picking. Not now, of course. Everything this far north is done by the end of August. There's a large patch of Saskatoons that grows on your property not too far from that beach." She points at the strip of sand on the other side of the lake. "That's where I pick to make the jam I sell in the store. Cecelia and Dad picked them every year."

"When I could get away," Gerry says.

Louise rubs her dad's shoulder.

"I don't think sending her out berry picking is such a good idea," Wilson says. "The woods are different, very disorienting. People have gotten lost, wander for days at a time before they're rescued. Most make it out alive; some don't. Remember that woman about five years ago? Got lost and her body wasn't found for a month. Finally found her in the far corner of the woods, close to the farmer's field. Died from exposure."

"I remember," Gerry says. "And she was a seasoned mushroom picker. Went out two or three times a week all summer. There were multiple sightings, but after a while she began hiding from her rescuers. Woods can make you crazy if you wander around in them for too long."

"Doesn't take much. One foot off the path and these woods can swallow you as easily as the lake can," Wilson says. "Can't see the path you were on once you've left it; all the trees look the same, all the paths blend in with the forest floor. And it's impossible to walk in a straight line when all you see is trees. Need the horizon to guide you. End up going in circles."

"As long as she leaves markers, she'd be okay," Louise says. "I've done it hundreds of times and not gotten lost. After a while you learn to recognize certain trees, broken branches, rocks."

"But you were raised here," Gerry says, "and Cecelia taught you how to find your way. Like Wilson said, one step off the path and suddenly everything looks the same and you're lost. Cecelia and I even got lost once. We walked in circles for a while until I got the bright idea to mark X's on the trees as we passed. Eventually we found our way out."

"Well," I say, cutting off this conversation about me getting lost in the forest, "I can promise you that I have no intention of going berry picking in the woods by myself."

"Next summer we'll go together," Louise says. "We can make some jam. The Farmers Alamanac is calling for lots of rain next year; berries should be plentiful."

"Did you know that lightning helps plants to grow?" Debby says. "I read it on Google. Something about the heat of the lightning interacting with nitrogen and oxygen."

"Lightning is the last thing we want living so close to the woods," Gerry says. "When there's a storm, I don't sleep all night."

"What year did lightning strike the tree that burnt down the cabins?" I ask.

"'49," he says. "I was on the volunteer fire department. We were lucky only three cabins were lost. I thought the whole place was going to go up in flames."

"Arson was never suspected?" Robert asks. "I mean, she had a lot of enemies by that point, am I right?"

"A few," Gerry says. "But no, arson was never suspected. And I was witness to the storm. It was a bad one. Watched lightning crack around the lake for hours."

Thinking I hear something in his voice, I look at him but see nothing other than the grief for the loss of his friend I've always seen.

I hear the boys' boisterous voices as Sheryl and the kids round the corner of the cabin. Sheryl has her towel wrapped around her. "Going to change," she says, looking at her husband. "I'll be right back."

"And no dipping your hand into the cookie jar while you're inside," Robert yells to her back with a smirk on his face.

I feel the hair on the back of my neck rise. That's the same thing his father would have said to me when we were young. I see Gerry look at my son, wanting to say something, but knowing it isn't his place.

"I don't think I ever told you," I say, trying to take the tension out of the air. "A few months ago, right near the beginning of the renovations, I found some money in the cabin. The day the cookstove was taken out and stored in the shed. I found it on the floor where it sat in the kitchen."

"How much?" Chip asks.

"Not a lot, just a one-hundred-dollar bill. I asked the guys if it belonged to any of them, but they said no, Wilson doesn't allow large amounts of money on the worksite."

"Worked for someone long time ago where a fight broke out," Wilson says. "One man accused another of stealing his money. Someone got killed. Decided that if I was in charge, I'd not allow my employees to bring more than twenty dollars to work. Just makes common sense."

"This was old money," I say. "Paper. Not in circulation anymore. The only people who would be carrying around those kinds of bills would be collectors."

"Could have been Cecelia's," Gerry says. "During the depression, there were so many bank-runs, it gave people a bad taste in their mouths. Even into the latter half of the depression, people were still keeping money at home, afraid the bank would close and they'd lose everything. My own father kept cash under his mattress for years until Mom finally talked him into putting it in the bank. Cecelia, however, took it to a whole other level. Right into the sixties, she still didn't trust banks. Probably because her own father lost his fortune that way. Used to hide her money all over the cabin; the cookstove in the summer, was a favourite spot. That's where the whole hidden treasure rumour got started. Everyone knew she didn't trust banks. When she died, people began looking. Been looking ever since," he says. "I think your one-hundred dollars is the first anyone's found."

Robert stands and runs into the cabin. We hear him banging around in the kitchen. He returns a few minutes later. "It's empty," he says.

"Son," Wilson says. "Do you really think we're so stupid as to not check the cookstove before we hooked it up? Young people nowadays, think everyone older than fifty is brain dead."

Robert blushes.

"Lots of hiding places on one hundred acres of land," Gerry says. "Could be anywhere. Though with the cabins that burnt down, Ruby's renovations, and countless people over the years searching everything from the old cabins, to the outhouses, the beach, and the woods, it seems unlikely it's still here. And knowing Cecelia, she could have given it all away. She was a generous woman. Gave money to whoever asked, and sometimes even if you didn't. But in its heyday, when this place was quite successful; I don't know if she'd have been able to give it all away."

Chip is sitting forward in his chair. "You mean there really might be money buried out here?"

"If it's here, it might not even be cash anymore," Gerry continues. "She told me once that she didn't like the way cash depreciated and was thinking of investing in gold."

"What does that mean?" I ask. "One hundred dollars from fifty years ago is still worth one hundred dollars today."

"But it can't buy as much," Robert says. "That's what she meant by depreciating. That's why it's good to invest, Mom. Not just keep your money in the bank."

"He's right," Gerry says. "She told me she could buy a gold bar for around ten grand. A lot of money, but she was doing well for many years. I could see her buying a bar at the end of each summer, especially in the fifties when running this place was less expensive."

"And today," Robert says, "a bar of gold is worth around five-hundred grand. If she did buy gold, that's a pretty good take on your investment."

"Do you remember the contract your father signed when he bought the place?" Chip says.

"I have it around here someplace," I say.

"I read it to you that first day we were out here last year. It said whatever is found on the property, whether in sight or hidden, belongs to the new owner of the property."

"I suppose that means if you find Cecelia's hidden cache, whatever it may be, belongs to you," Gerry says.

I glance at Robert; his eyes are wide.

1949

Cecelia and I come to a stop when we see two men standing in the fading light where the property line for the resort ends. The long shadows of the trees are streaking across the sand and cutting across their faces making it difficult to tell who they are. Because Cecelia and I are in the shadows, they don't see us and continue their conversation.

One man hands the other an envelope. He opens it and looks at the contents. "Don't you trust me?" the first man says.

The second man peers into the envelope. "You never told me who the other person is." The voice sounds like Eric Prentice.

"That's because I don't know," the first man says. He turns his profile to me and in the setting sun I see that it's Bart Dunlop, the hotel owner. The gossip is that he complained to town council that Cecelia's resort is costing him his business and she should never have been given a licence to build the place without them consulting him first. He looks towards the cabins. "Never seen the resort from this angle. Pretty little places." He turns back to Eric. "Note said I should contact you, that's all. What's it to you anyhow?"

"I told you, she's a menace," Eric says. "Her and that damned resort." He angles his hand to his brow to shade his eyes as he looks across the water.

Before I can stop her, Cecelia is stepping out from behind the bushes.

"Eric, Bart," she says. "Fancy seeing you two here. Not that I mind you being on my land, you're welcome to hike these woods anytime. Gerry and I were doing some berry picking." I step out behind her. "It was a good summer. Bushes are loaded," she holds up her full pail. "I'll bring you some jam when I'm done canning. Hope you enjoyed last year's batch?"

She looks back and forth between the men, not flinching, not cowering, and I see just how strong a woman she is, just how determined.

Mr. Dunlop is looking at his shoes. "Oh, yeah, yeah," he says. "The Mrs. and I loved it, thank you." He doffs his cap. "Have a nice evening now," he says then rushes to his car parked up the road. After a moment of trying to stare her down, Eric follows, but not before muttering, "Stupid bitch. If I were you, Johansen, I'd be looking over my shoulder."

"Cecelia," I say once the men have left. "Why did you let them know we were here?"

"Remember the day, years ago," Cecelia says, "when a bear came near the cabin we were building? You're the one who told me to never sneak up on a predator. You said it's better to let them know you're there so they have a chance to run away instead of charging you. Well, I was hoping the same principle would work with those two."

Chapter 20

When I woke up this morning, I decided to go for a walk around the lake, something I did last spring to get myself out of the Honeymoon Suite for a few hours, but haven't done since. When I asked Wilson what he thought, his advice was threefold: *buy a can of bear spray and don't be afraid to use it, wear a bell, and for God's sake, stay out of the forest.*

I left the cabin at ten this morning, a backpack stuffed with bear spray, a sweater, a flashlight, two bottles of water and three granola bars wrapped in plastic bags, strapped to my back. I have four bells, each twist-tied to a zipper pull, and I jingle like Santa Claus with every step I take.

I've followed the road which becomes narrower the farther around the lake I go, and have made it to the strip of sand that I can see from my front yard.

I put my binoculars to my eyes and focus on my cabin. It looks nice from this side, sitting among the evergreens, rustic and inviting, the kind of cabin I always imagined owning. I leave the beach to cross the road and peer into the maze of tree trunks that make up the boreal forest surrounding the lake. I have not, nor do I have any intention of, stepping across that invisible line that separates the civilized world from the wild. Becoming one of the statistics that Gerry and Wilson were talking about is not at the top of my to-do list.

Standing on the edge like this, the woods don't seem menacing at all. I hear birds chirping, squirrels chattering and see butterflies flitting between branches and dapples of sunlight playing on the forest floor. On the surface, it looks welcoming and inviting, like something out of a fairy tale. But, if you look past the trees that line the road, past the chattering squirrels, and the birds taking flight... If you allow your imagination to take you into the deep, dark centre, you can almost hear the forest pulsating; feel it's heartbeat, as if all the trees are one living thing, working together to lure you inside, hoping to swallow you whole, just as Wilson said.

I'm taking a step backwards to continue on my way, when something catches the corner of my eye, but when I turn back, whatever it was, is gone. I start walking, and again I see something in my peripheral vision. I turn my head just as a silver braid vanishes behind the trees.

"Missy," I call. "Is that you?"

The only sound I hear is the caw of a crow circling the treetops. I'm staring into the forest, when a white streak flashes between two trunks, then as if someone is nudging me forward, I find myself entering the forest. At first, I'm worried the path will disappear the moment I cross that line, like Wilson said, but when I look back and see the road just paces away, I defy his warning and stay where I am. From this vantage point, the forest doesn't seem nearly as threatening as it did from the road and I stand still, listening for Missy's footfalls as she tramps across the centuries old carpet of pine needles.

I step further in and call, "Missy, are you in here?" but again I hear nothing. I look back, and still seeing the road, step even further in to try one more time to find her. "Missy, do you need help?" I call, and again hear nothing. Deciding that even if it was her that I saw, she likely knows these woods better than anyone around, I turn to exit the same way I entered, only to find that the path has disappeared and all I see are trees.

"Oh, come on now," I say. "It can't happen that easily. It was right there just a minute ago."

I step towards the spot where I'm sure I entered, but there is no edge of the forest, no road, no beach in the distance. I try another direction and another, and still another, but with each step, the air around me becomes darker as I move further into the forest and the trees block out the sun.

"This is crazy," I say to myself, the sound of my voice, deadened by the tall pines. "I didn't go that far off the road. How could it disappear so quickly? Missy!" I yell. "Are you in here? I need some help. I seem to have gotten myself lost." She doesn't come to my rescue nor does she respond. "Well, this is a fine mess you've got yourself into," I say. "Just don't panic. The key is keeping your wits about you." I find a log, sit down, take off my backpack and remove a bottle of water then look at my watch; ten forty-five. "Eight hours to find my way out before the sun sets."

—

Eight hours later I'm still lost, and panic set in long ago. My shirt and pants are soaked with sweat, and grime from tripping over roots and broken branches hidden under the thick layer of pine needles, is caked on my face and hands. I suppose I should be thankful I haven't broken a bone, or hit my head on a rock. I'm shivering in my damp shirt; the warm fall air having cooled down with the sunset and the deep shade of the forest, and I remove my sweater from my backpack. Weariness takes over so, using my backpack for a pillow, I curl up under a tree. I don't wake up until I hear a voice whispering in my ear.

"Wake up, Ruby."

"Hello," I say.

"Why are you here, Ruby?" the voice says.

"Is that you, Missy?" I say.

"Why are you here?" she repeats.

"Because I followed you into the forest. Where are you? I can't see you."

"Look between the trees, you'll see me."

I squint into the forest. Gradually she takes shape. "Missy," I say.

"I'm so glad to see you. I'm lost. I stepped off the trail and got lost."

"You're not lost," she says.

"I'm not?"

"You're closer than you think. You'll find your way. You just need to figure out why you're here."

"I don't know what you mean," I say.

"Wake up," the voice says. "If you don't wake up, you'll die."

I open my eyes and struggle to my feet, my legs as weak as jelly, and look towards the spot I thought I saw Missy. There's no one there. It was a dream, just a silly dream. I start walking, occasionally, hearing a noise as if someone is following me, but I see nothing except black when I squint into the night.

I've no idea how long I walk—it's too dark to see my watch and time feels different when you can't see your own hand in front of your face. It's as if everything has disappeared and the only living being on earth is you. After what seems like days, the sky begins to lighten, and I find myself standing across from a small clearing. A tree marked with an X partially obscured by growth, is carved into the wood directly in front of me. Further on I see another tree with a faint X, then another, and still another. I start to run, not stopping until the road I left yesterday afternoon is visible through the trees. I'm stepping out of the forest when my legs give way and I fall to the ground.

—

"Ruby, Ruby," someone is shaking my shoulders. "Can you hear me?"

I open my eyes. Darren is kneeling beside me. He lifts a whistle to his lips, and blows. I'm on my back looking straight up between the trunks stretching towards the sky, and seeing the trees from this angle is making me woozy. I attempt to sit up, but a wave of dizziness knocks me back to the ground. The night has turned to daylight, and the sun is high in the sky.

"Careful," Darren says. "Sit up gradually. How long have you been lying here?" he asks, putting a bottle of water to my lips.

"I'm not sure," I say. "Where am I?"

"By the beach on the other side of the lake."

I hear footsteps, then four bodies, their faces in darkness with their backs to the sun, come into view. They stand around me, peering down at my prone body,

"What happened?" I ask. My voice is hoarse.

"I called the cabin a few times. When you didn't answer, I drove out to see if you were alright," Louise, one of the bodies in darkness, says, then kneels beside me. "I couldn't find you, but your car was there. I drove around the lake looking for you. When I still couldn't find you, I got worried and called Wilson. The five of us have been searching for you all day. I've been down this road three times already."

"I went for a walk," I say.

"Why are you on the ground? Did you fall?" Blair asks.

"I don't think so," I say.

Darren places his hands on my head feeling for goose eggs. He turns my face towards his. "You don't have any bruises, no bloody nose. Eyes look alright." He holds three fingers in front of my face. "How many do you see?"

"Three, I see three," I say. "I'm fine. Feel more stupid than hurt. I remember going for a walk, then I left the road and went into the forest."

"When was that?" Jim says.

"Must have been yesterday morning because it got dark and I spent the night in the woods, and now it's light."

"But what day was that?" he asks again. "What day did you leave your place to go for your walk?"

"Yesterday morning, Tuesday."

Louise and Darren, still kneeling by my side, glance at each other. "This is Sunday, Ruby," Jim says.

"No, it's not," I say. "It's Wednesday. I spent one night in the woods, then found my way out. I haven't been wandering out here for five days." No one says a word. "Have I?"

"Let's get you up off the ground," Darren says. He puts his arm around my waist and helps me to my feet. I'm weak and he holds on to me as he leads me towards Louise's car.

"I told you not to go into the woods by yourself," Wilson says. "Don't know about Louise, but my crew and I won't always be available to help. If you're going to pull stunts like this, at the very least, get yourself a dog. Have more common sense than most people I know."

"I didn't want to go into the woods," I say. "I saw Missy and thought she was in trouble, so I went to look for her. Which was dumb, I know. It was as if the road disappeared the moment I stepped onto the forest floor. I found the trees Gerry and Cecelia carved with X's and started running. That's the last thing I remember."

Darren opens Louise's car door and sits me on the passenger seat. "If you feel dizzy or confused, or anything unusual today, or even tomorrow, you go to the hospital. You hear me?"

"I'm okay," I say. "I didn't hit my head."

"People often don't recall hitting their heads when they fall. And you've had a frightening experience, easy to forget details. So, if you feel anything at all," he repeats, "dizziness, confusion, a headache, promise me you'll go and get a CT scan. I'll even drive you."

"I promise," I say. "Thanks, Darren."

Wilson has stopped on his way to his car and is looking at his son. For a moment I think he's going to compliment him, but then he says, "We're leaving, Darren. Get in the car. You need any more help, Louise?"

"We'll be fine," Louise says. "I can manage from here. Thanks."

"You need to talk to her," he says as he and Darren get into his car.

Louise drives me home, not saying too much, just glancing occasionally my way. She helps me inside and sits me on the couch then plops down beside me. She smiles at me, then looks away, then turns back and smiles again, much like she was doing in the car.

"Would you quit looking at me. I know I shouldn't have gone

into the woods. Wilson told you to give me heck. Just get it over with."

"Not going to give you heck," she says. "Everyone makes mistakes. You found your own way out which is probably more than most people could have done."

"Then what? Why do you keep looking like you have something to say?"

"You saw Missy? That's why you went in the woods?"

"I thought I did. I must have been seeing things. I feel so stupid after all the advice you and everyone gave me about staying out of the forest."

She pats my hand. "It can happen to anyone. Dad and Cecelia got lost out there, and they'd been in the woods dozens of times. It's the way the woods are; disorientating. Like being in an avalanche; hard to tell which way is up."

"I hadn't any intention of going in. It just kind of happened."

"Quit beating yourself up." She pauses. "I think, Ruby, that it's time I told you something," Louise says. "Something I should have told you that first day we met last spring when you came into the store for supplies and said you'd spoken to Missy."

"Okay," I say.

"You know Dad brought me out here a lot when I was a little girl. I told you that, right?"

"You did."

"It was wonderful. Swimming, playing with the kids whose parents brought them here year after year, wiener roasts, sing-a-longs, everything a kid could want. Had more friends than I knew what to do with. Mom was a city girl, she didn't like the lake, didn't like the outdoors. Only moved to the country because she married Dad. She had a few friends, went out for tea, listened to music, played bridge, that kind of thing. But mostly she liked to spend her time with a book. She was a good mom, loved me to death; just different than Cecelia. Mom taught me to paint, how to play the piano, how to be a lady, while Cecelia taught me to swim, how to shoot, and how to find my way in the woods so I wouldn't get lost. When I was here, at the lake, Cecelia was a second mother to me."

"Sounds like a wonderful childhood," I say.

"I was a lucky girl to have two such wonderful women in my life." Again, she pauses, and I wonder what she's wanting to tell me that's causing her such unease. "Have you noticed anything different about Missy?" she finally asks.

"What do you mean?" I say,

"Does she seem different than you and I? Talk different, dress different, act different; that kind of thing?"

"Well," I shiver and wrap the throw I keep on the back of the couch around my shoulders. "She's well spoken like she went to an exclusive school, and she always has on the same clothes; overalls, white shirt, and plaid jacket. But I don't think she has a lot of money."

"She used to be quite wealthy. Owned her own very successful business."

"What business was that?"

"Hospitality," she says.

"Oh," I say. "Just like Cecelia."

"Yes," she says, looking me in the eye. "Exactly like Cecelia. Do you see what I'm saying?"

"That Missy and Cecelia had similar lines of work?"

Louise sighs. "When I was little, I had trouble saying her name. Cecelia didn't slip off my tongue easily."

"It's not an easy name for a child to pronounce."

"Dad suggested I call her Miss C."

"I suppose that's easier."

"Say it fast," Louise says.

"Miss. C.," I say. "Missy. That sounds like—"

"Exactly," Louise says. "Missy. Now do you see what I'm saying?"

"What are you trying to tell me?" I ask, not sure I want to hear. "Just spit it out."

"I'm telling you that you've been talking to a ghost. Missy is Cecelia's ghost."

I pull my chin in and look at her with hooded eyes. "Give me a break! Missy is not a ghost," I say, trying not to laugh at my friend.

"I've stood two feet from her, had entire conversations with her. I've *smelled* her."

"What does she smell like?" Louise asks.

"Like smoke and water. Like she's been standing around a camp-fire at a lake."

Louise cocks and eyebrow.

"She lives in a cabin at a lake," I say. "Lord knows there's times when I've smelled like smoke and water."

"Ruby, you saw the cabin before it was destroyed by the storm. You know that no one could have lived there; it was uninhabitable. The only one who lived there was a ghost."

1949

The storm is loud and I lie in our bed alone, watching the room light up with each crack of lightning. I hate thunder storms. Give me rain, give me sleet, give me blizzards, anything but lightning; I'd be happy if I never saw it again.

Lila has already gotten up with the pretext that I was keeping her awake tossing and turning. I'm sure she used my restlessness as an excuse to go downstairs to read. "You worry about her too much," she'd said as she left the room. "She's a big girl, she can look after herself."

I've stayed in bed, trying to sleep. Lila's right; I am worried. It would only take one strike to set a tree on fire and burn down the entire resort. Finally realizing that getting back to sleep is impossible, I eventually get up and place a chair beside the window to watch the show.

"Daddy," I hear my daughter say and I turn. She's standing at the bedroom door, the light from the hallway behind her. "I'm scared."

"Shush," I say, crossing the room. I pick her up. "Don't be scared, Lou. It's only a storm, it can't hurt you."

"Then why don't you like storms, Daddy?"

"Because lightning can start fires."

"But you said storms can't hurt you."

"You're safe inside with me and your mom." I sit in the chair and put my daughter on my lap. "You see that wire outside the window? The one hanging down the side of the house? It's attached to a rod on the roof. If lightning strikes our house, it will go through the rod and down the wire then into the ground."

"So our house won't catch on fire?" she asks.

"That's right. So our house won't catch on fire."

"What's that?" she says. Her face is pale in the darkness.

"What's what, sweetie?"

"That." She points out the window towards the highway.

I squint at where my daughter is pointing and think I see something, but with the rain, it fades into the blur. "Come," I say, "you can sleep in my bed." I tuck her in and pull the covers up to her chin, then give her a kiss on the cheek. "Go to sleep now, little one. In the morning the storm will be all done and we can splash in some puddles."

I rush back to the window, but I see nothing. A crack of lightning streaks across the sky, lighting up the road, thunder booming immediately after. The storm is right on top of us.

I crawl back into bed and try to sleep. An hour later I wake to the phone ringing and Lila back in bed with me; Louise is between us. I reach for the receiver. "Hello," I say.

"Gerry," Hank says. "We've got a fire at the resort. Pick you up in five."

"Who was that?" Lila says after I've hung up.

"Hank," I say. "Fire at the resort, probably a lightning strike. Hank's picking me up." I lean over and give her a kiss; her hair is damp.

"Left the window open in the truck. Went outside to close it," she says.

"You stay here with Mommy," I say to my daughter. "I'll be back soon."

"Okay, Daddy," she says, then rolls over and snuggles into her mom.

Chapter 21

The phone is ringing. I'm at the water's edge, looking across the lake admiring the gold and red leaves mixed in with the boreal forest, and I decide to let it go to voice mail. When I return to the cabin an hour later, I check the machine. Aunt Bernice's voice is asking if I could please call her back and I kick myself for not answering.

"Ruby," she says without saying hello, as if she knew it was me calling.

"Aunt Bernice," I say quickly. "Is everything alright?"

"I'm good, I'm good. Had that bit of a cold this past summer, but still kicking, as they say."

"Why are you calling? Do you or Aunt Marjorie need some help?"

"No, no, dear. Everything's okay. Sorry if I scared you. I had a dream. I want you to make sure you lock your doors, that's all," she says.

"Lock my doors?"

"Yes. When you go out. Make sure to lock your doors when you go out."

"Alright," I say, thinking about the times I've gone out and left them open, something I'd never have even thought about doing in the city. With no one else but Missy living out here, I've never been worried about break-ins and fumbling with my arms full of groceries to find my key, felt unnecessary. "Why?"

"I saw the cabin in disarray, like someone had been searching for something. Sorry, I wasn't going to call…"

"I told her not to," Marjorie interrupts on the other line. "Said it would only scare you. But then I thought, some of her other dreams have come true so…"

"So I called," Bernice says.

"Well, I'm glad you did," I say. "It's good to hear from you. Sorry I haven't been into the city to visit."

We talk for an hour, sharing stories about the neighbourhood, about their friends, and about what I do all day long at the lake. Near the end of the conversation, feeling guilty about ignoring them for the past few months, I blurt out, "I've been thinking about hosting Christmas this year. Nothing's written in stone yet, but would you be able to join us if I do?"

"If you host Christmas this year, my dear," Bernice says, "my sister and I will be there with bells on."

Chapter 22

I open the back door to find my husband standing on the step, a bottle of wine in his hand. I'm not surprised he's here because I've just got off the phone with Louise, who warned me a man fitting my husband's description had been at her store asking directions.

A month ago, over a bottle of wine, I confessed to Louise the story of my marriage, and asked her to let me know if a man in his early-sixties with a crew cut and an arrogant attitude, stops and asks directions to my house. She then confessed to me that she's also a victim of domestic violence, and her ex-husband beat her for years. Each time, when he was done, he'd cry and tell her he'd never hit her again, that it wasn't her fault, and he would change if she'd just give him another chance. Then the next time she did something he felt was wrong, he'd strike her again. Any indiscretion could set him off, she said. Leaving the heat turned up when they went out, spilling a glass of milk, not getting the laundry done; any little thing, no matter how insignificant, would cause his temper to flare.

After years of staying out of his daughter's affairs because she'd asked him to, Gerry intervened and told his son-in-law to leave. Her dad told him if he refused to leave, that at some point he could count on dying, and was losing his life worth staying married to his daughter? It wasn't a direct threat, just that he would die. He explained to his son-in-law, dying could mean slipping in that old clawfoot bathtub that needed replacing and hitting his head. He could fall down those steep stairs to the basement and break his neck. Electrocuting himself when he was replacing that old light fixture in the living room ceiling, or even cutting off a limb while trimming the overgrown trees in the backyard then bleeding out. And, he said, any of these things could happen when he least expected them, as accidents tend to do. He said all of this in a calm voice, as if he and his son-in-law were the best of friends, and he was simply looking out for his welfare. Louise laughed when she told me that part, as that is so much the way Gerry is; calm, cool, and collected, but you know when he says something, he means it. Her husband packed up that day and never returned.

After I heard her story, I felt silly for complaining about my marriage, and explained to Louise that I'm not a victim of domestic violence, just a victim of my own stupidity in marrying the first man who said he loved me, and her married life had been far worse than mine. She pointed out that mental abuse is just as cruel as physical violence, sometimes even worse as the victim doesn't see herself as a victim so she doesn't tell anyone. And because of that, the guilt she feels in leaving is greater than if she leaves because she'd been punched in the face or pushed down the stairs. She ended her story by telling me that I'm not stupid. I'm not sure if anyone had ever said that to me since my mother died.

"Ruby," Steve says, flashing me a fake smile. "You're looking great. Have you lost weight?"

"What do you want?" I ask.

"Now, is that any kind of a greeting?" he says without answering me. "We haven't seen each other since you sold our house, and all you can ask is what do I want?"

I keep my arm blocking the doorway.

"I came to see if you were okay, of course," he continues. "I assumed you were buying another house in the city. I had no idea you'd moved here. You've fallen off the map these past few months."

"No one knew. I wanted to do it on my own."

"That's what Robert said. Told me you didn't share any of your plans with them until after you'd already made the decision to move and put the house up for sale. My, my, you're becoming quite the independent girl these days, aren't you?"

I attempt to close the door but he puts his foot across the threshold.

"When Robert said you'd renovated the cabin your dad gave you, I was shocked. Didn't think you had it in you to live out here all by yourself. Thought for sure you'd buy some apartment style condo in the city and have your children look after you the rest of your days. I decided I'd better drive up to see what I could do to help, make sure you haven't taken on more than you can handle."

"I do not need your help," I say. "I'm doing perfectly fine. The last thing I need is for you to check up on me."

"Come on, Rubes," he says, looking over my shoulder into the kitchen. "Be nice. I'm just worried about you, that's all." He holds up the bottle of wine. "I've brought your favourite. Let me in, give me the grand tour."

"It's eleven in the morning," I say, nodding at the bottle.

"I sincerely hope I didn't drive all the way out here just to be turned away at the door. At least let me use the bathroom. It's a long drive home."

I sigh, then step aside and allow him to pass.

"Wow," he says. "Look at this place." He stomps his boot on the floor. "Real hardwood. You've always wanted that. Must have cost a bundle. And granite countertops." He slides his hand over the smooth stone. "Kudos to whoever picked this out. Very classy."

"I picked it out," I say.

"You picked it out?" he says. "When we lived together, you were too scared to decide what kind of coffee you wanted at Starbucks, let alone redecorate the house."

"You mean you wouldn't allow me to redecorate the house," I say.

He ignores me and begins opening cupboard doors until he finds where the wine glasses are kept and takes out two. He twists the top off the bottle and pours us both a glass then picks them up and moves to the living room, setting one on the coffee table. He stands in front of the window, his glass of wine in hand. "A cabin at the lake, something you always wanted. Good for you, Ruby." He turns to look at me. "I'm happy for you."

"Why are you here, Steve?"

"I already told you. To see how you're doing. You are still my wife, after all. I have a right to find out if you're ok."

"I thought you were going to arrange for a lawyer and get the ball rolling for a divorce? I thought you'd had enough of looking after me and couldn't wait to be free."

"Yeah, well, I guess, at the time, I was tired of doing everything. Thirty-five years is a long time to be the one everyone counts on to keep a roof over their heads and food on the table. But then I thought," He stops when he glances at my untouched glass of wine. "Have a drink with me, Ruby," he orders. I pick up the glass. "But then I thought," he continues, "what kind of a husband am I if I can't even look after my wife? Especially out here in the wilderness, where having a man around might come in handy. Someone to chop the wood, light the fires, fight off the bears." He turns in a circle. "This place is great. Whoever your decorator is has done an excellent job."

I say nothing.

"Yes," he continues. "Very tasteful yet cozy at the same time."

He sets down his glass on the coffee table and points towards the staircase. "Do you mind? Gotta take a whiz."

"Go ahead," I sigh. "But then I want you to go."

He starts up the staircase, pausing on the bottom step. "Creaks," he says. "You should get that fixed before it gets worse."

"I like it," I say. "Gives the place character."

While he's gone, I put a coaster under his glass and take mine to the kitchen and dump it down the drain.

I hear the toilet flush, but he doesn't come down right away. When he does, he's gushing about the view. "I don't know who your contractor was, but what a great idea to have a balcony outside the bedroom window." He picks up his glass, noticing the coaster, and pulls back a large swallow, then sets the glass down on the wood, ignoring the coaster.

"There was already a balcony when I bought the place. I had it rebuilt. It was the idea of the original owner, a woman, who ran the resort for thirty-four years."

"Was it now?"

"She did. She made her own way in the world. I liked the idea of living in the place she originally built."

He faces me. "Is that what you're trying to do; make your own way in the world? Got to be careful about that, Ruby, you don't want to run home with your tail between your legs. You know you're not the independent type. I think you need to give some thought to us getting back together before you get in over your head."

I knew that's what was coming, knew it from the moment he walked in the back door. Robert likely told him how much this place is worth, and he arrived here today to put an end to the separation so he can move back in and convince me to sell, then take over managing my money yet again. I'd be willing to bet he has his suitcase in the trunk of his car.

"I do not need for us to get back together," I say. "I'm doing fine on my own."

He feigns surprise. "Surely you remember it was only a trial separation," he says. "We needed to give ourselves some cooling down time. I don't know about you, but I miss our life. Miss watching television with you, going out for lunches, having a drink together before supper."

"We haven't done those things for over thirty years, long before we separated. And a cooling down time were your words, not mine."

"We had thirty-five years together, managed to have three kids. We must have done something right. I've decided I don't want our marriage to end."

He moves towards me, I step backwards. "It takes two to make that decision, Steve. What if I've had enough of this marriage?"

"You don't know what you're saying," he says. "You need me."

He reaches for me but I duck out of his way. "If there's something I've learned in the past year and a half," I say, "is that I don't need you. Thanks to your leaving, I've realized I'm perfectly fine on my own."

He smirks and I want to slap that arrogant grin off his face. "Of course, you need me, Ruby. We both know that. You can't do anything without me."

"I've done all this," I say. "Renovated the cabin, learned to drive, learned how to pay bills. Even made friends without your help. It's not as complicated as you made it out to be. As a matter of fact, I think my job of keeping the house clean, making the meals, and raising our children was far more labour intensive than your job ever was."

"I was a police officer," he says in a patronizing tone. "I put my life on the line every day."

"And I agree," I say. "Being a cop is hard, there were days I worried if you'd be coming home. But until you've changed a diaper on one kid, while making supper for a spouse who had to have things perfect, climbed up the ladder to retrieve your son's running shoe from the roof, or entertained ten kids for your daughter's birthday party that you had to have finished before your husband came home from work, you've no idea what hard work is. Did Robert tell you I managed to avoid being attacked by a bear, or that I made it out of the woods by myself? I didn't have you to tell me what to do then, and I don't need you to tell me what to do now."

He's turned towards the window and I realize my words are falling on deaf ears; just like they did when we were together.

"What else did Robert tell you?" I say.

"I don't know what you mean?"

"What did our son tell you that prompted you to make the five-hour trip up here when you haven't worried once in the past year and a half about how I'm doing? Did he tell you how much this place is worth?"

"It's worth a lot?"

"Don't play innocent with me. I've always been able to tell when you aren't telling the truth, much as you like to think I walked around in a daze for thirty-five years." I shake my head. "All those affairs you had. You think I didn't know? I turned the other cheek just so I'd have a home to live in, just so I wouldn't have to figure out how to survive by myself. Good old Ruby, sweeping all the crap under the rug because she was too afraid to make it on her own. But I knew what you were doing; it was written all over that smug face of yours."

"I had no affairs," he says. "That's your inferiority complex telling you that. You've never felt as good as others, have you Ruby? I blame your dad. Too involved in his own life to look after you. It is true, however," he says, "that Robert told me how much this place is worth, but honestly, that's not why I'm here."

"My father left this to me," I say. "The will stipulated you're allowed no financial gain from this property unless I agreed to it. The only way you'd be able get your hands on any of it, married or divorced, would be if I signed the papers allowing you access, which I can assure you, won't be happening. Not like when you stole half my inheritance."

"Is that any way to talk to someone who loved and supported you for thirty-five years? Without me, you would have stayed in your father's house until the day you died. I'm the one who bought you a house, gave you a life, gave you a family, allowed you to grow up. Without me, you'd have nothing."

"Grow up!" I yell. "I was a child when you married me, and until a year ago, I was still that dependent child, waiting for you to tell me how high to jump. You may have taken half the money my father left me, but you are not taking half of my house. This belongs to me and to me alone!"

"Calm down," he says, patting the air, trying to placate me as if I'm a child. "The only reason I've come out here is because I love you and I thought you might need a bit of help. There was no ulterior motive."

"I find that hard to believe."

"What if I ask you to marry me again? Would that make you believe that I love you and only want what's best for you? We could renew our wedding vows. Don't you think the kids would like that?"

"Renew our wedding vows!" I say. "Our kids are ages thirty-four, thirty-two, and twenty-nine. If they can't manage the fact that their parents are not together anymore, then they're the ones who need to grow up. Now," I say, walking into the kitchen. "It's time for you to leave." I place my hand on the back door knob.

Instead of following, he sits on the couch. "Robert told me something else."

"You know, Steve, I don't want to hear. All I want from you is to leave me alone." I open the door. "I'm a different woman than I was last year. I'm not afraid to look after myself. I've discovered that I'm just as capable as the next person, even though you liked me to believe I wasn't."

"He said there's possibly gold out here," he says, talking over my voice. "Hidden on this land by the crazy lady who used to own the place."

"That's only our son's obsession with becoming wealthy." I say. "Something you instilled in him. Always talking about money, always telling him that a measure of a man's worth is how much money he makes, always counting every nickel and dime. This cabin was totally rebuilt and nothing was found. Trees were taken out, trenches dug, walls rebuilt and floorboards torn out exposing the ground below and nothing was found. Not to mention all the people who've searched the property in the last fifty years and found nothing. And Cecelia wasn't crazy. She was smart and strong. She made a life for herself out here in the woods after she was abandoned by her family just because she had a baby out of wedlock!" By the time I stop talking, I'm shouting.

"Like I said, crazy," he says calmly, making me sound like a shrew. He pulls open the front door and steps outside.

I grab my coat from the hook at the back door and follow him.

"Wow," he says, walking towards the lake. A thin coat of ice shimmers across the water. "Look at this view. How much property do you own?" he asks.

"Everything you see," I say.

He whistles as if he didn't already know. "You'll be a wealthy woman when you sell, Rube."

"I have no plans to sell," I say. "As a matter of fact, I've been thinking about expanding, not leaving."

He spins towards me. "Expanding. How so?"

"Nothing," I say, regretting my knee-jerk reaction. "Just something Jess and Debby said to me a while back."

"And what did our darling daughters tell you now? That you should open your own resort or something foolish like that?"

I keep my mouth closed.

"That's it, isn't it? That's what they told you? Takes a lot of brains to run an operation like that. You'd need a man around to help."

"I think I could manage," I say.

"You should do it, then," he says. "If you think you can do it, then you should."

"I should?"

"Sure. Run your own business. See what it's like to actually have a job. Maybe you'll appreciate what I did all those years."

"Steve," I say. "I appreciated you. Of course, I appreciated you. You gave me a roof over my head, food on the table. It's just that I want to…."

"Make your own life," he says. "Be," he makes quotation marks, "independent."

"So far, it's only a thought. I have no intention of running out to start renovating the cabins tomorrow."

"Go for it, Ruby. See what you can do. Everyone gets their shot, maybe this will be your fifteen minutes." He heads back to the cabin, lifting his empty glass in the air. "One more for the road."

"No, Steve. I'd like you to go now."

"I think I'll stay the night. Too much driving here and back in one day." He opens the front door just as a wind blows through the front yard, causing the trees to sway and pinecones to fall from the trees.

"Storm's coming," I say, looking up at the clouds blowing across the lake as I join him on the step.

"That came up fast," he says putting his hand to his brow to look at the darkening sky. "Didn't look like a storm when I was driving in."

"Storms can sneak up on you up here. It's having trees on all sides. You don't know the storm is on top of you until it hits."

"A little bit of rain won't hurt us." He grabs me around the waist. "That might not be so bad, hey? Being stuck out here, rain beating on the windows. Kind of romantic. Chance to test out that new bedroom of yours."

"Plough wind, Steve," I say, pulling out of his grasp.

Another gust blows across the yard and he looks between the tree tops at the blue sky. "Plough wind? This far north?"

"Oh yeah, for sure. Already had one earlier this summer. Turned two of the cabins to rubble. Took out one hundred-year-old trees. I hid in the new addition for hours."

"Really?" he asks looking me in the eye. "A plough wind? You get lots of them here?"

I nod, trying not to blink.

He lets go of me and looks at his watch. "I just remembered. I have an appointment. First thing in the morning. Need to get home. Can't waste any more time checking up on you," he says as if his driving up here was my idea.

We walk around the side of the cabin to the backyard.

"Don't take any wooden nickels, Ruby," he says as he climbs into his car. "You know how gullible you can be."

"Married you, didn't I," I say. "Can't get more gullible than that."

He looks directly at me and shakes his head. "You've changed, and believe me when I tell you, it's not in a good way." He slams his door and speeds away, shooting dust and gravel in his wake. The moment he's out of sight, the winds calm, and the sun returns.

Chapter 23

I've chopped some wood and am stacking it in the box I keep in the back porch when Wilson pulls into the yard. As I've seen him do countless times, he hops out of the truck with the agility of a man half his age.

"Wilson," I say, "good to see you."

"Thought I'd better drive out; make sure you're ready for winter," he says without any of the preamble most people begin their conversations with. "Big storm coming next week. You need to be prepared."

"Are you sure? I didn't hear anything about a storm on the weather channel."

Once again, he looks at me like I'm the stupidest person in the world. He nods at the axe in my hands. "You need to keep that in the back porch, maybe even two in case one breaks. And get them sharpened; there's a business in town that sharpens skates, take it there. You need a good supply of chopped wood and kindling in the back porch, more than you have in that little box. Enough to last you a week, two if you have the room."

"But I have a furnace, and an electric fireplace, and a phone," I say.

"And you live by yourself in the bush. You never know what can happen. What if you lose power or the lines freeze? What if the propane truck can't get here? What if the phone lines go down? You already lived through a storm; you know what a helpless feeling it is to be here alone with the power out. You can't just call someone to rescue you, or run to the neighbours for help. You need to think ahead if you want to live out here. Always have a backup plan."

He walks to the woodpile near the outhouse. "This needs to be closer to the cabin. Should have been moved weeks ago. Two or three storms from now, you'll never find it, or you'll never get to it." He picks up a log. "Some of this is too green; needs to be separated from the stuff you can burn now." He enters the shed, removing two snow shovels, and the two extension cords I bought at Carnations'. "Do you have snowshoes?" he asks.

"There's a pair of Cecelia's hanging on a hook on the back wall, just in front of the car."

He disappears inside and returns with the old-fashioned snow-shoes in hand. "Once the temperature drops, always keep your car plugged in, even if it's parked inside. That shed is uninsulated. And buy yourself some winter tires. Highway is no place to be without winter tires. What about a battery charger?"

"A what?" I ask.

He sighs and opens the passenger door of his truck, lifting a small metal box with a cord attached, off the seat. "This is a battery charger," he says. "You attach it to your battery when your car won't start." When he sees the confused look on my face he says, "I'll show you how to use it before I leave. Make sure you keep a spare set of keys in the coat you plan on wearing this winter, and don't leave the cabin without that coat on. Trick Cecelia taught me when I was a kid. It's one thing getting locked out in the summer, but in the winter, you could lose a limb, not to mention, your life."

"You've never said you and she were friends."

"That's because we weren't. I was a boy; she must have been in her fifties. Gerry brought me out here a couple of times to help with a few things." He hands me the shovels. "Keep these in the back porch all winter. They won't do you any good in the shed. Snow can climb half way up those doors if the wind is blowing the right way. Even the front and back doors of the cabin can be blown in. Have to chop your way out."

"Okay," I say, a bit worried about that last sentence.

"Have you stocked up on groceries yet?"

"Not yet," I say. "I can do that today."

"You'll want enough for a minimum of one month, two if you have the room. Southside is only a couple of kilometres away, but in a storm, it may as well be a hundred miles."

For the next half hour, Wilson and I restack the woodpile closer to the cabin, separating the green from the seasoned. When we're done, he drapes an orange tarpaulin over the top of the pile that's ready to use, tying it to stakes he's pounded into the ground. Then while I stock the back porch with the items he tells me I'll need this winter, he finishes chopping three times as much wood as I've already chopped.

"Wilson," I say.

He grunts.

"Do you think there's another woman living out here, maybe on the other side of the lake?" I ask.

"Only woman I know who's silly enough to live out here by herself, is you."

"Do you know about the ghost?"

"No time for such things," he says.

"But you told Louise to talk to me. That day I got lost in the woods and saw Missy, you said she should talk to me."

"About not going in the forest alone," he says. "You want to talk to people who aren't there, that's your business."

"Last spring, why didn't you want to look in the Vereschuk's cabin when we were searching for a place for me to stay during the renovations?"

"Place was over a hundred years old. Storm took it, didn't it? That should tell you something."

"Not because you believed it was haunted?"

"I already told you what I think about that. Now," he holds the battery charger up. "Do you want to waste my time talking about ghosts, or do you want to learn how to use this thing?"

—

The sun is low on this cloudless day in October, and after Wilson has left, I drive to town for supplies. The road is still free of ice, and with the little bit of snow that's fallen so far, I can't help but hope that Wilson is wrong, and winter will hold off for a few more weeks. The winter after Steve left, my kids brought me my groceries, took me to my appointments, made sure I didn't have to drive anywhere until spring. I don't know if they did this for their peace of mind, or mine, but I accepted their help gratefully, and from the first snowfall to the spring melt, I hobbled myself, my fear of driving on icy roads so great. So now, because my winter driving experience is minimal, I'm hoping Mother Nature gives me a few more weeks reprieve. I arrive at Carnation's to find Gerry inside sitting beside a space heater.

"Gerry," I say, "I was worried when I didn't see you on the porch."

"Cold enough out there to freeze the balls off a brass monkey," he says. "This is where you'll find me for the next six months, God willing."

"Don't say that, Dad, it's bad luck to joke about dying. And you know you could stay home. You'd be more comfortable at the house," Louise says.

"This is where I plan on buying the farm," he says. "In my chair, in my store, talking to my customers. So don't tell me what to do, woman!" He looks at me and winks. "You're looking well, Ruby. This country living seems to agree with you."

"So far, so good," I say. "Wilson said there's going to be a storm next week. Thought I'd better stock up on supplies."

"If Wilson says there's going to be a storm, then you'd best heed his advice. Walking barometer, that man."

"Say, Gerry," I say. "I was poking through the shed the other day and remembered the canoe up in the rafters. I'm thinking about next year maybe taking it out. Do you know if it's still usable?"

"I'm closing up now, Dad. You ready?" Louise says, interrupting his answer.

"Oh, I'm sorry," I say, looking at my watch. "I didn't realize how late it is. I'll let you go; we can talk some other time."

"You go," Gerry says, turning to his daughter. "Ruby can walk me home."

"If you're sure?" She looks back and forth between her dad and me.

"I'm sure," her dad says.

"Don't forget to lock the back door when you leave."

"Guess I've passed into that age where your children start treating you as the child," he says after his daughter has gone.

"I'm jealous of your relationship," I say. "Never had that with my dad."

"I'm a lucky man," he says. "I've had a good life and a job that I loved, both here and at the resort. I would have liked it if I could have worked for Cecelia for a few more years, and I truly believe that if she hadn't died, Sunset Lake Resort would have been popular into the seventies, eighties, and even the nineties; but I've had a good run, longer than most." He stands and pushes his walker to the window. "Some days I can't believe I'm as old as I am." He turns to me. "You said something about Cecelia's canoe?"

"Do you think it's worth taking down? Checking to see if it's sea worthy?"

"Depends. Can't recall if she repaired it or not."

"It needed fixing?"

"Had a hole in the bottom. 1955. The guest canoes had already been locked up in the shed for the night. Cecelia kept hers beside her cabin; she often went out for a late-night paddle. One of the guests borrowed it. He took his son to the other side of the lake. It's wilder over there, lots of broken off trees hiding beneath the surface, lots of floaters to maneuver around. The bottom of the canoe caught on something beneath the surface, tore a hole in the wood and the canoe sank. Young boy fell overboard, got tangled with tree roots under the water."

"Oh no," I say.

"He didn't drown, thank God, but it was a close call. Cecelia was pretty upset. Talked of shutting down the resort, but calmer heads prevailed. She consulted a lawyer who contacted the father of the boy. He agreed to settle out of court, for a fee, of course. Don't know how much she paid him, she never told me, but the man never said anything to the press. The publicity would have ruined the resort's reputation.

"I suggested, just to be on the safe side, that she get rid of the canoes, so she did. All but hers. She kept it in the shed up on the rafters where it is now. Only took it out when the resort was closed during shoulder season in the fall and spring." Gerry pauses. "It's funny; the next day I went to the spot the canoe sank, but there were no submerged tree trunks, and the truth of the matter is, canoes don't puncture easily. Tip sure, swamp definitely, but puncture, not that easily. Hell, I've rowed over rocks and nothing's happened. It's almost as if, since only Cecelia used that particular canoe, someone had purposely made a weak spot, intentionally wanting the canoe to sink with her in it. But we left it at that and went on with the business of running the resort. It's good she didn't close. She would have missed being open during the most prosperous years."

"The fifties, you mean?"

"The boom began when the war ended," Gerry says, "but during the fifties, those were the busiest years. Across the country, lake resorts became the place to take your kids for the summer. You didn't have the responsibility or the expense of owning your own cabin, but you could still have the enjoyment of living at one for the summer. Nowadays, of course, people have fancier holidays to go on, but back then, this was the cat's meow."

"I wish my parents had brought me out here," I say. "You and your family must have had fun, the resort being so close."

"Lila didn't like it at the beach. She'd go out once in a while if I begged her, but she wasn't really a lake person. I think Cecelia intimidated her, which was silly. But it was what it was." He rubs his hands over his face. "Now," he says, "if you'll be so kind to escort an old man home, I'd like to have my supper."

—

I pull into the yard and notice tire tracks in the skiff of snow. The backdoor is open, and from the step I can see the kitchen has been ransacked. With my heart pounding, I enter my cabin. Dishes have been pulled out of cupboards and lie in broken shards on the floor. The fridge has been emptied, and the cookstove, disassembled. The door to the addition is open and inside I see food that was once frozen, laying on the floor. I tiptoe past puddles to unplug the empty deepfreeze then return to the kitchen. In the living room, one of the front windows has been smashed, and the front door also stands wide open. Furniture has been pulled away from walls, and walls have holes in them as if they've been hit with a sledge hammer. On rubbery legs, I climb the stairs to find my bedroom and bathroom in much the same disarray. I grab the phone on my night table and dial Louise.

"I've been broken into," I say, my voice cracking.

"What?" she says. "Is that you Ruby? I can hardly hear you."

Between sobs I say, "Someone's been in my cabin and torn it apart."

"Stay where you are. I'll call the police and be right there."

1955

I'm putting Louise to bed when the phone rings. Lila calls up the stairs. "Gerry, you're wanted on the phone. It's Cecelia. You only left there a couple of hours ago. Can't she live without you?"

"I'm sure she only wants me to add some items to her grocery list," I say. "Next weekend a big party is coming out. They want a wiener roast on the beach and she's running low on hot dogs."

"She asks too much of you," Lila says. "You're my husband, not hers."

"I guarantee you, my love; Cecelia would never want to marry me." I give my wife a kiss. "And be grateful for her business, it's what's keeping us in business. I take the receiver from her.

"Hello."

"Gerry," Cecelia screams. "There's been an accident you need to come out here, right now!"

Chapter 24

"Do you keep anything of value out here?" the officer asks.

"I don't own anything of value," I say, "unless you consider my grandmother's tea service, valuable."

"No expensive paintings, sculptures, that kind of thing?"

I look at him, wondering if he thinks he's stumbled onto some sort of art theft ring. "I own nothing valuable," I repeat.

"Well," he says, glancing around the room, "it looks to me as if someone was searching for something."

"I have no idea what that could be," I say.

"Holes in the walls, things torn apart. Yup, someone was definitely looking for something. Do you have any enemies?"

"I have no enemies."

"Were you out?"

"I was."

"Did you lock the doors when you left? It's the kind of place, out here all by yourself, where people might consider just leaving the door unlocked."

"Of course it was locked," I say, thinking about Bernice's warning.

"Where's your husband?"

"In the city. We don't live together."

"Divorced?"

"Separated."

He jots something down in his notebook and I wonder if he's

writing down that some stupid woman decided to live by herself in the woods without a man to look out for her.

"I have no idea who could have done this." Tears roll down my cheeks. Louise hands me a tissue. "Sorry," I say. "This is a bit upsetting. My new cabin is," I look around me, my hands in the air, "ruined."

"Not ruined," Louise says. "Wilson will be able to fix this up in no time."

"Isn't this the place where that woman was supposed to have hidden some sort of treasure a hundred years ago?" the cop says. "Maybe someone from town came looking for it?"

"It is," I say. "And not a hundred years ago. She died in 1965." The officer can't be more than twenty-five years old and I'm sure 1965 likely seems like a hundred years ago to him.

"Okay then," he says. "I'll talk to my supervising officer, but I'm pretty sure that other than sending a patrol car to drive past a couple times a week, there's nothing else we can do for you. You need to file a claim with your insurance company, and you're good to go." He tips his hat and leaves.

"You should stay with us tonight," Louise says. "At least until you have the window fixed. I'll help you clean this up tomorrow."

—

"I thought you were going to get a dog?" Darren says as he boards up the window.

Louise was here bright and early to help me sweep up glass, and throw things out. I called my insurance company and they said if I take pictures of the damage and send them in, I can go ahead and get the damage repaired. He said from what I've told him, they will most likely be issuing a cheque, but it could take a month or two. So, because I don't want to stay at Louise's place for a month, I called Wilson and he said he'd send Darren out today to board up the hole and repair the damage. He's ordered a new window, and as soon as it comes in, he'll install it for me.

"Your dad suggested I get one, but I haven't got around to it yet. I guess if I'd listened, I wouldn't be in this situation now."

"Do you know who would have done such a thing?" Darren asks, looking around at the damage.

"The cops thought maybe someone from town who's heard about Cecelia hiding treasure out here."

Darren laughs. "I doubt that. When we were kids, a couple of my friends and I would come out here every Hallowe'en to look around. Don't know why we picked Hallowe'en, but we did. We'd dig holes in the beach, as if no one else had ever thought to look there. Search through the bush, sure we were going to find something in a tree or under some broken limbs and become instantly wealthy. We were even in the cabins a few times, but they were pretty spooky. Just sort of ran through them screaming, then told the other kids we looked in them but didn't find anything, as if no one else had ever thought of doing that. I think this place has been pretty thoroughly searched over the years," he says.

"Then who could it be?" I say.

He taps the wood that's now replacing the broken glass. The cabin is dark without the natural light and I hope the window doesn't take too long to arrive. "If this damage was done by someone looking for treasure, then it's someone new to hearing about the possibility of money being hidden. Who've you told about the one hundred dollars you found during the renovations?"

"Just the people at the party last summer," I say.

"What about your husband? From what you told me, he's interested in money. Would he wreck your house looking for it? Are your children in contact with him? I seem to remember the subject coming up last fall at that wiener roast. Perhaps one of your kids said something to him?"

I'm quiet, realizing who could have done this.

Darren meets my eyes with a knowing look. "I think, Ruby, that you should get yourself a dog, and soon. There's a pound two hours north of here. Go and look and don't come back without one."

Darren leaves and I make a phone call. The answering machine picks up and my husband's voice tells me to leave a message. At the beep I say, "I want to thank you, Steve, for thirty-five years of putting a roof over our heads and food on the table for the kids and I. For looking after a woman who thought she was incapable of looking after herself. For waiting patiently for the inheritance that never came to fruition. But I no longer need to be married to you. I've discovered that I am more than capable of taking care of myself. Tomorrow I'm calling my lawyer and filing for divorce. And if you refuse, I will make sure all your cop friends know what you've done. I'm sure break and entry is illegal even for a police officer." I hang up.

Chapter 25

"This one is cute," I say. "Don't you think, Jess? What breed is it, do you know?"

"Maybe a lab cross? I've heard labs are easy to train, but not that ferocious. What about this one, Mom? Looks ferocious but at the same time, kind of friendly."

"Maybe," I say. "There's this one too. Nice welcoming face. How much is he?" I ask the assistant whose name tag says Brianna.

"The puppies are all the same price. Doesn't matter what size or what sex. Only time the price is different is if they've already been spayed or neutered which usually means it's an older dog. They're cheaper because we don't have to pay to have the procedure done. You can't adopt a dog without it being spayed or neutered."

The day after Darren repaired my window, door, and walls, I called Jess to see if she'd accompany me to the pound to help me pick out a dog. I told her to call her sister to see if she wanted to join us, and that after we get the dog, the two of them are welcome to stay overnight and I'd make them supper. This morning, the girls arrived in Debby's SUV, then the three of us drove to the pound.

When the kids were young, many times they asked for a dog, but Steve said no, claiming he was allergic. I knew he wasn't allergic, but was afraid of dogs, having been bitten when he was a child. He didn't tell this to the kids because he felt it would undermine his authority to admit to a weakness. I'm hoping his fear of dogs is something that will benefit me.

"How do you tell which one would make the best guard dog without being the kind of dog that would attack its owner?" Debby asks.

"I suppose a dog who's been abused by its owner might not be the best choice for you," the assistant says. "As well as a power breed. They need someone who knows how to handle dogs, especially if you've never owned a dog before. Have any of you owned a dog before?"

"We haven't," I say. "Do you have any recommendations?"

"Well," she says, biting her lip. "There's Bull over here. Pitbull cross. He would make a great watch dog."

She points to a hulking brown dog standing at the back of his cage. I reach out my hand, and he curls his lip and growls.

"But like I said, perhaps not the dog for you." She stops by a cage with a medium sized white dog standing near the door and wagging its tail. On the cage door, under the number 428, it says, Daisy. "She's a poodle, golden lab cross. They're called labradoo-dles. Non-shedding if you're allergic. Very docile. More like a big lap dog."

"She looks very sweet," I say as Daisy licks my hand through the wire cage. "But she might be too gentle. I live alone in the country and need a dog who's going to tell me when there's someone in my yard. A dog who will scare away a potential burglar."

"Here's one, Mom," Debby says. I look at the tiny dog licking her hand.

"Too small, Debs. Something bigger, but not too big."

"Mom," she says. "Just tell me what kind of dog you're looking for."

"A dog that's not too big and not too small. A dog who will warn me when someone's on my land, but a dog that lets the people in I want to see."

"In other words, a dog that doesn't exist," Jess says.

"The dog does exist," Brianna says. "It's the training that makes the dog, not the breed. If you prove yourself to be the leader, then the dog will respect you and listen. Then and only then will you have the perfect dog. That said, there are dogs that train easier than others."

I stop by a cage in the far corner. "What about this one?" I look for a name but all I can see is number 117. "Why doesn't he or she have a name?"

"Oh, I'm sorry, he's scheduled to be euthanized this evening." She looks at her watch. "I told Mike to take him out of here an hour ago. He's not supposed to leave these dogs here for visitors to see."

I stare at the poor animal crouching in the corner of its cage. "Why is he scheduled to be euthanized?"

"Nothing he's done, just been here too long. Over eleven months now. We don't have the funds or the room to house dogs for longer than that. He's been adopted a couple of times, but always returned to us after a few weeks. Not affectionate enough was the complaint both times. And he's a border collie, very intelligent, but needs a lot of interaction. Unless you have the time to exercise this breed a lot, or are taking them home to heard your flock of sheep, they don't tend to be adopted as easily as dogs who are happy laying in front of the fire all day. It's sad we have to put them down, but it's the reality of running an animal shelter. They don't all find their forever homes."

"What was his name before he landed on death row?" I ask.

"His name's Scout. He's…" she flips the pages, "…seven years old, just about eight. But like I said, he's not up for adoption anymore."

I kneel and look Scout in the face. His tail gently wags on the cage bottom, before he turns his head away, as if he knows his time is up. "I want this one," I say. "I'd like to adopt Scout."

"I'll have to go and talk to my supervisor. The papers to have him put down have already been drawn up."

"You do that," I say. "My daughters and I will wait here while you get it all sorted out. Could you open the cage, please? I'd like to pet him."

—

Two hours later, the girls are in the front seat of Debby's car, with Scout curled up in the back seat beside me as we drive home to Sunset Lake. He came with me willingly but still hasn't given me any affection, not even a lick on my outstretched hand. Nor has he stood up to look out the window with his tongue hanging out like I've always imagined dogs do in cars; as if he doesn't trust the fact that he's been adopted and thinks I'm simply taking him for a car ride then dropping him back off at the shelter. We pull into the yard and I open the car door.

"Come on, Scout," I say. "You're home. This is where you're going to live now."

Tentatively, the dog steps off the seat and out onto the soft ground. Immediately, his nose goes down and he begins sniffing. He lifts his leg next to the tire.

"No, no, Scout," Debby says. "Not on my car."

"Over here, boy." I lead him to a spot near the back fence. "Good boy," I say when he goes where I've pointed. "You are clever, aren't you? Come on, lets go inside."

As I'm unlocking the door, the four of us crowded on the back step, the dog turns his head towards the south side where the Vereschuk's cabin used to sit, and whines. I quickly open the door. "Come on boy, let's get inside before we all see a ghost."

Chapter 26

Scout is curled up in front of the fireplace, and the girls and I are about to sit down and have supper when I decide I need to talk to them.

"What's up, Mom?" Debby says.

"I've something to tell you." I look at each of their faces in turn. When they were children, the thought of divorce would, on occasion, cross my mind, but along with fear of being alone, I didn't want my children to see me as a failure. Today, I pause, hesitant to tell them, not because I think it will hurt them, but because I don't want them to think less of me.

"What is it, Mom," Jess says.

"I'm filing for divorce. Your dad and I will not be getting back together."

"Mom," Debby says. "I don't think any of us thought you and Dad would be getting back together. Well, except maybe Robert."

"I'm sorry," I say.

My youngest puts her arm around my shoulders. "Mom, it's okay, really. You don't have anything to be sorry for. We could see how unhappy you were. Even as kids, we knew." Jess nods. "And we're adults now, it's not like the family has been torn apart. Besides, we know it was Dad who instigated the separation."

"You do?"

"You'd never have struck out on your own unless you were forced into it. Dad leaving, and you inheriting this cabin was the best thing that could have happened. Grandpa may not have given you much when he died, but in giving you this place, he gave you your freedom. Hiring contractors. Living at a lake by yourself. Chopping wood. Driving to and from town to buy your groceries. We're proud of you, Mom, not disappointed."

My eyes well with tears and I give her a hug.

"And don't worry about Robert, he'll come around. Sheryl will whip him into shape."

We decide to eat our meal while watching the movie Sixth Sense. It's not a movie I'd have chosen, but it is close to Hallowe'en and Debby insisted.

While we eat, I feed Scout on the rug in front of the fireplace. He nibbles at the bowl of food, then curls up on the rug to sleep. Occasionally, I see him open his eyes at a sound, or a movement, wary of his surroundings. Once, he even walks to the window and barks into the night as if seeing something, until Jess tells him to quit scaring her and go and lie down.

"Mom," Deb says when the movie is over and we're loading the dishwasher. "What did you mean when you said, *let's get inside before we all see a ghost?*"

"When did I say that?"

"When you were unlocking the back door. Scout whined and you said, *let's go inside before we see a ghost.*"

When I don't explain, she says, "Are you going to tell me or not?"

"Not," I say.

"Did you see a ghost?" she asks. "Is that what you meant? You saw a ghost at that cabin where you said Missy lives, and you thought Scout might see one too?"

"Of course not. There's no such thing as ghosts. And that cabin is long gone, nothing left but a pile of dirt where Wilson cleared up the debris."

"Mom, I'm old enough to not freak out if you tell me you can talk to dead people, that's okay."

"Debby, for heaven's sakes, I don't talk to dead people, and I don't see ghosts. This isn't the movies."

"Was it Cecelia?" she asks. "The woman who fell off the roof? Is that who you saw? Is that why you got a dog?"

"I told you; I didn't see a ghost. And I got a dog to scare away burglars, not ghosts. I was broken into, remember? Quit bugging me."

"There's something you're not telling us," Debby says. "I can hear it in your voice. You know I'll figure it out, I always do. You may as well just tell me."

She's right. At Christmas, no matter how much I told her no, my youngest would sit under the tree and shake, and sniff and listen to each package until she guessed what was inside. I'd even disguise the package with double wrapping paper or put things inside the box to try and fool her, but even then, nine times out of ten, she'd figure it out. I admired her tenacity and wondered how long it would take her to guess right, whereas Steve would always get angry and threaten to throw all her gifts out if she didn't quit snooping. His warnings didn't stop her, and Debby would wait until her dad was out of the house to continue her investigations.

"Okay, okay," I say. "Louise told me that when she was little, she had trouble pronouncing Cecelia, so her dad told her to call her Miss C."

Jess whips her head around. "Miss C?" she says. "You mean Missy? The person who lived at the cabin that's not there anymore? The one we tried to visit?"

"That's who she meant," I say.

"But that would mean you've been talking to…"

"A ghost," Debby finishes.

"I have not been talking to a ghost," I say. "Missy is as real as you and I. It's the same as the rumour that there's treasure hidden out here; it's just a tall tale, an urban myth. Small towns are full of them." I yawn and stretch. "Scout and I are going to bed." I give each of my daughters a hug. "Thanks for helping me today."

—

I wake to the sound of my dog barking. I've given the girls the front bedroom which is larger, and taken Scout to the small bedroom with me. In the night, curious about his new abode, the dog must have left my room and wandered down to see the girls.

"Scout, for God's sake, quit barking," Debby says, her voice muffled. She's always been a stomach sleeper and likely has her face buried into the pillow. As a child I worried she'd suffocate herself but the doctor said she'd wake up long before that happened. "You're barking loud enough to wake the dead," the words becoming louder at the end of her sentence when she lifts her head off the pillow.

All is quiet for a couple minutes until he starts again. This time it's Jessica who says something. "Scout, are you okay?" When he continues to bark, I get up and enter the bedroom. Jess is sitting on the foot of the bed, while Debby is still under the covers.

"What's going on?" I say.

"Scout keeps barking. We can't get him to stop," Debby says from her face-down prone position.

I approach the window and scratch Scout's head. "What is it, pup? Do you see something?" I look down to the yard below. Missy is sitting in the Adirondack chair looking out over the lake. I glance at Jess sitting on the bed, but she won't meet my eyes.

Chapter 27

The night after the girls have gone home, snow arrives, just as Wilson predicted. In the morning when I open the inside door, a drift is pushing against the screen, and a small pile has collected between the doors. I force the snow off the back step with the screen door, then shovel a spot near the cabin for the dog to relieve himself. Ignoring the job ahead of me, I close the door on the mountain of snow, and make Scout and I some breakfast.

An hour later, I'm outside shovelling a path to the shed, the dog tunneling through the drifts, seemingly happy to have something to do, when Wilson pulls up in his truck, a snowblower in the back. I hear a low growl from the dog.

"No," I say. "No growls."

"Don't tell him that," Wilson says as he steps onto the snow. "He's only doing his job. You want him to warn you of strangers, not lick their hands. If you don't want him to growl at specific people, you need to teach him that he can trust that person."

"How do I do that?"

"First, you lightly tap his nose with your knuckle while saying no in a sharp voice. Never hit a dog. If he does something wrong, it's not his fault, it's yours."

"I would never hit my dog," I say, offended.

"And don't be using that high-pitched girly voice women like to use when talking to dogs. Calling your dog cutie or sweetie or any of that crap won't get you anywhere. After you tap his nose and he stops barking, you tell him he's a good dog and give him a treat. Once he's learned who to trust, he'll never forget. And don't act afraid; he's sensitive to everything you do, especially this breed. They're very intuitive to what their owners are feeling. That's why they're easy to teach. Eventually, he'll learn to think on his own."

I run inside and grab a handful of kibble. When Wilson steps close to me and Scout barks, I do as Wilson instructed. Scout sits and lifts his paw. I give him the piece of dog food and tell him he's a good boy.

"I didn't know he knew how to do that," I say.

"He's a rescue. Likely been at more than one family; probably knows more than you think. Too many people adopt this breed and expect them to be a house dog, then take them back to the pound when they start tearing up the house out of boredom. He's not the kind of dog who wants to lie around all day and do nothing. He needs lots of exercise."

"That's good. I need lots of exercise too."

"And never feed him his meals outside. Dog food is as much a bear attraction as garbage."

"Good to know," I say.

"Most of the bears are hibernating for the winter, but it's never too early to get in the habit of doing things the right way." Wilson pulls a bag out of his pocket and removes a bell.

"Bought him this," he says. He takes off Scout's collar and attaches the bell.

"That's very kind, Wilson. Thank you."

"Not being kind, did it to keep him safe. Make sure you walk him around the lake, on the road to town, even through town; all the paths you normally take. Introduce him to as many people as you can." He pats Scout's head, Scout licks his hand, something he's not done with me yet. "And always keep him on a leash when you take him out of the yard. The last thing you want is for him to wander off by himself. I'll come back next week and we'll go for a walk in the woods. You need to teach this guy what paths to take. He'll learn pretty quickly which way is home. Border collies are a smart breed. Don't waste a lot of time being affectionate. Need a job if you want them to be happy."

"He has a job. To protect me. And I'd love to go for a walk with you next week."

"We're not going for a walk; we're teaching the dog how to save your ass." He jumps onto the bed of his truck and lowers a ramp, then rolls the snowblower to the ground.

"I know you don't like being complimented," I place my hand on his shoulder and feel his body tense, "but I want to thank you for all your help with the house, the yard and now with the dog. Because of everything you've taught me, I'll be fine."

"Didn't come out to tell you how to train your dog, came out to blow some snow. Dog was here and I saw you didn't know what you were doing."

He pulls the rope on the snowblower and blows out the driveway. When he's done, he says, "Nice meeting you, Scout." The dog lifts his paw. "You look after her, you hear me. She needs all the help she can get."

—

I'm trying to stay awake so I can show Missy to Scout from my bedroom window. I want to teach the dog that when he sees her, he's to wag his tail and not bark and I'm hoping to be able to do this without having to introduce Scout directly to her. So far, in the past few days, either I've fallen asleep, or she hasn't made an appearance.

It's two in the morning on my fifth night of trying, when I see Missy step into the yard. Immediately Scout barks. I have a piece of wiener in my hand and tap his nose, telling him no in a sharp voice. He sits down and whines, then lifts his leg as if wanting to shake a paw. Missy looks in our direction, then disappears down the side of the cabin and into the woods behind the beach.

Chapter 28

November passes in a series of days; some clear and calm, the sun sparkling off the snow like diamonds and caressing my cheeks with its warmth, and some days, the wind howling off the lake sending pellets of snow stabbing my face like needles. By the time December arrives, the snow in the yard has drifted up to the windowsill and the picnic table and firepit are buried under its cold blanket. Across the lake, I can see a huddle of ice fishing huts with smoke curling out their stovepipe chimneys. The snowplows have been out three times to clear and sand the road behind my cabin as well as the highway into town. I've driven to the store once—Louise invited me to her house for my birthday—but that's the only time I've had the car out of the shed since the first storm. On the way to the celebration, I gripped that steering wheel like it was a lifebuoy ring, but on the way back, I felt a bit more at ease and was hopeful that Jessica was right and it would only take a few more times for me to become a confident winter driver.

I've fallen into a pattern of, on the nice days, getting up early, then sitting wrapped in my quilt on the balcony drinking coffee until noon. After lunch, Scout and I go for a long walk in the sun and come home to an early supper. On the stormy days, I start a batch of bread in the morning while Scout curls up in front of the fireplace. By three in the afternoon, the bread is in the oven and, if the snow has stopped, the two of us are outside shovelling. Even Scout enjoys coming back inside to the smell of fresh baked bread. Wilson has been out a few times to walk with me, and to shovel, or check the furnace and water tank, but other than my birthday party, he's the only other human I've seen since the first snowfall.

In my time alone, where all I've had to look after is myself and Scout, I find myself missing my family, and decide to make good of my promise to Aunt Bernice and host Christmas. When I phoned Louise and invited her and Gerry for Christmas dinner, I heard him in the background saying *It's the most wonderful time of the year*. He may be right as I'm feeling anxious for the season to begin.

—

"So lovely out here. Reminds me of my own youth," Aunt Marjorie says as she watches my grandsons build a snow fort on the beach.

This morning, eight extra people have packed themselves into my small house. My family are on borrowed cots and air mattresses which are spread out in every room, while my aunts have the guest room. Everyone but Robert doesn't seem to mind. He's complained more than once about leaving behind a perfectly good bed to spend Christmas out here in the bush. I've heard Sheryl tell him to quit being a baby and start setting a better example for his children.

The weather forecast was for a pleasant Christmas Eve, with the temperature hovering uncharacteristically around zero and I decided I'd like to have a wiener roast in the front yard of the cabin for my family. So, after asking my guests to pack warm clothing, yesterday, Wilson arrived with his snowblower and cleared a section of snow in my front yard. I then dug out the fire pit, spread a camping carpet on the ground, and set out lawn chairs.

"We used to have wiener roasts on Christmas Eve as well," Marjorie continues. "When the weather was cooperative. At that salt water lake on the edge of town. Remember, Bernice?" She stands and wiggles her bum near the flames.

"I do," Bernice says. "The entire town would meet there at noon. The men would build fires on the beach, and the women would unload coolers of food onto the picnic tables."

"We'd have a mid-afternoon wiener roast, then play with our friends until dark while the adults sat in chairs around the fire," Marjorie says. "They'd have to drag us home to go to Mass. Only thing that pulled us away was knowing that if we didn't, Santa wouldn't come."

"I don't even remember being cold, we were having so much fun," Bernice says rubbing her mittened hands together in front of the fire. "The years go by so fast; I can't believe I've gotten so old."

"Speak for yourself," Marjorie says. "I'm a year younger than you."

"Some say that a life well-lived goes by fast," Bernice muses.

"They also say, only the good die young," Marjorie says.

"I always wanted to do something like this when the kids were young," I say.

"Why didn't you?" Bernice asks.

"Steve said it would be more trouble than it was worth."

"Well, I for one, think this is the best Christmas Eve I've ever had. And Steve, pardon my French, can go suck an egg."

Sheryl, who's standing further from the fire pit as she keeps an eye on her sons, yells, "Stay off the ice," at Bruce, and Michael, who have stopped building a snow fort and are toeing the ice at the edge of the lake.

"Quit your worrying," Robert calls. "Let them be boys, you're turning them into sissies. Come and sit with us by the fire."

Sheryl walks away hesitantly, looking behind her one more time before grabbing a handful of Cheezies then sitting in a lawn chair. Robert scowls at her.

"You said this used to be a resort?" Marjorie says.

"From the mid-thirties to the mid-sixties."

"The name we saw on the shed when we pulled into the drive-way," she glances at her sister, "was that the owner?"

"It was," I say. "Cecelia Johansen. Do you know the name?" I ask.

"Just wondered," Marjorie says.

"She had no husband, no job, it was the middle of the depression, and she was young, only twenty. Many of the men in town thought she was overstepping her bounds building this place without a man to run the business. But she followed her dreams. She was a strong, independent woman," I say.

"Much like you," Bernice says to me.

"I'm the furthest thing from strong. And I'm just learning to be independent at sixty-four."

"Never too late," Marjorie says.

"There used to be cabins all the way to the end," I say, pointing towards the north end of the row where the land sits empty. "In '49, lightning struck a tree which caught three of the cabins on fire, and the years and weather have condemned the rest. If I hadn't restored this one, it was scheduled for the chopping block. The ones remaining either have to come down within the next couple of years, or be restored."

"You should restore them and re-open the resort. Wouldn't that be exciting!" Bernice says.

"That's what I told her," Jess says.

"Too expensive." I look at Robert; he's shaking his head. "Tearing them down is my only option."

"If you want something bad enough, there's always a way," Bernice says, glancing at her nephew.

"What made the resort close?" Marjorie asks.

"Cecelia died and none of her family wanted to keep it running, so it was put up for sale. That's when Dad bought it."

"Tell them how she died, Mom," Debby says. Then without waiting for me to say something, she says, "She was building the second storey and fell off the balcony. Hit her head either on the way down, or on the ground, no one knows for sure. Died right there."

"Oh my," Bernice says. "That poor woman. What an awful way to lose your life."

"That's what happens when you're a woman living alone this far from civilization," Robert says. "You get into trouble and there's no one to help you."

"Things can happen in the city too, Robert." Bernice's scolding is quick, acerbic, and blunt. "Don't talk to your mother like that. She knows what she's doing."

We're looking up at the balcony, imagining what it would be like to fall over the edge, when one of the boys starts to scream. Sheryl jumps to her feet.

"He wrecked my snow fort," Bruce shouts. "He did it on purpose."

"Quit your fighting," Robert yells, "or you'll have to sit in the car and miss Christmas."

"Some believe that she didn't fall but she was murdered," Debby says. "And," she continues, "supposedly, this place is haunted by her ghost. They say she buried a fortune out here. People have been searching for years to find it, but so far no one has."

"Really!" Bernice says.

One of boys starts to scream again. Sheryl attempts to stand, but Robert grabs her arm, forcing her to stay sitting. When the child keeps screaming, Robert stands up to give him heck. "How many times do I have to tell you to quit," he pauses. "Where's Michael?" he says.

Before the rest of us can react, Sheryl is out of her chair and racing towards the beach. "Michael," I hear her shout. "Michael, where are you? Quit playing games."

"The fort fell on him," Bruce shouts, pointing at a pile of snow. "The fort fell on him and buried him."

Scout is digging at a drift, the snow flying backwards between his hind legs, and Sheryl falls to her knees and starts digging along with the dog. As the rest of us approach, Michael appears from behind a tree.

"Surprise," he says. "I wasn't buried, I was hiding!" He points to the tree. "Over there," he screams, jumping up and down.

"Then we pretended the fort fell on him," Bruce finishes. "We fooled you!"

"That's a terrible joke," Aunt Bernice says as her and Marjorie hobble up later than the rest of us. "Darned near gave me a heart attack."

Sheryl stands and turns her back to us as she wipes away the tears. I give Scout a hug and tell him he's a good boy.

"Some day, young man," Bernice says, bending close to Michael's face, "that kind of a prank is going to come back and bite you on the butt. You ever hear about the boy who cried wolf?"

I see Michael sheepishly glance at his dad, looking for approval.

"Michael, you shouldn't be doing things like that," Robert says, trying to hide his smile. "You scared your aunts, your grandma, and your mother." As we're heading back towards the cabin, he gives his son a high five.

—

It's Christmas day, and the turkey, which has been roasting in the oven since nine this morning, is making the cabin smell wonderful. Sheryl, Jess, Debby, and I, are in the kitchen making salads and doing last minute chores, while watching out the living room window at my grandsons playing in the snow. They were up at six this morning and immediately wanted to play the video game Santa brought them, but Sheryl told them if they got some fresh air, they could play after supper. They've been given strict instructions to play no practical jokes, and to not leave the yard, and if they do, they will lose all video game privileges for an entire year.

"This was such a good idea, Mom," Jess says, taking a tray of buns to the dining room. "Christmas in the country. I love it."

"You would," Robert says, finishing his chore of hooking up the video system to my television. He sits down and pops in a game, ready to play with the toy himself, but Sheryl reads him the riot act and he puts the controller down. He grabs a pickle off the tray I've already put on the table. "You've always been a tree hugger. Me, I like putting the boys to bed early on Christmas Eve and having a couple of drinks, Christmas day lounging around in my housecoat followed by Christmas dinner, to bed early, then boxing day shopping. Had my eye on a TV but I'm sure it will be sold out by the time we get home." He takes another pickle off the tray.

"We do not need another TV," Sheryl says. "And instead of eating all the pickles, why don't you make yourself useful and go and talk to your aunts rather than complaining about being here in your mother's beautiful home. And just so you know, I think it's nice to have a change. Teach the boys that Christmas is about more than getting gifts. It's about family."

Robert wanders to the living room to socialize, and I wish Sheryl would talk to him like that when he's criticizing her weight.

The back door opens and as he always does, Wilson enters without knocking. He stops in the porch, as if reluctant to enter and have to say Merry Christmas. Darren steps into the kitchen, giving me a kiss on the cheek. "Merry Christmas," he says then hands me a bottle of wine.

Wilson holds up a snow shovel with a ribbon tied on the handle.

"What's that?" I ask.

"It's Christmas, isn't it?"

"You bought me another shovel?" I say.

"Collapsible shovel." he says. "You keep it in your trunk."

"Oh, Wilson, that's so thoughtful. I didn't get you anything."

"Instead of feeling guilty about not giving me a gift, give me your car keys," he says.

"What?"

"Keys. Give me your keys. I'm putting this," he shakes the shovel, "in your trunk. Won't do you any good stuck in some closet which is where you'll put it the moment I go home."

I grab the set of keys off the hook by the back door. "Thank you," I call to his back.

While he's opening the shed, a car parks on the road behind Wilson's truck, and Louise and Gerry climb out. I hear them call Merry Christmas to Wilson, who waves his hand over his head without returning the greeting.

"Merry Christmas," Gerry says, when he enters the porch pushing his walker in front of him. He gives me a kiss and hands me a tin of homemade fudge.

—

After much laughter, many toasts to a prosperous new year, and Robert quizzing Gerry every chance he could get about where Cecelia might have hidden her money, supper is over and my grandsons have been excused to play their video game.

I'm loading the last of the plates into the dishwasher when Debby says, "I was driving past your place the other day, Aunt Bernice, and noticed some garbage bags on your driveway. Sorry I didn't stop and help you with them, but I was already late for work. I drove past on my way home, fully intending to stop and help, but they were already gone. Did you get them taken out to the trash?"

Bernice glances over her shoulder at me, then, out of the corner of her mouth, says quietly to my daughter, "We did."

"Were you cleaning out your basement?" Debby asks, not taking the hint.

Before her sister can answer, Marjorie interjects. "That's right. We were cleaning out the basement. We decided it's time to start downsizing. Who knows how long we'll be able to live on our own and we certainly don't want to leave everything we've collected over the past fifty years, for you guys to clean up. We left them there to go through the contents before we threw them away."

"On your driveway? In the snow?" Debby persists. "Why wouldn't you go through them in the comfort of your house?"

"Because we didn't put them there," Bernice says quickly before Marjorie cuts her off again. "That witch, Julia did."

"Julia dropped some garbage bags on your driveway?" I say. "Why would she do that?"

"Who knows what that woman thinks?" Bernice says while Marjorie pokes her with her elbow.

I look at each of my aunts in turn. "What was in them?" I ask.

In unison, Marjorie says, "A lot of garbage," while Bernice says, "Things of your dad's."

I stop mid-step on my way back to the table with a bottle of wine and a tray of squares. "Which was it? Garbage or things of Dad's?"

"Both," Marjorie sighs, helping herself to a brownie. "She's moving."

"Who's moving?"

"Your…," Bernice glances at Bruce and Michael who are engrossed in the video game and not listening to us, and whispers, "… wicked step-mother."

Marjorie nods. "Apparently, she wants something cozier. Last I heard she sold the house your dad had built for her, for five-million and is looking at a smaller house in an exclusive area by the river."

Bernice snorts. "If you can call four-thousand square feet, small. And it's not the size of the house that prompted her to move, it's the man she's seeing. He lives in the same gated community. It seems she's found herself another fish to fry. As if the ten million your dad left her isn't enough."

"So," I ask, cringing at the fact my father was an easy target, "what does Julia moving have to do with dropping off Dad's things on your driveway?"

"I figure instead of throwing them out, she decided to make a point that she doesn't like me very much, and gave them to us," Bernice says.

"It's not like she didn't give us warning," Marjorie says. "She called the night before and said she had some of Arthur's things she thought you might want and since she didn't know where you were living now, asked if she could bring them by our place for us to give to you. Of course I said yes; it's not our place to turn them down; there might have been something you wanted as a keepsake. I thought it would be a box, or something small, not the fifteen bags she piled out there for all the neighbours to see. Didn't know she was pulling one over on us until we began opening them up."

"We had to go through every one just in case there was something important," Bernice says. "You never know with that woman; she could have mixed something important in with the used underwear."

"I'm sorry you had to deal with that," I say. "You should have called me or one of the kids to help."

"We didn't want to bother you. You'd just had a storm; the roads wouldn't have been plowed yet, and I know the kids lead busy lives.

We don't have anything else to do. We managed."

"What kinds of things did you find in the bags?"

"You know, the usual stuff people throw out when they're cleaning house. Old clothes, half empty bottles of shampoo, tubes of toothpaste, worn-out shoes, jock straps, combs, brushes, pens that didn't work. Bags and bags of paid bills and receipts that were never shredded. Like I said, garbage," Marjorie says.

"There was one thing mixed in with the papers that was interesting." Bernice says. "More interesting now than it was a couple of days ago."

Again, Marjorie pokes her sister in the ribs.

"Quit that," Bernice says rubbing her side.

"Your mouth is flapping again," Marjorie says.

"She has to know," Bernice hisses at her sister.

"And I have every intention of telling her. I just thought perhaps someplace less," she looks at the faces glued to hers, "crowded."

"We should have said something yesterday," Bernice says, "when the subject came up. Then it would be all over and done with."

"What is it you're trying to avoid telling me?" I ask.

Bernice opens her mouth then closes it again, perhaps worried her sister is going to poke her in the ribs. Neither woman says anything.

"What did you find?" I say. "Just tell me, for heaven's sake."

"A document," Bernice says. "We found a document."

"What kind of document? Architectural stuff?"

Instead of answering, Marjorie says, "You know your dad was an orphan, right?"

"I do," I say.

"And that he was born in an unwed mother's home?"

"I know," I say haltingly.

"And because he was never adopted, he was raised in the orphanage that sat next door to the home run by the same order of nuns."

"Mom told me some of that," I say. "Mostly, the subject wasn't talked about."

"From the time he was young," Marjorie continues, "he was determined to find out who his parents were, but the nuns told him they didn't know. All they knew, they said, was that his mother arrived on their doorstep three months pregnant and with a large amount of money her father had given her. They said they didn't know either her name, or the name of the man who got her pregnant."

"Tight lipped old gals," Bernice says. "They knew more than they were letting on." She shakes her head. "As an adult your dad searched library records looking for recorded births, visited churches to see if the nuns took him there to be baptized, but could never find anything."

"Then when you were ten," Marjorie says to me, "he found something."

"Really?" I say. "He found out who his parents were?"

As is her way, Marjorie takes the long way around. "Shortly after he and your mother married and he was trying to make a name for himself as an architect, he made his living purchasing old houses and turning them into showpieces. I believe flipping is the word they use nowadays, though your dad would do more than change the carpet or put in new windows. He'd rebuild them using the same architectural features from the original house, restoring them to their original beauty. He was a talented man. Could bring those houses back to life as if they were living, breathing things. Cold towards people, but loved buildings."

"I remember," I say.

"He was hoping to make enough money so he could open his own architectural firm, but he was struggling," Bernice says, taking up the story. "He was so particular about restoring the houses to their original state, that he put too much money into them, and was barely making a profit."

"Then in 1965," Marjorie says and I feel like I'm watching a tennis match as I look back and forth between the two women, "the orphanage closed and was put up for sale, and your father bought it. When the demolition crew were clearing out junk, they found bags and bags of records of all the births that had happened at the home since the day it opened, tucked away in a cupboard in the basement. They turned them over to your dad."

Bernice takes over and I sigh, knowing if I interrupt, it will only prolong the story. "They were simply shoved into a bag and not in alphabetical order, so he began the arduous task of reading each file. Your mom showed me his office one day. Every surface was covered in files and I remember kind of admiring him for his tenacity. After weeks of searching, he found something." She takes a drink then pauses. No one says a word, not wanting to interrupt her train of thought. "I recall, it was shortly after that when things seemed to turn around for him and his business began to thrive. He moved you and your mom out of that one-bedroom apartment, and bought the house you were raised in."

"So, what did he find?" I ask.

"A file," Marjorie says. "He found a file that went by the name of, Baby boy Arthur, born April twenty-second, nineteen-thirty-one."

"Apparently," Bernice interrupts, "the nuns would go through the alphabet once, then start back at the beginning. Both for the girls and the boys."

"Okay," I say, trying not to become impatient. "That was Dad's birthday."

"There was no father of the baby named on the card, nor was there any record of where the mother's family was from or who they were. The file said that the baby was never adopted and was raised by the nuns. Because the girl's father had paid them to not divulge the last name, the nuns gave the baby the last name of Daniels as the orphanage was on Daniels Avenue. It was the only baby boy born in nineteen-thirty-one who was named Arthur and raised in the orphanage. So of course," Marjorie raises her palms, "he knew he'd found his own file." She pauses. "The thing is," she says when she starts talking again, "there must have been one nun who had a guilty conscience."

"What do you mean?"

"She jotted down Arthur's mother's name. Your grandmother's

name. She wrote it in the file. Apparently, she couldn't let this baby grow up without knowing who his family was."

"Who was she?" I ask, when Marjorie stops talking yet again. "What was her name?"

The two women look at each other, seemingly afraid to go on with the story.

"What?" I say. "You've come this far, tell me who she is."

"Cecelia Johansen," Bernice blurts out leaving Aunt Marjorie with her mouth hanging open. "Your father's birth mother's name was Cecelia Johansen."

"You mean my Cecelia Johansen?" I say. "The one who built this house? The one who owned Sunset Lake Resort? The one who died?"

"Do you think it's the same woman?" Bernice asks. "Could there be two Cecelia Johansen's?"

"The question to ask is," Marjorie says, "did Cecelia Johansen, the original owner of this place, have a baby boy and give him up for adoption? Does anyone know?"

Gerry glances at me; I nod. "She did," he says. "Cecelia got pregnant without being married and had a baby at an unwed mother's home. Her family was angry and embarrassed about the pregnancy and kicked her out. They wanted nothing to do with the child and nothing more to do with her. It happened just before I met her."

"Oh my," Marjorie says, glancing at her sister. "It was a different time."

"It was," Gerry says.

Everyone around the table is quiet. Marjorie finally says, "We had no idea she had anything to do with this place until yesterday when we saw the name on the shed. We didn't know what to say."

Marjorie places her hand on my arm. "I would have said something sooner, dear, had we known."

"I suppose that's why your dad bought the place. He was trying to make a connection to his family," Bernice says softly. "And that's why he gave it to you."

"This is crazy," I say. "My biological grandmother is Cecelia Johansen?"

"That explains a lot," Gerry says. "I always said you reminded me of her."

"I wonder if Grandpa knew about the treasure," Debby says.

"And if he found it," Robert says.

1963

"They say it started out back in the garbage can. I heard someone say something about a cigarette," I tell my wife. Louise is in the kitchen putting candles on a cake.

"Place was a fire hazard," Lila says. "Bart couldn't afford to keep up on repairs after the resort opened."

"Happy birthday to you, happy birthday to you, happy birthday dear Mom, happy birthday to you," our daughter sings as she enters the dining room, the cake glowing with candles.

Lila is slicing us each a piece when the phone rings. She looks at me as if to say, 'don't you dare.'

I hold out hands in supplication, then walk to the phone. "Hello." I listen for a moment, keeping my eyes on Lila who has her eyes glued to mine. "I can't," I say. "It's Lila's birthday. I'll come out in the morning." I listen again. "I understand. I'll be right there." Before I can explain, Lila has thrown the knife down and is leaving the table. "The pool arrived this afternoon," I say to her back as she races up the stairs. "The man who assembles it has shown up a day early and needs a hand."

Lila stops on the stairs. "The pool arrived today? I thought it wasn't coming until tomorrow. I thought you said Cecelia was going to be in town this afternoon?"

"I guess her plans changed when the pool was delivered. If I don't go and help her now, I'll be even longer tomorrow because I'll be doing it by myself, and I know nothing about putting a swimming pool together."

"Do you also jump through hoops like a trained dog? Every time she calls, you roll over on your back to have your stomach scratched."

After she's gone upstairs, Louise says, "It's okay, Dad. You go. Missy needs your help. We can have cake tomorrow."

Chapter 29

I'm at Carnation's General Store today because I want to ask Gerry some questions that I couldn't ask at Christmas with my family in the room.

I find him in his usual place; sitting by the space heater just inside the front door, but today, instead of talking to everyone who comes into the store, he's asleep, his chin resting on his chest, snoring ever so slightly. I quietly take a basket from the stack beside his chair, and pick out what's on my shopping list.

"He's been doing that more and more," Louise says, nodding at her dad as she rings through my groceries. "Having afternoon naps."

"Well," I say, "he is one-hundred and two. I think he's earned a sleep in the afternoon."

"What are you two hens flapping your lips about?" Gerry says. "I wasn't sleeping. Had my eyes closed. Ruby," he says, sitting up straight, "good to see you. Then at my age it's good to see anyone." He gives Scout, who's come up to him and nuzzled his hand, a pat on the head. "That was generous of Wilson to give you a Christmas gift. Don't think I've ever seen him do that before."

"What, give a friend a gift?"

"Give anyone a gift. I've known him for over fifty years and he's never given me a thing. You must be softening him up. So," he says, "have you, what do people say nowadays, processed the information yet?"

"You mean, about Cecelia being my grandmother?"

He raises one bushy eyebrow.

"I don't know what to think about that," I say. "What do you think?"

"Stranger things have happened," Gerry says with a shrug.

"So, you agree my father bought the orphanage to find out who he was?"

"It goes without saying," he says.

"Then when he found out who his mother was, he bought the resort after she died?"

"The universe works in mysterious ways."

"Quit talking in clichés. Do you, or do you not believe that my dad left me the resort because he knew Cecelia was his mother?"

"I do," he says. "I believe your dad left you Sunset Lake Resort in his will because he wanted you to know who your grandmother was." He pats my hand.

"Why didn't he just tell me?"

He shrugs. "You tell me. You knew him, I didn't."

"That's the thing," I say. "I didn't know him. He and I barely knew each other. He was distant and cold, never wanted to get to know me, never wanted to talk to me."

"Perhaps he was a man of few words and this was his way of talking." Gerry cocks his head at me. "Or maybe not," he says with a shrug. "We'll never know for sure. All parties who could tell us are dead and gone."

I pull up a chair and sit beside him. "Do you think you ever met my dad? Did he ever meet Cecelia?"

"I never met anyone by the name of Arthur Daniels, I can tell you that. And if Cecelia did, she didn't tell me. Then again, she never outright admitted to me that she had a baby, so she certainly wasn't going to introduce me to her son. And there were always people coming to the resort to talk to her about one thing or another. Salesmen for everything from boats, to clothing, to grocery supply companies; hard to remember everybody. She even bought that pool you had taken out, from a travelling salesman." He taps his chin. "I remember the day she told me about that purchase. I thought it was a crazy idea; tried to talk her out of it. Told her the salesman had bamboozled her. The lake was right there, why would she need a swimming pool? But she was adamant and it turned out she was right. The adults loved it. They could let their kids swim after dark, while they partied on the patio around the pool. She was always one step ahead of me, that woman. Trouble was, the pool was delivered during Lila's birthday party. Cecelia called and asked me to come and help assemble it. Lila wasn't happy. In hindsight I suppose I shouldn't have gone running. But all I could think about was having to figure out how to put that damned pool together myself, so I left," he says. "Sometimes it's difficult to see the trees for the forest until it's too late." He wipes a tear from his eye. "Sorry. Got off track. What were you asking? Something about Cecelia meeting your dad?"

"Did you or Cecelia ever meet my father? Was he ever at the resort?"

"Like I said, there were so many people coming and going all summer, it's difficult to remember everything." He pauses. "Though I do remember someone." He scratches the top of his head. "It was September of '65. I remember because Cecelia and I had finished the staircase to the second storey the day before, and I was upstairs, pounding subfloor in place so we could get the wall studs and roof on before winter. A car pulled in beside the shed, and a man got out. At first, I wondered what this slick, good-looking guy could be selling, then realized he was too polished to be a travelling salesman. Tall, handsome, mid-thirties, kind of aloof, rather abrupt."

"It certainly sounds like my dad. He was always cool towards people."

"Kind of got that impression from what you've told me about him."

"Do you think it was my father?"

"Couldn't say for sure. But I'm quite sure he was the only person who Cecelia never introduced to me."

"If that was my dad, why didn't she leave the cabin to him, instead of him having to buy it after she died?"

"Probably because she died less than a month later. Likely would have gotten around to doing something about it had she lived longer, but paperwork wasn't her thing. I balanced the books, paid the bills, then gave her the net cash at the end of each month for her to look after."

"What would she have done without you, Dad?" Louise says from behind the cash register. "You practically ran that place."

"I was only the numbers man behind the scenes. She was the ideas person. I would never in my wildest dreams have thought a resort in this neck of the woods would be as successful as hers was. She had a dream and took a chance. That was her personality. All in or all out."

"So, Dad came out to the resort to confront his mom?" I ask. "He wanted to know why she abandoned him?"

"There was no indication that they'd had a confrontation. I saw her enter her cabin then exit a moment later with an envelope in hand. I'd seen her do that many times with people who came out to borrow money. She always had cash around the house and always placed it in a small brown envelope when she gave it away."

"Do you think she was under duress? Did she look like she was being forced to give him money?"

"My recollection is that she was happy to see him, excited even, and under no duress at all. But given that was fifty-two years ago, my mind might be playing tricks on me. But I'll tell you this, if she *were* under duress, *that* would be something I would remember. So, no, I don't think she was." He scratches his chin. "Do you want my opinion?" "I do," I say.

"If that was indeed your father that I saw that day, I think the money was Cecelia's way of trying to make up for all the lost years. I know she carried a lot of guilt around for having given him up. I think she was trying to be a mother."

I pause, hesitant to ask the next question I have. "Do you..." I begin then stop.

"Do I what?" Gerry says.

"Do you think my father could have killed her?" I look at my hands fidgeting on my lap. "Do you think he might have killed her for more money?"

He places his hand over mine. It's warm. "I do not. If he could get the money for nothing, as I think he did that day, why would he want to kill her?"

I breath a sigh of relief. "Thanks, for listening, Gerry. I'd better be going. Heading to the city bright and early."

"Visiting your kids?" he asks.

"Actually, I'm killing two birds with one stone."

"She's serving that husband of hers divorce papers," Louise says from across the store, "then staying overnight at her son's house. You sure you don't want us to look after Scout? It's no trouble, really."

"No, it's fine. My grandsons are looking forward to seeing him. We can take him for a walk, burn off his energy as well as theirs."

"Drive carefully."

"Break a leg," Gerry calls to me as I leave.

1965

A car pulls into the yard and parks behind my truck. A man gets out.

"You, up there on the roof," he calls across the yard. "Can you tell me where to find Cecelia Johansen?"

"And you are?" I mumble, squeezing a row of nails between my lips.

"Someone who wants to talk to Cecelia Johansen."

I laugh and pull the nails out of my mouth. "Dining hall." I point with my hammer. "She's busy planning next season's menu with the chef. Doesn't like to be disturbed."

He lifts his hand in a wave as he's walking away, and I'm reminded of Cecelia with his determined strides, hands loose and swinging easily by his sides; a man comfortable in his own skin. A minute later, Cecelia emerges from the dining hall alone and enters her cabin.

"Everything okay?" I ask when she exits her cabin, an envelope in her hand.

"Everything's fine," she says.

"Who's the stiff?"

Her eyes flash. "No one that concerns you."

I pound the last nail into the subfloor, then climb down the stairs to the main floor, leave by the back door and put my tools in the shed. I get into my truck and wait for the stranger to pull out from behind me. A moment later, he and Cecelia exit the dining hall.

"Goodbye," Cecelia says, giving him a hug. "Come back anytime. You're always welcome here."

He backs out of the driveway as do I. In my rear-view mirror I see Cecelia turn to watch us drive away, then I follow him to the highway where he speeds up in the direction of the city.

Chapter 30

It's still dark this time of the morning, and I'm thankful the road is clear as I drive past the general store, and turn onto the highway. I look at my watch, 6:30 AM; five and a half hours before I'm meeting Steve at the restaurant. I told him I'd rather just give him the papers then go to Robert's house and spend time with my family, but he insisted we have one last lunch for old times sake, like we used to do when we were first married. Reluctantly, I agreed, thankful that at least he agreed to meet with me. I pat the manilla envelope lying on the passenger seat beside me. Finally, I'll be a divorced woman. Finally, I'll be able to say I'm truly on my own.

Not used to getting up this early, Scout is already asleep in the back seat and I put on a CD to listen to on the way there. The roads are dry, and I make good time, arriving in under five hours.

The restaurant he's chosen is a fancy place nestled in a high-end shopping district on the opposite end of the city; a place I've never driven before. I'm nervous driving in the unfamiliar neighbourhood; likely the reason Steve chose this place to meet, he's always enjoyed being spiteful. I pull into the parking lot.

I'm still in the car, the door cracked to get out and allow Scout out to relieve himself, when a red Mustang pulls into the entrance on the other side of the lot with Steve behind the wheel and immediately my temper rises. During our thirty-five years together, I wasn't allowed to have a new dishwasher when ours broke, but he was allowed a new car every twenty-four months. He would never be caught dead in a car as old as mine. I take a breath trying to calm down. Mustn't get flustered before I see him. He'll see me as vulnerable and walk all over me if I appear upset.

Steve parks his car in the far corner of the lot, then climbs out from behind the wheel. I'm about to get out of the car and wave and call his name when a woman gets out of the passenger side of the mustang; it's the same woman he had with him at the coffee shop. I stay in the car gently closing the door, and Scout lifts his head, hopeful I'm done what I came here to do and we can go. I'm slouched down, my eyes just above the dashboard, and witness Steve give this woman a kiss right there in the parking lot! When they're done, she walks across the lot heading for the strip mall next door. Steve calls, "Have fun shopping."

"Did you see that, Scout?" I say to my dog. "My husband, someone I've been married to for thirty-five years and still am, I might add, someone who claims he still loves me, is seeing another woman. You should know, boy, that I'm a bury my head in the sand kind of person." I hold his muzzle in my hand and look into his eyes. "I have a habit of pretending everything's okay, just so life can go on as usual. So, if you ever want to misbehave, know that I will most likely not discipline you." I scratch him behind the ears. "You could be the worst dog in the world and I'd forgive you." I'm quiet for a moment. "What should I do? Should I confront him? Do I say, here's the divorce papers, and by the way who was that gorgeous woman you were kissing in the parking lot?" Still, Scout remains silent. "You're right, I won't say a word. What do I care if he's fooling around on me? I'm filing for divorce, it's no skin off my nose if he wants to get himself a girlfriend young enough to be his daughter." Scout barks. "I know, I know. I need to go." I shake the envelope. "I'll be back as soon as I'm done giving him this. I'll eat fast, I promise." Scout barks again and I get out of the car.

I enter the restaurant area. It's crowded and noisy, and I don't see Steve. A waitress approaches.

"Good afternoon, Ma'am," she says. "Are you meeting someone? At lunch time we don't have room for single seatings; I'm sure you understand."

I smile at this snooty waitress and say, "I'm here for the Steve Phillips reservation."

She checks the electronic pad she has in her apron. "Right this way," she says. She leads me to a table then pulls out a chair and I sit down.

"Ruby," Steve says in a loud voice. "You made it."

"I did."

"I guess better late than never," he says.

"It's only ten after twelve," I say. "Many times, you were two and three hours late for things I'd planned. And you didn't have to drive for five hours to get here," I say, my voice rising, and bite my lip, wishing I didn't let him get under my skin.

"Now, now," Steve says, "let's not be tacky."

"Speaking of tacky—" I say, then stop, biting my tongue. I won't do it. I don't care if he has a girlfriend, he can have ten girlfriends for all I care, likely does. I place the envelope with the divorce papers inside, on the table. "You know, Steve," I stand, "I think I'm just going to go. I've lost my appetite. Here's the divorce papers. Just sign and mail them back to me."

"Come on Ruby, eat with me. One last meal together. It's been a tough year for me. I need some cheering up."

"It's been a tough year for you?" I repeat. "What's that mean?" I sit back down.

"Job, finances, that kind of thing. Been struggling emotionally lately."

I scowl at him.

"You have to admit, you always promised we'd inherit millions of dollars when your dad died. It's been tough on me. Sent me into a depression."

The waitress approaches. "Can I get you a drink?" she asks.

"Water," I say.

"I'll have a Scotch," Steve says.

"Have you decided what you'd like to order?" she asks.

"Not yet. Come back in five, okay?" Steve says, giving her a wink.

She leaves us alone. "Did you or did you not tell me that I'd be rich when your dad died?" Steve says.

"I might have mentioned it, I don't remember."

"That's how you got me to marry you, by promising me I would be wealthy one day."

"Got you to marry me?" I sputter. "I did nothing of the sort. If I remember right, it was you who couldn't wait to marry me, couldn't wait to get your hands on my dad's money."

The waitress brings us our drinks, then leaves when she realizes we're having an argument.

Steve smiles. "Whose idea it was doesn't really matter, Ruby. The point is," he says, pausing for emphasis, "we got married and you assured me that upon the death of your father, we were going to inherit millions, so naturally, I didn't save as diligently as I should have. I spent more on you and the kids than I would have had I known we weren't going to inherit the money. Now, I find myself in the sticky situation of not having enough to live on. I've had to take a job as a security guard."

"You're not a cop anymore?"

"Mandatory retirement at 60. I've had to cut back my lifestyle significantly. I've been considering talking to a lawyer."

"A lawyer?" I say. "There's no need. I've already had the papers drawn up." I tap the envelope.

"Not about the divorce, Ruby. About suing you because I don't have enough money to retire on."

"What?" I laugh.

The waitress reappears. "Are you ready to order now?" she asks, likely tired of us taking up a popular table at lunch and not ordering any food.

"Ruby," Steve says. "There will be no divorce papers signed today until I've decided what I'm going to do." He smiles at me, placing his hand on my arm. "Do you understand?" His voice is condescending, patronizing.

"Of course, I don't understand," I say shaking his hand off. "You're thinking about suing *me*? It's *me*," I pat my chest, "who should be suing *you*. All the years of you depriving me, all the years of telling me to make do, all the years of you making me feel worthless, and you're going to sue me?" I stand up, knocking my water over. "The only reason you're doing this is because you found out my house is worth two million dollars, and that there may be money hidden someplace on the property." Patrons have stopped eating and are staring at our table.

"You're making a scene, Ruby. Sit down and stop making a fool of yourself," Steve says, his voice sharp.

"Let them stare, I have no intention of sitting down. You're the one who's making a fool of himself. You think you can get what-ever you want by bullying me? What about the one-hundred and fifty thousand I gave you out of my inheritance? What about the two-hundred and seventy-five thousand from the sale of the house? How the hell can you be suffering when you're driving a brand-new Mustang?"

"You saw?"

"I saw her too."

"I needed a new car," he says. "And she's a friend."

"A friend with benefits," I whisper.

"I didn't get a house given to me like you did; I had to buy some-thing to live in when you sold our house out from under me."

"I did not sell our house out from under you," I say with bared teeth. "You weren't even living there, you walked out on me, re-member? And you agreed about me selling. You told our son to tell me, and I quote, "*that sorry bitch can do whatever the hell she wants to do with the place, as long as I get my share of the money from the sale.*" Steve opens his mouth, but I'm not done. "Believe me Steve, when I tell you this, you will never get another dime out of me. My father gave me that cabin, and I have no intention of selling it and letting you get your hands on the money. And if that means I have to stay married to a sorry loser like you until one of us dies, then so be it."

I stomp out of the restaurant, then stand beside my car pound-ing my hands into the roof. Scout sticks his nose out the crack in the window, not understanding what's happening. Steve exits the restaurant, divorce papers in hand, then throws the envelope into the back seat. He climbs behind the wheel and pulls up to the lady's clothing store next door. The woman he brought with him, exits the store carrying three shopping bags and gets back into the Mustang. She leans over and gives my husband a kiss, then they drive out of the parking lot.

In a spur of the moment decision, I decide to follow them. Maybe if I can talk to him without getting angry, I can make him understand that the two of us don't belong together anymore, that we've gone our separate ways, that staying married will only ruin both our lives. We drive through traffic, me a few cars back as we weave between lanes, then turn onto the freeway that circles the city. I feel my skin crawl when I see her reach over and rub her fingers down his cheek. We exit the freeway into a new area, then Steve turns into a gated community where the houses must cost half a million each, and parks in the garage of a two-storey condo. I pull to the curb half a block away and watch them emerge from the garage, Steve carrying the shopping bags from the expensive lady's wear store. He finds the key for the door on his keyring, and they enter the condo together.

"Well, Scout," I say. "Looks like that husband of mine has either bought himself a new condo, or is living with a woman." Scout whines, pawing the car door. "Oh, Baby, I'm sorry, I forgot to pee you!" I open the door and the two of us climb out where the poor pup pees the moment his paws hit the sidewalk. I'm filling his water bowl on the side of the road, when the woman exits the house. She's taking her mail out of the box when she turns and looks at Scout and me. She frowns, perhaps remembering me from the coffee shop.

I duck as she runs inside, then, dragging Scout into the back seat before he's finished peeing, I jump behind the wheel and pull away from the curb, leaving the water dish behind. In my rear-view mirror, I see Steve and his girlfriend running out of the condo, staring after my retreating car.

Chapter 31

I pull into Robert's driveway but sit in my car as I try to compose myself. I'm blowing my nose when there's a knock on the car window. Scout barks once at Sheryl who is standing on the driveway. I roll down my window.

"Are you okay, Ruby?" she asks, reaching through and scratching Scout's head. "We saw you drive up and the boys got so excited for Grandma to be here. They've been talking all day about you and the dog coming to visit. When you didn't come inside, I told them they'd better let me talk to you in case Grandma is sad."

"I'm not sad," I say. "Just collecting myself after my lunch with Steve. I mean, I'm divorcing the man anyhow, I'll be fine."

She rubs my shoulder. "I'm sorry. I can't imagine how hard this must be. Come on," she opens the car door. "The boys can play with Scout in the backyard while we have a drink. If ever there was a time to have a drink, this must be it."

—

"He actually said he's not signing the divorce papers because he's trying to decide if he's going to sue you?" she asks.

"He did," I say.

"And he's suing you because…?"

"He thought he was going to become a rich man when my dad died so he didn't save a dime. So now he's broke and he's blaming me."

"In my experience, people who blame others for their predicaments are trying to justify their own actions, even if in their hearts, they know they're wrong. They just can't admit it to themselves. Makes them feel superior to believe they aren't in the wrong."

"He's blamed me our whole marriage. Whenever something didn't go right it was because of me."

"But this," she holds out her hands. "I mean, to blame you for him not saving enough money for retirement? No lawyer is going to take his case. He's bluffing. Didn't your dad's will say he couldn't touch the cabin?"

"It did," I say. "But he thinks if we stay married, he can sway me into selling and giving him some of the money."

"But he's the one who asked for a separation, not you. He's the one who left."

"I know. But at the time he didn't realize how much land I had actually inherited; neither did I. Now that he knows it's a hundred acres and worth two million dollars, he wants to stay together."

"And he thinks threatening to sue you will keep you from divorcing him and signing the papers? The man's off his rocker. I'm sorry, Ruby. I shouldn't have said that. Sometimes my mouth talks before my brain thinks."

"But you're right," I say. "That's exactly what he thinks. And," I say with my finger in the air, "he has a girlfriend."

Sheryl pulls her chin in and looks at me. "He's talking about not signing the divorce papers, yet he has a girlfriend? Well, that proves he's loony. You know what you should do?" she says. "You should hire a detective. Get some pictures of them together. Isn't that how they do it in the movies? That should be enough for you to get a divorce. You wouldn't even need him to sign if you could prove infidelity. I had a girlfriend who did that. Divorce came through before the creep had his suitcase packed."

"I'd sooner stay separated than to hire a detective to sneak around taking pictures of my husband and his girlfriend. It just seems so, tacky. I've already given half of my inheritance, and I have no intention whatsoever of giving him half the cabin or getting back together with him, no matter what he's deluding himself into thinking. So," I shrug, "what harm does it do if we just stay separated? It's not like I have a bunch of boyfriends lined up who want to marry me."

"I'll tell you what harm it does; he'll always think he has control over you as long as you two are married. It's that generations way of thinking; the man is in charge." She glances at me. "I guess I shouldn't talk, hey?"

"Why *do* you let Robert bug you about your weight?" I say. "You stand up to him about so many things, but not that."

"I don't know. I suppose because I think he's right. He's a good provider, a good father. And except for that one topic, he's kind to me. I just get tongue-tied when he brings it up."

"I let Steve talk to me like that for years. He made me think I wasn't capable of being independent. He'd tell me that I needed him, that I'd never make it on my own. Took me a long time to realize I'm just as capable as the next person. And now, here I am, living at a lake all by myself. Don't let that son of mine make you think you have to be skinny in order to be beautiful. I think you're beautiful just the way you are."

She pulls me to her chest and gives me a bear hug and I wonder how I got so lucky to have such a beautiful soul in my life.

"And forgive him," I whisper into her ear. "He didn't have a very good role model growing up."

"We need to get you out of this mess," she says refilling our glasses.

"I don't know how. Until he signs, I'm still Mrs. Steve Phillips."

"We'll talk to Robert. He's good at finding solutions to problems."

On cue the front door opens and Robert walks in. "What's wrong?" he asks when he looks at his wife and I marvel at my son's intuitiveness.

"Your father wouldn't sign the divorce papers. He's trying to decide if he should sue your mom of all things. Can you believe it?"

Like a whirlwind, two boys and one dog enter the back door; all blurred colours whirring around as if they're melting into one. When they see their dad, they run to him, vying for his attention, my dog jumping at their heels.

"Guess what, Dad?" they say in unison.

"What?" Robert says, first picking up one then the other and giving each a kiss on the cheek.

"Scout knows how to give a high-five!" Bruce says. "And he's trained to walk by my side if I tell him to." The boy stands tall and says with authority, "Walk straight." Scout heels by his side and waits to be told what to do.

"And," Micheal says, "he comes if I call his name, but if I say *stay* and hold out my hand like this, he stays. He also knows the command to sit when I just wave my hand up like this. I don't even have to say anything." He demonstrates and Scout, obligingly sits.

"Well, isn't he a smart dog?" Rob says.

"Can we get our own dog?" Bruce asks. "A border collie like Scout? Can we, can we?"

"I don't know," their dad says. "I'll have to think about it. That's a lot of responsibility. You have to walk a dog, make sure you feed him, take him to the vet for shots. Do you think you can do that?"

"Yes," they say in unison. "We can do it, Dad."

"Supper time," Sheryl says, stopping the negotiations. "We'll continue this conversation after the boys are in bed."

"You're going to talk about getting us a dog?" Bruce asks.

"No, we are not. We are talking about something that Grandma, Dad and I were discussing before you came barrelling inside. Go wash up and take your seats."

———

I've helped the boys with their teeth, got them into bed, then read them two bedtime stories. I'm now looking out the window in the family room watching the snow that wasn't supposed to start until tomorrow night, begin to fall.

"I hope this snow doesn't amount to much," I say. "I'd like to go home tomorrow."

Robert is quiet as he sits in his chair.

I sit in the chair closest to the fireplace. "Are you okay, Rob?" I ask. "You've been awfully quiet since supper. Did I say something wrong? I'm sorry for imposing on your family time."

"No, Mom. You didn't say anything, of course not. And you're not imposing."

"You're probably just tired," I say. "You work hard all day then you have to come home to having your silly old mom staying over. I'm sorry to put you and Sheryl out like this."

"Mom, would you stop? You're not putting us out. Sheryl and I would have you here anytime, hell, come and live with us if you want. All·I want for you is to be safe and happy."

"Then what's wrong?"

He looks the other direction, as if he's embarrassed to tell me whatever it is he has to say. "Dad and I were just talking, that's all."

"What do you mean?" I say. "You and your dad were just talking?"

"It was just a joke," he says.

"Robert," Sheryl says, passing me a glass of wine. "What did you do?" She sets a bowl of chips beside me but takes none for herself.

He shrugs. "I made a suggestion," he says showing his wife his palms, "that Dad should tell Mom that he can't sign the papers yet because he's trying to decide if he should sue."

"You did what? You suggested to your dad that he sue your mom?"

"I was only joking! I didn't think he'd actually go through with it," he says. "But," he says, "I mean, you can't blame Dad for being upset. He was supposed to inherit millions when Grandpa died."

"What?" Sheryl says, throwing her hands in the air. "You think your father should blame Ruby for what her dad did? We are responsible for our own behaviour, Robert. How many times have you told the boys those very words. Sometimes I don't know who I'm married to. How many times have I told you to quit acting like your father? Time and time again, you remind me of him, and not in a good way. Maybe now you'll listen to me."

"We'd had a couple of beers." He looks at the beer in his hand

and places it on the table. "I was only thinking of you living out there all by yourself, Mom. I worry about you. And Dad seemed so lonely."

"Without consulting her?" Sheryl says. "You decided what your sixty-four-year-old mother needed without talking to her? She is an adult, you know. More of one than you are at the moment."

"I thought they'd get back together. I thought they still loved each other."

"You thought, you thought, you thought. Is that all you can say?" Sheryl says. "You didn't think, that's the trouble. You need to make this right. You need to talk to your dad, make him sign those divorce papers and give your mother the freedom she deserves, or I promise you, you'll be sleeping on the couch for the rest of our married days." She glances at me. "And I swear, Robert, if you don't stop bugging me about being overweight, I'm going to file my own law suit!" She grabs a handful of chips and stomps out of the room.

Chapter 32

The door opens and Scout's tail begins wagging so fast, I don't think it's ever going to stop.

"Hey, pup," Wilson says, as he walks into Carnation's. "He's soft," he says to me. "You've turned him into a pet, not a guard dog."

"He's a good boy," I say as Scout licks the man's hand.

Wilson scratches the dog behind the ears. "You should have left him with me instead of dragging him halfway across the country in a storm."

"The forecast was for snow to start today, not three days ago," I say. "Anyhow, I'd already made plans to stay overnight with my son and daughter-in-law, just stayed a few days longer. My grandsons were looking forward to spending time with the dog."

Three days after I left my cabin, I'm finally home, the worst storm of the winter dropping twenty centimetres of snow on the city and more in the country. The plows cleared the highway last night and I left the city this morning.

"Gotta go," Wilson says. "Dropped in to make sure you two got home alright. No time to stand around and chat." He gives Scout a pat on the head and leaves.

"He seems to like you, Ruby," Gerry says.

"I think it's more like tolerates me," I say. "It's the dog he likes." I take a basket and begin to pick up a few groceries. Gerry leans his head back and closes his eyes.

"How did the meeting go with your husband?" Louise asks. "Did he sign? Are you now a divorced woman?"

"Not exactly," I say. I tell them what happened.

"What an ass," she says. "Does he really think he can sue you for that?"

"I've no idea. Robert's going to talk to him today."

"You two are forgetting," Gerry says from behind closed eyes, "he has to be able to justify it under the law. As far as I know, there's no law that states a spouse has to make good to the other spouse on a spoken word of inheriting a fortune from a wealthy parent. He's bluffing."

"Well," I say, "whatever happens, I've no intention of letting him back into my life. It took me thirty-five years to shake him off, there's no way I'm hitching myself to him again."

—

I walk into the cabin and the phone is ringing.

"Hello," I say.

"Mom," Robert says. "I finally got a hold of Dad. You don't have to worry about the lawsuit anymore."

I lean against the fridge and slide to the floor. Scout sits beside me and puts his head in my lap. "How did you manage that?"

"I told him I was ashamed to be his son, ashamed of talking about you behind your back, and ashamed of him. I said if he ever wanted to see me, Sheryl, or his grandsons again, he had to quit threatening you."

"And he agreed?"

"He did. You gotta admit, though," Robert says, "he really must love you."

"He doesn't love me, Rob," I say. "He wants us to get back together so he can talk me into selling the property then giving him some money. Did you know he has a girlfriend? They're living together. Now do you believe me that he doesn't want me back?"

My son is quiet.

"Did he say when he'd sign the divorce papers?" I ask.

"He said he wants to talk to you, didn't say when. I guess I'm now the product of a broken home."

"Our marriage was broken before we even said our vows," I say. "It's been broken for thirty-five years."

Chapter 33

It's a cold night this evening at the beginning of March, and I'm curled up in front of my fireplace watching tv, when Scout starts to bark.

"What is it, boy," I say, as if he has the capacity to answer. "Did you hear something?"

He twirls and runs to the back of the cabin, staring at the door, still barking. I check the deadbolt, then look out the porch window. I see no one.

"There's no one there, I don't know what you're barking at." I scratch behind his ears. "Probably just the wind in the trees," I say.

Scout stops barking, and we settle back in front of the fireplace. Ten minutes later I just about bite the rim off my wine glass when he starts barking again. "Okay," I say, "you're officially scaring the bee-jeesuz out of me." Once more, I follow Scout to the back door and peer out the porch window. A shadow runs past the shed. I back up. "You're right," I say. "There's someone out there. In two strides I'm at the phone and have the receiver in hand when there's a knock on the door. Scout is barking so loud; the sound is reverberating in the pipes of the cookstove.

"Ruby," a familiar voice shouts over the barks. "Let me in, for God's sakes. I'm freezing out here."

"Steve?" I hang up the phone without dialing. "Is that you? What the hell are you doing sneaking around my house?"

Steve rattles the door knob. "Let me in and I'll tell you. Just lock that damn dog up first."

His tone is angry and I don't move.

"Come on, Ruby, I'm not going to hurt you, I only want to talk to you. I said put the dog away and let me in." He rattles the knob again.

"Did you sign the divorce papers? Is that why you're here?"

"I just need to talk to you."

"There's nothing to talk about, Steve. Sign the papers, then leave them on the step."

"I'm not going to sign until we talk."

"You had your chance to talk and instead you threatened to sue me."

"Why do you want to divorce me?" he says. "We had a good marriage, didn't we?"

"You're the one who asked for a separation, not me, Steve. You're the one who walked out on me. You're the one with a girlfriend. What did you expect?"

"This is stupid." He pounds on the door; the wood shakes and I thank Wilson for installing bear proof doors. "Let me in," he shouts.

"I think it would be foolish of me to let you in," I say.

There's silence for a minute and I peek out the corner of the window to see what he's doing. He's still there, leaning against the side of the house. "When did you get the dog?" he asks quietly.

"The day after you broke into my cabin. He's vicious too. I've had him in classes and trained him to attack strangers. He's a pitbull. A big vicious pitbull with very sharp teeth and a bad attitude. Down Spike," I yell. Scout is standing by my side, wagging his tail cocking his head, wondering why I'm yelling at him.

"Didn't look like a pitbull when I saw him. Looked like a border collie."

"Yeah, well, he's got pitbull in him."

"Having a dog is a good idea, Rubes. You need protection out here. You live all alone in the bush. And it's not just because you're a woman. I'd be cautious living here alone and I'm a cop with a gun."

"I like being alone."

"You always did. I'd come home from work, wanting to tell you about my day, and all you wanted was for me to leave you alone. You barely listened when I told you about the people I'd arrested that day, or the close calls I'd had dealing with drunks. You weren't interested. You liked reading, and gardening, things you could do by yourself, things that didn't involve me."

"I only reacted like that because you made me feel as if what you were doing was far more important than anything I did at home. You never wanted to listen when I told you what the kids were doing, talk about my book club, or the plants I'd bought for the garden. You were out saving the world, while I was at home washing the floors."

"Cops can be arrogant. It comes with the territory or you'll get killed out there. Remember when we were first married and we'd go out for lunch on my day off? Then we'd go to a movie or shopping. I bought you a dress one time. Cost a lot of money."

"I remember," I say. I also remember him flirting with the sales-girl who told me the dress looked wonderful on me as she batted her eyelashes at my husband. I told Steve I would never wear the dress as I had no use for such a fancy piece of clothing. He insisted it was perfect and went back the next day and bought it, likely hoping to be able to talk to the same saleswoman again. It hung in my clos-et, never worn, the tags still dangling from the collar until the day I cleaned out my closet and moved here. Steve never even noticed.

"Those were good years," he says.

"Uh huh," I say.

"Then we had Robert, and you became busy with him. Then Jess, then Debby. I felt like I was left behind."

"It's not easy being a stay-at-home mother," I say.

"It's not," he says. "You worked hard. You raised three good kids." He rattles the knob again. "Can I come in now?"

I walk to the door and put my hand on the knob. Scout looks at me, then at the knob, then back at me, as if to say, *Maybe we shouldn't let him in, Mom.*

"I don't want to divorce you, Ruby, I still love you," he says, "but if that's what you really want, then I'll sign the damn papers."

"I thought that's what I wanted," I say.

"You can't think you know," he says. "This is something you need to be sure about. It's not like buying a pair of shoes. You can't take it back once it's done."

"Maybe you're right," I say.

"I am right, Rubes, I am. We should wait until you're sure this is what you want. Just remember that you're my wife and I love you. We must have had some feelings for each other or we wouldn't have stayed together for so long." His voice sounds further away than it did, and I look out the window; he's left the door and is peering in the window of the shed. "We can sell this place and find something in the city. Invest the money wherever Robert suggests. That boy knows his stuff, takes after his dad. We'll retire with a nice nest egg. Never have to worry about money again."

"What?" I say.

He's now kicking at the snow, pulling up buried branches. In one spot he bends forward and starts to dig with his hands. It's a spot where I cut off a sapling last fall, drilled holes into the stump, then poured in stump rot. When Scout came to live with me, I covered it with rocks to prevent him from getting into the chemicals. Steve removes the rocks, then turns away in disgust when he sees the tree stump. "I said," he says, "we'll sell this place and be set for life."

"I don't want to sell this place," I say. "I've made it into my home."

"Oh, yeah, yeah, we don't have to sell right away. Enjoy it for a couple of years. Heck, we can live here if you want. Wherever you're happy, I'll be happy. But you have to agree, we can't live out here until we're old and gray. Best to sell while we're still young enough to enjoy the profits. Tell me," he says, once again standing on the back step. "Did the treasure the previous owner supposedly stash out here, ever turn up?"

I say nothing and back away from the door. Scout stays by my side.

"Ruby, are you there?" he asks. "Did you find out where the old bat hid her stash?"

"There is no treasure," I say. "There never was any. It was all a hoax. Someone in town thought it would be funny to start a rumour." I pause; Steve is quiet. "I want you to sign the divorce papers, Steve," I say. "I want you to sign them then set them on the back step. Put a rock on top so they won't blow away. Then leave. I'm not opening this door until you're gone. It's late. Drive carefully. That road can be tricky in the winter."

It's quiet for a few moments and I worry he's not going to leave. Finally, I hear a car door slam and watch out the porch window as his taillights disappear into the night, his tires fishtailing on the snow. I open the door to find the divorce papers lying on the back step, a rock on top. I turn to the last page where he's scrawled his name.

Chapter 34

April is always a tough month on the prairies. Spring is in our sights, but the month can go either way; warm weather can cause the trees to bud and plants to sprout, or there could be more snow. This year it seems it's going to keep snowing and on April twentieth we have another storm. Scout and I are snowed in for a week. Finally, the first week of May with the temperatures on the rise and the snow melting, I leave Scout at home and head to town. Louise called and said I have some mail from the provincial government. She suggested the three of us meet for a drink at The Kernel after the store closes, where she can give it to me. I slide into the booth while Louise hands me the envelope.

"Looks official," Gerry says. "What is it?"

"None of your business," Louise says. "You need to quit being so nosey, Dad."

"You forget, old people can get away with asking questions others can't," he says to his daughter. "Apparently our," he taps his head, "ability to be appropriate dwindles with age."

"Ha," Louise says. "You know exactly what you're saying, don't try to pull that over on us, old man. Sometimes I think your brain works better than mine."

"It's just some information I requested," I say.

"About what?"

"Dad,…" Louise warns, glaring at her father.

"If you must know," I say, "I sent away for information on getting a government grant."

"For….," Gerry says, urging me to tell him everything.

"Opening a resort," I say with a sigh. "I was curious to know if they give individual people money, or if I need to be a corporation or something like that. And before you ask any more questions," I say holding up my finger to stop him from saying more, "I have no idea if I'm going to do it or not, just getting information. This is the first step in a long line of steps I'll have to take, if in fact I want to take them. If the government doesn't supply grants, then my inquiries end with this. I am not a rich woman. And even if they do give money to individuals, I still haven't decided if I want to go through with it. I have no idea how to do such a thing and the thought of trying to figure it out, scares me. But if I do decide to move ahead, there's still lots of, as you would say, Gerry, rows to hoe. This is the first step, that's all."

We order some drinks and food and for the next hour, talk about everything from the town's population decreasing when another family moved to the city this past winter, to how high the lake might rise from the run-off this spring, to whether it's going to be a good farming season. Not until we're finishing our meal, does Gerry go back to the topic of re-opening the resort. I tell him again that I'm not even sure if I have the capability of doing such a thing.

He wipes his mouth with his napkin then says, "Anyone can do anything if they set their mind to it. Just do your homework before you send in the application. Although there's something to be said about jumping in with both feet before you know how to swim. That's what Cecelia always did. Drove me crazy sometimes. She would just go ahead and do something without much thought as to whether she knew how or not. She built the cabins, opened a resort, took out ads in magazines, all without ever having done those things before. She just did it. If she failed, she'd try something else." He scratches his head. "You remind me of her," he says.

"Me? I'm nothing like her. I like to have my ducks in a row before I do anything."

"Not in that way," he says. "You are a planner, yes, I can see that, but you're tough like she was. You've just never been given a chance. That first day when you and your real estate agent stopped and I saw you standing beside your car, I said to myself, *I wonder what happened to that woman to make her take so long to live her life.* I could tell that you were out of your comfort zone; driving up here alone, doing whatever it was you were planning on doing. But I could also see the resolve in you. Someone who was willing to push herself that much, had to be tough."

"From your chair on the step you could see all that?"

"You've blossomed so much since then. Cecelia would be proud to have you as the owner."

"Are you saying I'm a late bloomer, Gerry?"

"Through no fault of your own."

"Well, I don't think I'm as tough as she was, but thank you for the compliment."

"I hope you re-open," he says. "Put this town back on the map."

"We'll just have to wait and see," I say. "I haven't even applied yet."

"The speed the government works, don't count on me being around." He taps the envelope. "Open it," he says.

"Now?"

"The older I get, the more I think there's no time like the present."

I pick up the envelope, take a breath, and tear it open. Inside there are papers explaining what I need to do to qualify for a grant, a letter outlining the details of how to apply for the grant, and a page attached for me to fill out telling them what my plans are and how large of a grant I think I might need. Suddenly, feeling overwhelmed, I shove everything back in the envelope.

Gerry places his warm hand over mine. "It's okay," he says.

"I'm no good at this," I say. "Paperwork stresses me out. I can't do it." I shake my head. "I'm nothing like Cecelia. I'm the total opposite."

"You think she wasn't afraid? I can't count how many times I witnessed her questioning herself. Crying when she thought she was alone, then telling me it was just the onions she was cutting, or she'd gotten a bug in her eye. She even told me once she should have married when she had the chance and lived the easy life. But she kept going because she loved it out here."

"It's too bad she died," I say. "It was a real tragedy."

"It was certainly the last thing any of us expected. That's why you have to push through your fear; life's too short to not try doing something you want. And," he says, "I think that deep down this," he points to the envelope, "is something you really want."

"That's the thing; I don't know," I say.

"You'll never know unless you try," Gerry says.

"And with that," I say, "I'm taking my envelope and going home. Thanks for the beers and burgers."

1965

I hang up the phone. "Can't get through. Snow must have taken down a line someplace. I'd better drive out and help her cover the wood, make sure she's alright," I say to Lila. "Crazy weather. Goes from warm and sunny to six inches of snow in a day."

She doesn't hear me. "Lila," I say, "Are you listening? I'm driving out to the lake."

"I'm sorry," she says. "What did you say?"

"I said I should drive out to see if Cecelia is alright."

She turns around. "You're going to the lake? Is that what you said?"

"Three times now."

"No," she shakes her head. "You stay here with me. I don't want you driving on that narrow road in this blizzard, and neither would Cecelia if she were here to tell you."

"Are you okay?" I ask.

"I'm fine," she says, her back, once again to me.

"You seem upset about something. Did something happen? Is Louise alright? Did she have a fight with her friend?"

"Nothing happened and Louise is fine," she snaps.

"Doesn't sound like it," I say.

"I don't want you taking a chance driving out to the lake when there's no need, that's all. Cecelia will manage fine by herself, just like she always has. All that will happen if you go out there is you'll get stuck and leave me to face the storm alone."

"Okay, okay, I'll stay here." I put my hand on her shoulder, she shrugs me off.

"I'm sure she managed to cover the wood by herself," Lila says. "She's lived out there for thirty years and managed everything from blizzards, to thunderstorms, coyotes, and bears. I'll bet she's cozy and warm in front of her fireplace, a glass of homemade wine in one hand and a plate of rabbit stew in the other. You know how self-sufficient she is. It would be a waste of time for you to take a chance driving there."

—

"Snowplows are here," I call to Lila. "Stores not busy, I think you can handle it by yourself for a while. I'm going to check on Cecelia," I say quickly, then slam the back door before she can talk me out of it.

I throw my snowshoes on the passenger seat then hop in my truck to follow the trio of plows, passing the phone company on the side of the highway repairing the pole that came down two months ago. I stay behind one of the plows as it leaves the highway to clear Sunset Lake Road, then park behind Cecelia's cabin, the yard too deep with snow to pull in.

"Want me to wait?" the driver calls from his perch high up in the plow. "Make sure you get back alright?"

"I'm good," I say. "Thanks." I wave goodbye as he heads back to town.

It's quiet out here, with barely a breeze and I marvel at how much snow has collected on the ground and in the trees in the past two months. My eyes fall on the swimming pool. Snow has drifted up the sides, and filled the inside with snow, causing one of the panels to collapse and I sigh, anticipating the fight I'll have with the company Cecelia bought it from, to get someone up here to fix it. The outhouse is buried halfway up the outside walls, and there is no path shovelled to the woodshed. As a matter of fact, the only tracks I see in the yard are those of deer, rabbits, and coyotes. There are no footprints or snowshoe tracks anywhere and I try not to dwell on the fact that something might have happened. I buckle on my snowshoes, step up onto the three-foot-high snowpack, and make my way to the back step, praying that Cecelia is alright.

The door is inaccessible, buried to half its height in snow, and I call from the bottom of the step. "Cecelia, it's me, Gerry. Are you home?"

There's no answer so I walk across the top of the drifts to the front yard, telling myself that because of the high quantity of snow, she's likely using only the front door this winter to make less shovelling for herself, and is clearing snow from the step right now, or gone ice fishing or hunting, or even bundled up and sitting in the front yard with a steaming cup of coffee, admiring the wonder of nature spread out before her.

I round the corner of the cabin and all I see is white. If it wasn't for the trees rising out of the snow, their trunks dark slashes across the pale-blue sky, I wouldn't be able to tell where the lake ends and the sky begins. The front door is as snowed in as the back, and I climb the step, wrestling the shovel out of a drift.

After clearing off the step, I yank open the door and call, "Cecelia," sending crows flying from the treetops. She doesn't answer. I step inside. It's cold and I can see my breath. A cup and a plate sit on the coffee-table with a partially eaten piece of toast on the plate. A mouse is nibbling on the corner of the toast and the coffee table is covered in dust; something Cecelia would never allow to happen. I run into the kitchen, calling her name, then the bedroom, even up the new stairs to the unfinished top floor, but she's nowhere to be found. I return to the living room and step back outside, the snow muffling the sounds as I shout her name across the lake. I look for her ice fishing hut that usually sits directly in front of her cabin about two hundred yards out, but she hasn't erected it this year, and other than deer, rabbit, and coyote prints, there are no other footprints on the lake.

My eyes stop on the outline of the picnic table, chairs, and the fire pit, all buried to the top in snow. Other years she's used that picnic table and firepit all winter long, having wiener roasts and hot chocolate, even sitting out here at night when the northern lights are strung across the sky like Christmas lights. I start to get the feeling that something's terribly wrong.

The snow must be three feet deep across the front yard so, worried about what I might find, but knowing I have to try, I break a dead branch off a tree. Then, walking across the top of the pack, I begin poking the end into the snow, all the way to the ground, with each stab, praying I don't hit anything. I've poked my way down the path she takes when she's on her way to the shore, across the front of the yard beside the fire pit and chairs, then the perimeter closest to the beach, and am back near her cabin, standing in front of the window just under the balcony, when the end of the stick hits something other than the ground. There's no shrub planted here, no table, no stump from a tree she removed. Cecelia's never been one to keep her house, or her yard cluttered with junk; everything is always put neatly away. With so many houses to manage, there's always been a place for everything and everything has always been in its place.

I grab the shovel, then start digging snow away from the spot, and have dug a deep hole when I feel the edge of the metal catch on something soft. With my stomach doing flip-flops, I take off my snowshoes and kneel, sinking to my hips as I dig the rest of the way with my hands. Cecelia's sheepskin winter coat with the fleece lining peeks through the white, and I pull myself back, my heart racing in my chest. As if I'm swimming, I take a couple deep breathes, then again lean forward and start to dig. I uncover her back, the snow by her sides intertwined in a lacework of reddish-brown crystals clinging to her clothing. I pull off my mitten and push my fingers into the snow, placing them against her neck, hoping against hope that I feel a heartbeat, but I feel only her skin, as cold and unyielding as marble. She's likely been dead for weeks, perhaps even months. She's on her stomach, her hands by her sides, her legs stretched straight out behind her. I look up; the balcony is broken and sagging, though, I'm unsure if it's because Cecelia grabbed onto it when she fell or if it's from the weight of the snow. I attempt to turn her over, but she's frozen to the ground.

I jump to my feet, and without bothering to put my snowshoes back on, slog through the hip deep snow to my truck, then drive like a bat out of hell back to town to tell the cops and call an ambulance.

—

I pull into his driveway, the edges lined with rocks, park beside the car that's up on jacks and pound on the door of his trailer. The door opens and he falls down the steps and into my arms. He reeks of alcohol. I push him back inside; he lands on his back. "What the hell?" Eric shouts from the floor.

"Did you actually think you could get away with it?" I ask, my voice calm considering how angry I am.

"Get away with what?" he asks.

"I found her, this afternoon. Buried under the snow."

"Found who?"

"You pushed her off the second storey then left her there to die."

"I did what? What are you talking about?" he slurs. He tries to climb to his feet, but I push him down again.

"You killed Cecelia. Don't try to deny it."

"Johansen is dead?" That gets his attention and he sits up straight.

"You know damn well she is. You killed her."

"I did no such thing."

"Quit your lying."

"Do I look like I'm in any condition to kill someone? I've been drinking all day. Never left this trailer."

"She didn't die today, you idiot. Coroner figures a few months ago. I just found her today."

"A few months ago? Like how long?"

"Couple of months maybe. Could be three."

"I've been in the city for the past six months looking for work. Nothing in this one-horse town for me since the lumberyard closed. Got back today when the plows cleared the highway."

"It had to be you, there's no one else."

"Are you kidding?" He pulls himself to his feet and flops on his couch. "She has more enemies than she could count. There's Dunlop, any one of the men she belittled over the years, and there must be some renters that she insulted."

"You need to leave," I say.

"I think you've got that backwards," he says pointing to the open door of his trailer.

"I want you to get out of town," I say. "If I see you around town again, I'll get a gun and shoot you."

Chapter 35

"I want to have a party," I tell Louise on the phone. "A birthday party for Gerry. And I want it to be a surprise."

"He's not really a party kind of guy. Hell, he wouldn't let me have a party when he turned one-hundred, I doubt he'll want one for his one-hundred and third. But," Louise says, "If I tell him it was your idea, he might be more willing to have one. Just let's not make it a surprise. He likes to know what's happening."

"Okay," I say.

"Keep in mind, every year, for the past few years, whenever I've planned a get together; birthdays, Christmas, anything, I've told myself to not count on him being around come that date. So, you can plan the party, but don't be totally sure that he'll be there."

"His birthday is only seven weeks away. He's as healthy as a horse, as he would say. He'll be here, I'm sure of it."

—

I'm pulling the second cake out of the oven, the first already cooled, wrapped in tinfoil, and in the deepfreeze, and have enough batter left for a third, when the phone rings, startling me and I drop the pan on the floor. "Damn it," I say, as Scout begins eating the ruined cake. I pick up the phone. "Hello," I say, trying to push the dog away before he eats the whole thing and gets sick.

"He's gone," Louise says.

"Louise, is that you? Who's gone?"

"Dad. He's gone."

"Gone? Where?"

"Gone," she repeats. "Passed away, no longer of this life, dead."

"Are you sure?" I ask, then realize I shouldn't have said that. "Sorry," I say. "With all his joking about dying, I feel someone should check for a heartbeat to make sure he isn't teasing."

"Believe me, that's the first thing I did. I've told him so many times that no one was going to believe him when it really happened. He was sitting in his chair, talking to Hank, and called me over. He said he loved me more than life itself, and that he'd had a wonderful life, and, even though the resort didn't reopen in his lifetime, he was glad to have lived long enough to meet Cecelia's granddaughter and see the cabin renovated. His last words were, *It's time I shuffled off this mortal coil.* Then he closed his eyes and that was it. I think he scared Hank more than he did me."

"When did this happen?"

"This morning, a couple hours ago. The ambulance just took him away."

"I can't believe it," I say. "Are you okay?"

"I don't think it's sunk in, but I'm good. I mean, who has their father with them until he's just about one-hundred and three? It's going to be odd not having him in his chair driving me crazy with his clichés, but I'm counting my blessings for having had him around as long as I did." We're both quiet for a few minutes until she says, "What should we do about the party next week?"

"I don't know. I suppose we'll have to cancel. Without the birthday boy, there is no birthday party." I look at all the food I have stacked around the kitchen. "Between the two of us, we have enough food to feed an army." I can feel Louise smile at the cliché. "What do you think we should do?"

"Years ago, Dad told me he didn't want a funeral. He asked for a memorial service. Out there. At Sunset Lake. Weather permitting of course. He wanted the guests to have a bonfire, then have his ashes sprinkled over the water. He wanted singing and dancing, and laughter. He didn't want anyone to wear black, and he didn't want anyone to mourn his death. It was his hundredth birthday when he made this request, and there was no one living at the cabin, so I told him yes, I'd be glad to do that for him. Now that you're living out there, I don't know what to do. Would you be interested in hosting something like that? We could change the birthday party to a memorial service. We'd keep the same guest list, but I'd have to expand it as customers of the store might want to say goodbye. We could still have a barbeque and wiener roast, then a bonfire on the beach. We could even sing happy birthday, make it a birthday party and memorial service in one. I think Dad would appreciate the irony, and it would be a shame to waste all the food we've bought."

—

Blair, Jim, and Darren, have finished constructing the bonfire that's to be lit at dusk, and are now unloading Wilson's barbeque from the back of Jim's truck, and placing it on the deck beside mine. Twinkle lights have been strung from the trees, and the picnic tables that I saved from the dumpster have been dragged outside the shed, cleaned up, and placed around my yard. I have a refrigerator full of potato salad, pickles, cheese, and coleslaw, as does Louise. Boxes of wieners, hamburgers, and buns have been taken out of the deepfreeze to thaw. I'm expecting the entire town to arrive on my doorstep in just a few hours.

"Anything else you want us to do?" Blair asks, coming in the front door.

"Nope," I say. "You've done enough for now, thank you."

"We're going home to get cleaned up. See you in a few hours."

"Don't forget," I call as he closes the screen door. "No black clothes. Gerry wanted a party, not a funeral."

—

At four o'clock, cars begin to park on my property, and by five thirty, every square inch of land behind each cabin has a car parked on it. Everyone is wearing their brightest coloured beach wear, and the gathering resembles a luau, not a funeral. Some of the people I know, some I don't, only having seen them shopping at Carnation's, getting gas, or standing in line for ice cream at A Scoop Above.

At five, Darren lights the wood in the firepit in front of my cabin, and the air becomes crisp with the smell of roasting hotdogs. Jim and Blair are manning the barbeques, flipping burgers, and teasing one another as I heard them do many times over the course of the renovations. Coolers filled with ice, water, beer, and wine, sit on each picnic table, and Louise, Jess, Debby, Sheryl, Darren, and I rush around, making sure everyone has a drink.

By seven, I've lost track of my friend, as well as my family, and find a chair in a relatively empty part of the yard, a hamburger, and a glass of wine in hand. I'm taking my first bite, when I overhear a conversation between two men sitting in the chairs in front of me. One man is in a Hawaiian shirt, the other, dressed in denim. I don't know their names, but I know them to be customers at Carnation's. They don't see me and continue with their conversation as if I'm not here.

"He knew where it was," the Hawaiian shirt man says. "You can count on it." He takes a bite of his hotdog.

"What makes you so sure?" denim shirt asks.

"How else would that store stay in business for the past seventy years?" He brushes crumbs off his brightly coloured shirt.

"You think he took the money and used it for the store? Doesn't sound like Gerry. My impression of him was that he was an honest man, not a thief," denim shirt says.

"Okay then," Hawaiian shirt continues as he takes another bite, "if you don't believe that," he says talking around the food in his mouth, "then how about this. He's the one who killed the Johansen woman, then took her money and pretended he found her already dead. He could have easily hidden it at home and deposited it in the bank little by little over the last fifty years."

"That's even more difficult to believe than your first scenario."

"That's what my dad always believed."

"Your dad also believed that aliens took him to their spaceship and did weird things to him, so I wouldn't go believing anything that man had to say. Isn't the money supposed to belong to the woman who lives here now? The one who's hosting?"

"That's what's supposed to happen," Hawaiian shirt says, "but tell me this; if you knew where the money was hidden, and no one else knew that you knew, could you keep your hands off that much cash if you could get away with it?"

"I suppose it would depend on the amount. How much are we talking about?"

"I've heard as much as a million dollars. And, rumour is that she might have bought gold with her money. If that's the case, it's worth a lot more than what it was when she bought it."

Denim shirt whistles. "I suppose that might be enough to tempt even the most honest person."

"I've seen people here tonight looking in the trees, under rocks, poking through the old cabins," Hawaiian shirt says. "I even saw a couple of people trying to get into some of those ancient outhouses." He pushes the last of his hotdog into his mouth then wipes his lips with the back of his hand.

Denim shirt tips his bottle back and drains it, then slaps his buddy on the shoulder. "Well, you won't catch me in an outhouse, but I might take a peek around later, just in case I get lucky. Right now," he shakes his empty bottle, "I need another beer."

"Another beer and another hotdog," Hawaiian shirt says. "Can't stand funerals, but at least they have decent food at this shindig."

After they've left, I go to find Louise. She's sitting by herself in a chair near the shore, looking out over the lake.

"How are you doing?" I ask as I place my own chair beside her and put my arm around her shoulders.

"Just thinking about Dad."

"One of a kind," I say.

"As honest as the day is long," Louise says.

"A diamond in the rough," I say and we laugh. "I just heard the craziest conversation I think I've ever heard."

"Oh?"

"I don't know if I should say. Don't want to hurt your feelings."

"You're not going to hurt my feelings, Ruby. And if that's what you think, then I imagine I already know what you're going to say."

"You do?"

"There are people in this town who've been saying it for years." Even in the dimness of dusk, I can see the disgust on her face. "Someone thinks Dad found the money that Cecelia hid, and took it. Is that what you heard?"

"That's what I heard," I say. "I don't know their names, two men, customers at the store. Isn't that crazy?"

She shrugs. "Dad and I heard all sorts of gossip over the years. The most popular being that he took the money to keep the store running, which is stupid. We've managed on our own; struggled some years, but managed, thanks to our loyal customers who don't want to see us close. I've also heard that he took the money to pay off the mother of a love-child he fathered in the seventies, or that he took it to pay off gambling debts. Or, and this is the stupidest one, that he killed Cecelia and took the money. He loved her; he'd never kill her."

"I hate gossip," I say. "It only shows how ignorant some people can be. If you can't say anything nice, don't say anything at all."

"Of course, our friends knew that he would no more steal money, than he'd cut off his own arm, and that's all that mattered to Dad. But there's always those who believe what they want to believe, and no amount of trying to persuade them differently, would make any difference. So, Dad didn't try. He always said, you can lead a horse to water, but you can't make him drink." She shakes her head. "I don't know why they'd come to his memorial if that's what they think."

"From what I saw, free food and beer. And the treasure. They said there's people even searching tonight."

"I'm not surprised. Money makes people do crazy things."

"Can I ask you something?" I say.

"Anything."

"Did Gerry believe there's treasure hidden out here?"

"I think he did, but he never said for sure. All he ever told me was that Cecelia talked about investing in gold and that she didn't believe in using banks. He said she gave lots of money away, so who knows if she even had any left to be able to buy gold." She looks at me and smiles. "But Cecelia was a smart woman. I'm willing to bet she did hide it out here someplace."

"But where?" I say. "I can't think of one place it could be. Everything's been demolished and rebuilt."

"Like I said, she was smart. She'd hide it in a place no one would ever think of looking. Maybe one day you'll find it," she says with a wink.

"My dad had a bar of gold," I say. "It was a payment for a job, but instead of cashing it in, he kept it in his safe. I suppose that's something else Julia got."

A commotion starts behind us and Louise and I turn to look. Bruce and Michael have picked up a wiener stick each and are pretending to have a sword fight. Sheryl grabs the sticks and says something about poking out their eyes.

Robert laughs, then to someone standing behind him he says, "Boys will be boys."

Ever so slightly, Sheryl shakes her head. "You're a better father than your dad was, Rob," she says quietly. "Don't act like him."

My son takes Micheal's hand, leading him away from the firepit, then bends down and talks to him face to face.

Louise and I turn back to face the lake.

"Parenting must be the hardest job in the world," she says.

"It is that," I say. "You learn as you go. I can tell you that I made lots of mistakes. There are days I wish I had a do-over. Many do-overs, actually."

"You did your best and that's what counts," Louise says. "Your kids aren't serial killers, or thieves, or drug dealers. They've got good jobs, have made lives for themselves. They're normal everyday adults with flaws and with virtues, and in this crazy world, that's all we can ask of anyone. So?" she says.

"So, what?" I ask.

"Have you seen Missy lately?"

"I haven't seen her for months."

Louise reaches into her pocket and pulls out a picture. "I was looking for pictures of Dad and found this in an album in the basement."

She holds a photograph up in front of me. It's tiny, with scalloped edges like they used to do in the fifties and sixties. It's also in black and white.

"Who's this?" I ask.

"Look closely."

I take the picture and hold it up to my face. It's getting dark and difficult to see, but the person in the picture is a woman with a long braid, white blouse, overalls, and a man's plaid jacket wrapped around her shoulders. Her skin is wrinkled as if she's spent too much time in the sun, and she has on a floppy hat. She's turning her head away, as if she doesn't want her picture taken.

"It's Missy," I say. I turn the picture back and forth in my hand.

"It's Cecelia," Louise says. "From nineteen sixty-five, about a month before she died. She was only fifty-two in that picture. Spent a lot of time outside, looked older than she was. But then, I think she had an old soul."

"It's Missy," I say, "the way she looks today."

"She didn't like having her picture taken, was always shying away from the camera, but Dad caught her one day when she was beginning the second floor on this cabin. Look in the background. See that pile of lumber? That's the wood she was going to use, the wood you and Chip saw in the backyard the first day you looked at the place. The lumber Wilson took to the dump."

I'm quiet.

"I think she's waiting," Louise says.

"For what," I say.

"For you to ask for help."

"With what?" I say.

"When I was a kid and I'd come out here, Cecelia would teach me all sorts of things. How to chop wood, how to start a fire, how to fillet a fish. Even taught me how to skin a rabbit. Not something I'd do today. But she was self-sufficient, and thought all women should know how to look after themselves. If Mom had known what I was doing when I was only ten years old, she'd have skinned me alive along with the rabbit. But Cecelia wasn't worried; she believed in me. She'd show me what to do, tell me I could do it, then give me the knife. If I asked for help, she'd show me again, but I knew that she wanted me to try on my own first. She'd be patient, not correcting, just waiting while I figured it out. Most times I did, but if I needed help, I knew all I had to do was ask and I wouldn't be made to feel bad because I needed help. I think that's what she's doing now. She's waiting for you to figure it out on your own, or ask for help."

"But with what?" I say. "I've nothing I need her help with. I feel like I'm doing fine."

"As Dad would say, your guess is as good as mine. But she's waiting. And when you finally do figure out what she's waiting for, that's when you'll see her again."

Wilson calls to us. "The sun is setting, ladies. Time to get this show on the road," and I wonder if Wilson isn't taking over saying Gerry's clichés.

Chapter 36

Darren, Jim, and Blair, each drop a match onto the kindling at the base of the bonfire, and within seconds, fire is licking up the sides of the wooden teepee and soaring out the hole in the top. Louise stands at the water's edge, her father's ashes at her feet.

"Thank you all for coming out here tonight," she says. "Dad would have loved this. His favourite thing to do in the world was to be at the store talking to his customers. Asking about your lives, your kids lives, your jobs. Seeing you all here tonight, enjoying this beautiful setting, would have made him the happiest man in the world." She's quiet for a moment while she collects herself. "I've heard some of you over the years say that you think my father was a dishonest man."

I hear a few whispers, and see Hawaiian shirt, who's standing at the back of the crowd, look the other way.

"I believe that the celebration of his life is not the right place to have to defend my father, so instead I'm going to talk about his character," Louise says. "If he accidentally short-changed someone, no matter if it was a nickel or ten dollars, he'd make sure you were reimbursed the next time you came in the store. If he found a dollar bill on the floor, he'd put that bill in a separate place in the cash-register until the owner claimed it. If he'd promised someone he could get something in the store, he would go out of his way to get it, even if it cost him more than he could sell it for." She wipes away a tear. "He loved being the wise old man who people came to when needing advice on anything from their kids, to their jobs, to what kind of a car to buy. Once, he even advised Bill," she points to a young man in the front row who's standing beside a woman cradling a baby in her arms, "that if he didn't hurry up and ask Donna to marry him, he was going to ask her himself. And that was just last year!"

Everyone laughs.

"He loved having been born and raised in this community, loved being from a small town. When you remember him, I want you to think of a kind, generous man who would do anything for any-body, a man who loved you all, and a man who felt like he was the town's custodian. Thank you for coming out tonight to celebrate his life." She bends forward and picks up the box, kicks off her sandals, wades out to her knees and pours the ashes into the water. I hear her mumble, "Bye, Dad. May you be as happy in death as you were in life." All around me I hear voices saying goodbye.

As the bonfire dies to glowing embers, people begin to wander back towards my house. Friends and neighbours are hugging and laughing, calling to one another that they'll get together again soon, and not be a stranger for too long. Everyone is in a loving frame of mind and I get multiple people saying thank you to me, and that this was the best funeral they've ever attended and this is exactly how they want their send-off to be.

—

Everyone but my family, Darren, Wilson, and Louise, have left and I'm standing on the deck, stacking bowls together to take in the house to wash, when a piercing scream fills the air. Scout starts barking wildly from the beach. We turn to see one of my grandsons yelling his head off as the other lies on the ground, though it's diffi-cult to make out who is who in the darkness.

"We're not running," Robert says, grabbing Sheryl by the arm as she begins to rush towards her children. "I told them that no one would believe them if they pretended to be hurt, and we're done answering to their pranks."

Darren, however, who's been taking leftover hamburgers off the barbeque and piling them into a Tupperware container, drops what he's doing and rushes to a picnic table. He grabs a cooler, pulls out the water bottles while he's running, and races towards the boys. Sheryl shakes free of Robert and chases after Darren.

"They're just fooling around," Robert yells to their backs. "They're going to laugh at you when you get there," and it crosses my mind that perhaps Robert is threatened by his kids making a fool of him, much like his own father was.

Ignoring Robert, Darren shouts to me, "Ruby, go and get your first aid kit."

I run upstairs and by the time I get back outside, all I can see are dark shapes on the beach, bending over the boys.

When I arrive, Darren is kneeling beside Bruce who has his hand immersed in the cooler. The boy is sobbing while Darren talks to him in a calm soothing voice, and Sheryl strokes her son's back. Wilson and Louise are dipping pails in the lake and pouring water onto the smouldering embers. Debby is holding onto Scout, and Jess is shining a flashlight on Bruce and Darren, while Robert screams at Michael.

"What the hell were you thinking?" he yells at his son. He points at the sticks lying in the sand. "I thought we told you to leave these alone. Now look what you've done; you've scarred your brother for life, maybe even made him blind! I tried talking to you calmy, rationally, but apparently you aren't grown up enough to be talked to as an adult."

I approach my son. "Rob, it's okay," I say. "You're scaring the boy. It was an accident. Kids have accidents."

He storms past me to stand by himself.

"I didn't mean to," Michael says to me. "We were just playing. He fell backwards. His hand went in the fire. I'm sorry."

I give my grandson a hug. "We know you didn't do it on purpose."

"His eye will be fine," Darren says, peering at the cut on the side of Bruce's head. He pulls a wad of cotton out of the first aid kit. "The

stick scraped his temple, but missed his eye. It's a superficial cut."
He dabs at the blood with the cotton ball then puts a small Steri-
Strip on the wound, closing the edges. "But you should take him to
the ER and have his hand looked at. I'll soak a towel with lukewarm
water and you need to keep his hand very loosely wrapped all the
way to the city. I'll give you a jug of water to keep the towel damp.
The longer he keeps the burn wet, the better."

Wilson stops what he's doing and is looking at his son with
something resembling respect.

"I thought you're supposed to use butter," Robert says. "Butter
and ice. That's what my mother always said. Sheryl, go and get some
butter and a bag of ice."

"No," Darren says. "Lukewarm water is your best bet."

"How do you know?" Robert asks. "What are you, a doctor or
something?"

"I'm a nurse," Darren says. "Well, just about. I start my last year
next week."

"Robert," Sheryl says. "Quit arguing and carry our son to the
car."

I rush forward and hug my son. "You're a great dad, Rob. You
can do this. Everything will be fine."

Robert picks up Bruce, as Darren talks to Sheryl. "Kids bounce
back from things like this easier than adults. He seems like a tough
little boy."

"He is," Robert says over his shoulder as he's carrying Bruce to
the car. "He's tough just like his grandma." He glances at me and I
smile.

We return to the cabin and I run inside to get Sheryl a blanket to
wrap Bruce in. "I'll call when we're done at the hospital," she says as
I hand her the blanket.

"Even if it's the middle of the night," I say.

Chapter 37

Louise, Wilson, and Darren, stay to help clean up the mess along with Jess and Debby, who are staying the night. By one in the morning, we have it in some semblance of order and I send the guys home and my daughters to bed.

"I don't know about you," Louise says when were alone, "but even if I do go home, I'm not going to be able to sleep. Is it alright with you if I stay for a glass of wine?"

"It's alright with me. Pour me one too," I say plopping down on the couch. She pours two glasses. "That was a very nice memorial speech you made."

"Thanks. Might not have been appropriate, but it felt good. Do you think Bruce is going to be alright?"

"Darren seemed positive, and I trust his judgment."

"He'll make a good nurse when he graduates. Did you see the look on Wilson's face?"

"I did," I say. "Hopefully he'll have more respect for his son now. He's not as tough as people say. He's even warmed up towards me. Told me the other day that I'd surprised him being able to live out here by myself. Likely as close to a compliment as he's ever paid anyone. That's one thing about your dad; he was always supportive of me."

"I miss him already," she says. "I know no one lives forever and I know he lived a good long life, but after being around for so long, it just seemed like he was going to be around forever. I don't know how I'm going to ever *not* miss him."

I pat her hand. "You'll always miss him, but time will make it less painful."

"Wouldn't it be nice if we could have do-overs?" she says. "Just like you said; do some small part of your life over again so you wouldn't have that particular regret."

"It would be nice," I say. "Ease some of the burden as we age."

"Did Dad tell you that Mom was jealous of Missy?"

"He mentioned it. Said Lila was intimidated by her."

"I think maybe she thought they were having an affair. Dad and Cecelia. They weren't," she says. "It was all in Mom's head. For some reason she thought Dad was under Missy's spell. Dad and Missy were good friends, that's all they were."

"That must have been so hard for your dad to find his friend dead in the front yard."

"I still remember him coming home," Louise says. "He was wild; ranting that Missy was dead and the cops believed she fell off the roof. He said she would never go on the roof in a snow storm. From the very beginning he believed that someone had killed her. At first Mom and I didn't know what to think, we'd only just seen her a couple of days before."

"You and your mom? The two of you were here before Cecelia died?"

"When we left, she was alive and well."

"I thought your mom didn't like coming out here."

"She didn't and I wish with all my heart that she hadn't come out here that day." Louise sighs. "She came out to confront Missy about trying to steal her husband from her."

"Oh dear," I say.

"Mom pushed Missy against the pool and Missy bumped her head on one of the steel posts between the side panels. She didn't pass out, just had a bump. Missy talked quietly to Mom and Mom seemed to soften. She started to cry; said she was sorry. Missy told me to take Mom home. Missy had given me a few driving lessons that summer, so I loaded Mom into the passenger seat and drove us home. The next day we had a big storm and the phone lines went down. Dad couldn't get here to check on her for weeks. He found her two months later, dead in the front yard."

"What are you trying to tell me?"

"I didn't know anything about head trauma at the time; I was only fifteen and unless you were into sports, I don't think too many people were aware of the damage it can cause. It wasn't until a few years later, when I heard about a football player that had died when he hit his head, that it dawned on me that might have been what happened to Missy. I'm not sure if Mom ever figured it out before she died. We never spoke of that day."

"And you've carried this around with you all this time? You never told your dad?"

"Never told Dad, never told anyone. All anyone knows is that Dad found Missy dead in the front yard, and that he was never the same. For years I regretted leaving her after she bumped her head, wished I could do that part of my life over. I considered going to the police and confessing what I suspected happened, but truthfully, it was already fifteen years after the fact and Mom was dead and gone. Missy believed in the code of the country; you look after your own, and saying something to the authorities about the fight would have killed Dad, ruined Mom's good name. Missy was dead and gone, and I thought, why drag others down, it wouldn't bring her back. Best to let the dead rest in peace."

1965

I'm walking home from school, feeling a nip in the air and looking at a sky that's threatening snow, wondering if I can squeeze in one more swim in the pool after the store closes tonight, before Cecelia empties it for the season. The past two years, winter came early so we only got to use it to mid-September when the first frost arrived. This year, however, winter has held off, and it's already the first week of October. Missy told me she was going to empty the pool the minute frost was in the forecast, but last week, I was still splashing in the water, wishing summer would last forever. I run down the alley and see our truck pull out of the garage with Mom behind the wheel. "Mom," I call, "where are you going?"

She stops and rolls down the window. "To Meg's house. She wanted some help with, uh, some help with her kitchen. She's got new cupboards and doesn't know where to put everything."

"Okay," I say, drawing out the word, thinking that's an odd reason to be going out this time of the day. That would normally be something she would do in the morning after I'd gone to school when she has coffee with her friend, or something the two of them would do on a weekend evening over a glass of wine. She's always home when I get home from school then we cross the alley to help Dad in the store. "Is something wrong, Mom?"

"Nothings wrong, Louise," she says. "I'm fine. Go home. You'll have to make your own snack today."

I race across the alley towards the store.

"Where are you going?" Mom shouts out the car window. "I told you to go home."

"To help Dad, I can grab a bag of chips in the store." Friday afternoons are one of the busiest afternoons of the week. It usually takes all three of us working just to keep up.

"No," she says abruptly. "I mean, not today. It turned into a quiet day. You should go and do your homework. And I don't want you having chips as your snack."

"Are you sure you're alright, Mom?"

"Quit asking questions. I said I'm fine and I'll be home as soon as I can. Now let me leave. Amy's going to wonder where I am."

"I thought you said you were going to Meg's?"

"I mean, Meg's," she says, looking flustered. "Quit bugging me!"

I open the gate, then turn to watch Mom as she exits the alley. Thinking she's acting odd, I race to the front yard and continue to watch as she pulls onto the street, but then she turns the opposite direction she should take if she were going to her friend's house. She follows the road to the highway and turns left at the Sunset Lake sign. "What the hell," I say to myself. Mom rarely goes to the lake, and never alone. The only times are if Missy has invited the whole family to sit under her Christmas tree or have a barbeque and a swim. I can't remember once in my fifteen years, when Mom has gone to the lake by herself. Feeling like Mom or Missy might be in trouble, I race out of the yard, and turn onto the highway, following Mom down the road.

When I was very young, and Dad didn't have to take supplies out to the resort, which didn't happen too often, he and I would walk to the lake if it was a nice day. We'd hold hands and talk while I told him about my friends, about school, about my piano lessons, and I remember them as being one of the happiest times in my life. But this afternoon, all I feel are knots in my stomach. I hold my face to the sky, hoping it doesn't snow today.

When I arrive at the resort, our truck is abandoned on the road behind the shed, with the driver's door standing open as if Mom were in a hurry to get out. I hear voices coming from the yard.

Afraid I might be interfering on the women's private conversation, but wanting to make sure everything's okay, I creep towards the back of the shed and find Mom, her back to me as she talks to Missy who's standing between the pool and Mom. Missy is holding a wrench as if she was going to open the valve to empty the pool. Her canoe is sitting beside the cabin. Her reward at the end of a busy day; a canoe trip around the lake.

I'm about to step forward and ask if I can have one more swim before the pool is emptied, when Missy's eyes meet mine. She shakes her head, warning me to stay back. Mom turns, ever so slightly, but she doesn't see me. A white flake lands on my nose and I look to the sky; it's beginning to snow.

"Thought you got rid of the canoes," Mom says. "Didn't some kid just about drown?"

"Repaired it," Missy says. "Got rid of the others. Father didn't press charges."

Mom nods, her lips pursed. "Of course you did," Mom says.

"As they say, money talks. You're good at dodging bullets, aren't you, Cecelia? So good at dodging bullets." She shakes her head. "Remember the day the hotel burned down? You told Gerry you were coming to town that afternoon. Had some things to pick up at Garrets Hardware you said. Then you ended up here instead with a dozen witnesses getting that," she points to the pool, "monstrosity delivered. Everyone knew you didn't want any competition; everyone knew you wanted that hotel to close."

"That's not true," Missy says. "Bart could have competed if he'd renovated his place; it was falling down and outdated. How could he expect people to stay there at his inflated prices when just down the road there was this place?"

"You be quiet." Mom says.

"You put a good man out of business," Missy says.

"It was you who put him out of business, Cecelia. You and your," she waves around her, "family resort, of all the stupid things. This is what put him out of business, not me."

"What is it you want, Lila?" Missy says.

"I want you to admit you've been trying to steal my husband from me. Then I want you to close this place down for once and for all, and leave. Go back to wherever you came from."

"I can't admit such a thing," she says, "because it isn't true."

Mom laughs. It's a deep laugh, so guttural it doesn't even sound like my mom. "Knowing the way that man shares every aspect of his life with you, I'm quite sure he told you he waited to propose to me because he wasn't sure if he was in love with me. I think we both know, hell, the entire town knows who he's really in love with. But, because he'd been stringing me along for years, he did the honorable thing and proposed. He's an honourable man."

"He is an honorable man," Missy says. "And you're wrong. He waited to propose because when he came back from the war, he had no way of supporting a wife. He wanted to wait until he'd started the store. He wanted to wait until he was established. Not because he felt obligated to you, not because he was waiting to see if I'd marry him, but so he'd be able to support a wife and family. You must know that I have no intention of marrying."

"Are you barren?" Mom suddenly asks Missy, as if the idea has just occurred to her.

"I am," Missy says. "I had a baby when I was very young and the doctors tied my tubes. Barbaric, but that's what my father requested and like you said, money talks. I woke up and the nuns told me I'd never have another child."

"That explains a lot," Mom says. "He wanted a family so he chose me over you."

"He chose you because he loves you," Missy says. "And you have a beautiful daughter."

"I do have a beautiful daughter. And now you're trying to steal her away too, pretending like you're her mother, teaching her things, allowing her to stay overnight. You know what she told me?"

Missy shakes her head.

"She told me that she's the luckiest girl in the world because she has two mothers." Mom steps in Missy's direction. Missy backs up, moving closer to the pool, trying to avoid a physical confrontation. "Can you believe that? Two mothers, of all things. I'm her mother, you're just a, what are you, Cecelia? A whore? A slut? No," she says. "I know what you are. You're a mistress, that's what you are."

"I'm not trying to steal your daughter," Missy says. "And I am most certainly not Gerry's lover. We're friends and that's all we've ever been, all we'll ever be."

"I was doing laundry today and putting some clean clothes in her drawer when I found something," Mom says, not hearing what Missy said. "Want to guess what it was? Something you gave her."

"I don't play games, Lila."

"No, I suppose you don't." Mom sticks her hand into her coat pocket. She pulls out a wad of money. "This," she says. "This is what I found. I counted it. Do you know how much this is? Sure, you do, you gave it to her. Who else around here could afford to give her this much money? Who else flaunts their wealth, giving cash out right and left to anyone who asks?"

I kick myself. I was supposed to give that money to dad and I forgot.

"Are you trying to bribe her into loving you now? Is that what you're doing?" Mom says.

"It's for her post-secondary education."

"So, you're not only keeping our store afloat with all your purchases, as well as paying my husband to work for you, you're also giving our daughter money for her education? Don't you think her dad and I are capable of doing that on our own? Why must you always condescend to us?"

"I'm not condescending to you," Missy says. "I only wanted to help."

Again, Mom steps threateningly towards Missy, but Missy has no room left to move out of the way, and presses her palms against the side of the pool.

"If you had your way, I'd be out of the picture," Mom says, "and you and Gerry could live happily ever after with Louise as your daughter. Did you know not a day goes by when I don't wonder if my husband is going to come home and ask me for a divorce? Not a day," she says absently. "Do you know what that feels like? Fifteen years of worrying that some day I'm going to be alone?"

I decide to speak up. "No, Mom. Dad would never leave you. He loves you more than anything. He's always worried that you're unhappy."

"What are you doing here?" she says, glancing over her shoulder. "I told you to go home. You don't belong here; this is between Cecelia and me."

"Listen to your daughter," Missy says. "She knows what she's talking about. Gerry loves you; he loves both of you."

"I told you to be quiet," Mom snaps.

"Mom, don't hurt her, please," I say, tears running down my cheeks.

"Give me one good reason why I shouldn't," Mom says.

"Because she's our friend."

"She's no friend of ours, Louise. She's been trying for years to take your dad away from me, don't you know that? And now she's trying to steal you as well. You're an innocent girl, you can't see the ways of adults. Especially adults as conniving her." She stares at the pool. "I hate this pool," she says, her teeth bared like a wild animal. "It represents everything I hate about this place. It's useless, it's in the way, and it takes you away from me. Remember the day it was delivered, Louise? It was my birthday. Your dad left my birthday party because she," Mom again points at Missy, "called and ordered him out here to set it up. He left my birthday party for her!"

Suddenly, Mom is running towards the pool, her arms stretched out in front of her, and begins pounding the sides with her fists, the sound reverberating through the water like a bass drum. Missy steps towards Mom, trying to calm her down, but Mom gives her a hard push. Missy's head hits the metal pole that separates each of the panels, holding them into a circle. Missy grabs the back of her head. Her eyes are closed and she has a painful expression on her face. When she pulls her hand away, there's a streak of blood on the palm. I run towards her to help, but Mom blocks my path.

"Leave her be," she says to me.

"But, Mom, she hit the head."

"I said," Mom says, her voice sharp, "let her be."

"I'm okay, Louise," Missy says. "Just bumped my head. I'll be fine.

"Was your child a boy or a girl?" Mom asks.

"What?" Missy says, rubbing the back of her head.

"You said you had a child. Was it a boy or a girl?"

"A boy."

"When?"

"1931."

"You were just a girl in '31," Mom says. "Not much older than my daughter is now."

"I was twenty when I gave birth."

"So young. That must have been difficult."

"It was," Missy says. "One of the most difficult things I've ever done."

"Where's the father?"

"The father raped me but I paid the price. My father kicked me out then told me the only way he'd help me financially was if I gave my son up. I was a child myself; I had no choice."

"I'm sorry for your troubles," Mom says. "No woman deserves that."

"Lila," Missy says quietly. "Your husband and I have never been lovers, nor will we ever be. I'm," she stops.

"You're what?" Mom says.

"I'm sorry," Missy says stepping towards Mom and placing her hand on Mom's shoulder. "I'm sorry you feel this way. But you need to know, your husband and I are friends, nothing more." Mom crumbles into Missy's arms. "Take her home, Louise. Don't tell anyone what happened here today and take her home."

"But your head," I say.

"I'll be fine," she says. "Just look after your mom."

Chapter 38

The envelope with the information from the government about applying for grants, is laying on the dining room table. It's been there since Louise gave it to me at The Kernel before Gerry died. I've picked it up many times, but then feeing overwhelmed, set it back down, too afraid to begin doing something I fear I won't understand how to do.

This afternoon I pick it up, grab a cup of tea, and head to the balcony. It's the end of October and it froze again last night. The lake looks very cold, very rough, and very uninviting with a thin layer of ice ringing the edge. In a month's time, the entire body of water will be frozen solid. I watch a deer walk up to the shore and take a drink then disappear into the forest the other side of the beach. Watching wildlife has become a hobby for me. I've bought myself a pair of binoculars and have seen bear, deer, coyotes, rabbits, and fox. The only thing I haven't seen is Missy, either standing on the beach looking at the sunset, or cutting through my front yard on her way to where ever she goes.

I turn on the deck heater, snuggle into my chair, pull the quilt up to my chin and open the envelope, removing the stack of papers. Immediately I stuff them back in, unable to comprehend even what's on the first page.

"I can't do this. Running a resort is too complicated for someone like me. Find someone else," I say, talking to no one. I throw the envelope onto the end table, tuck my legs under me and curl into a ball, the blanket pulled up to my chin. With the afternoon sun and the deck heater warming up the balcony like a sauna, I fall asleep and dream. I see Gerry and Cecelia clearing the land and building the cabins. I see kids playing on the beach and splashing in the water. I see parties, and wiener roasts, bonfires and new friends being made. I see Louise and Missy picking berries in the forest, then fishing off the pier. It's so real I can feel the water spray onto my face, taste the hot dogs, and feel the warmth of the fire on my skin. I hear Missy asking me why I'm here, and wake up just as the sun is setting.

I pick up the envelope and take it downstairs, then sit at the dining room table, the pages spread out before me. For three hours I fill out forms, answer questions, and tell the powers that be what my plans are. When I'm done, I reread everything I wrote, change some of the wording, then shove the papers into the envelope provided. I lick the flap, stick it closed, then plaster some stamps on the corner. Then, so I'm not tempted to change my mind in the morning, I load Scout into the car, drive to town and park in front of the mailbox outside of Carnation's.

"Come on, Ruby," I say. "Get out of this car and drop the envelope in the slot." But my body won't move. Scout cocks his head at me and whines.

Across the alley, the back door of Louise's house opens and she emerges. "What are you doing over there?" she calls. "Do you need something from the store?"

I open the car door. "No," I say. "Just trying to make up my mind about whether I want to mail this." I wave the envelope at her.

"Is that the application for the government grant?"

"It is," I say. "I'm procrastinating. Afraid of making a fool of myself."

She wraps her sweater around her body. "Thought you mailed that away long ago. You know what Dad always said to me?"

"I don't," I say. "But I'm sure it's something profound."

"He said, *It's better to have tried and failed than not to have tried at all.* I believe it was Alfred Lord Tennyson who said that originally, but don't tell Dad."

"They were wise men," I say. "Both Alfred and your dad."

"Do you want me to come and pry that envelope out of your hand and drop it in the box?"

"No," I say. "I can do it." Still, I stay in my car.

Louise lifts her hands in the air. "It's up to you, but I think you should bite the bullet and mail it. You only live once. God," she says, "I must be channeling Dad."

Scout and I get out of the car, then I hold the envelope over the slot.

"I can't stand here all day," Louise says. "It's cold out here."

I let go and hear the envelope hit the bottom of the metal box.

"There you go," Louise says. "Now we just wait and see what happens. And whatever it is, I'm sure it will be wonderful."

I drive home, grab a glass of wine, and run upstairs, ignoring the squeak in the bottom step.

—

Winter arrives with its usual force, Thanksgiving, Christmas, and New Years comes and goes. Gerry is deeply missed for these holidays, but as he would have said, *life goes on.* January, February, and March pass, and finally April arrives with everyone counting the days till spring, and still no response from the government.

Concluding that my application has been denied, I've made the decision to forgo rebuilding the resort and instead hire Wilson, Blair, Jim, and Darren to tear down the old cabins this summer, as the town requested three years ago. I'm walking down the stairs to give Wilson a call, when there's a knock on the back door. Scout races ahead of me. Louise is standing on the step, an envelope in her hand.

"Thought I'd make a personal delivery," she says, handing me a large brown envelope.

"Is that what I think it is?"

"It is."

I take it and walk to the dining room without opening it.

"Open it," Louise says. "They either accepted you or denied you.

Doesn't matter either way; at least you tried."

I tear open the envelope and read.

"Well?" Louise says. "Don't leave me in suspense."

"I guess, if I want to start the process, they'll grant me my application," I say. "I just have to meet with them and tell them my game plan."

"You mean you're going to open a resort?"

"It looks that way," I say.

Chapter 39

"The toilet in cabin number seven needs unclogging," Wilson says.

"Okay," I say.

"I think that brat flushed his stuffed toy," he grumbles.

"That's a possibility," I say.

"Kids get away with more than they did in my day."

"That they do," I say.

He grunts and leaves to go to cabin number seven.

"Could you fix the bottom step when you're done?" I call as he rounds the corner. "It's squeaking again; driving me crazy."

When he's gone, Louise says, "You'd think he'd be less ornery now that he's part owner of this property. How's his house coming anyway?"

"You can see it, right there across the water." I hand her my binoculars.

Louise has come out today to bring me the framed picture of the cabin I gave Gerry for his birthday a few years ago, and we're now sitting in the front yard enjoying a glass of wine.

"Oh yeah," she says. "Looks nice."

"I walked over there yesterday. Darren was helping Wilson lay flooring. Should be complete by next month. Darren said his dad told him he was proud of him. Said it was a mistake, pushing him away after his mother died."

"Wow," Louise says. "Guess you can teach an old dog new tricks."

"And," I say, "Darren got a job at a hospital north of here. He asked me if he could buy a couple of acres of land from me and build himself a cabin. His dad is going to help him build it. I told him I'd give him the land, but he said no, he wanted to do it himself."

"Sometimes in life, things just work out, don't they?" she says.

"I certainly couldn't have done this without Wilson or his money. Nothing like having a contractor as your business partner when you need total renovations done. I think the cabins turned out quite lovely. He may be an ornery cuss, but he has something of a decorator's eye in him. Don't tell him I said that."

It's June, and a few of the cabins are rented for the next two weeks, with July and August nearly fully booked. Louise, Scout, Jess, Chip and I have just gotten back from a long walk around the lake. Scout, who is now thirteen, is snoring at my feet.

It's my third full year of running the resort and I'm hoping this season does as well as the other two. So far, I've broken even the first year and made a slight profit the second, which for a start-up, I'm told, is considered a roaring success. The province has even installed a cell-phone tower. Some call it progress; I kind of liked being out of reach.

Bernice and Marjorie booked a cabin for a full month the first year, as did Robert, Sheryl, and the kids, as well as Debby and Jess. I told them I wouldn't take their money but they insisted on paying, with Robert stating that I'd never become a successful business-woman if I kept giving out freebies. The entire time he and his family were here, I didn't hear him once hassle Sheryl about her weight.

The following winter, Bernice passed away in her sleep, surprisingly, not her lungs, but her heart. It just quietly stopped beating in her sleep one night. Marjorie was so grateful to me for giving her sister such a nice last summer that she told all her friends, of which there are many, that Sunset Lake Resort was the best holiday she'd ever had, better than Hawaii and Mexico combined. Because of her spreading the word, the resort was booked all last summer.

My cell phone rings, "Hello," I say, walking to the picnic table and opening my bookings schedule.

"Another booking?" Louise asks when I hang up.

"That's the last of the cabins," I say. "I'm full all summer. Glad the kids booked early this year or they'd never get in."

"It's hard to believe it's your third year," Louise says. "Seems like it was yesterday you opened."

"Five years ago, this was all a dream. Seventy years old and I finally have a job."

"Did you hear?" Louise says. "A ladies' clothing store is opening in town. Hasn't been one of those since Missy was running the resort. This place is bringing people back, Ruby. Cecelia would be proud of you. I only wish Dad could have been here to see; he'd be busting at the seams."

"He's here," I say. "I can hear him saying something like, *what goes around comes around.*"

I wander to the edge of the water, wondering if my own father would be happy with what I've accomplished. Perhaps this was his intention; to force me into becoming independent.

"They seem happy," Louise says, watching Chip and Jess walking along the beach in front of the Vereschuk's. "Make a cute couple."

"They do," I say. They began seeing each other the winter after the year my cabin was finished, though they didn't tell me until just recently. I haven't seen Chip with a stick of gum since he and my daughter became a couple.

Wilson returns. "Going to fix the squeak now," he says, banging open the door and entering the cabin.

"Do you ever wonder if Cecelia's money is hidden out here?" Louise asks.

"Haven't thought about that for years," I say.

She's quiet for a moment. "She had an expression she used to say to me, told me it was our secret. Did I ever tell you?"

"No. I don't think you did."

"Don't know why I didn't think of it sooner. As a child, I thought it might be a clue, but you know kids; they think everything is a clue to something." She taps her chin. "I'll be danged if I can remember exactly how it went. Something about failing to recognize the answer, or taking that first step, maybe? Did Dad ever say anything like that to you?"

"That sounds familiar," I say. "I can't quite remember."

Scout has stood up and is looking at the beach. He's whining, wagging his tail, and lifting his leg as if shaking a paw. A shiver runs up my spine.

"You cold?" Louise asks.

"Feeling a chill. Going to get a sweater." I enter the cabin and inch past Wilson pressing the bottom step, a couple of nails tucked between his lips and a hammer poised over the tread, trying to figure out where he should pound the nail this time, then climb the rest of the way to the top. I sit on the edge of my bed, remembering that first day I was up here, standing on the unfinished second floor and seeing Missy in the front yard. I ran down those stairs and talked to her about renovating the cabin, and she responded by saying something that sounded an awful lot like what Louise just said to me. *A journey of a thousand miles begins with a single step?* "No," I say, "that's not right. *The road to riches is paved with gold?* No, that's something Gerry would have said. Crap, what the hell was it? All I can think of are that man's stupid clichés!" I press my fingers to my forehead. "Come on, Missy, tell me what you said."

"Did you say something to me?" Wilson yells from the bottom of the stairs.

"No, sorry, Wilson. Just talking to myself."

I step onto the balcony to clear my head. Louise has taken Scout to the beach and he's running through the surf, looking like a young dog, not the senior citizen he is. Jess and Chip have stopped on the beach to watch, but then Jess turns and looks towards my front yard. She tugs on Chip's sleeve and points at something. Chip shakes his head and turns back to watching Scout play in the water.

I turn to where my middle child pointed, and for the first time in a long time, I see Missy sitting in the Adirondack chair. I call her name, and wave, excited to see her. She stands and looks up towards me, nodding her head, then walks across the yard, disappearing into the forest. I turn to look at Jess and know she saw the same thing I did.

I hold my face to the sky and close my eyes, comforted by the fact that Missy is still at the resort. I try to imagine myself back here that first day. Standing near the edge, worried about falling, then seeing Missy. Her sunhat. Her silver braid. Her overalls and man's plaid jacket. Her clear concise voice. *Sometimes the secret lies in taking the first step, but we fail to recognize it so as a consequence, don't move forward.* My eyes pop open. That's it. That's what Missy said the first day I saw her and we were talking about me renovating the cabin. Could it be that easy? I leave the balcony and am about to ask Wilson to stop pounding nails into the step, when he appears in the doorway. He has a crowbar in his hand and an odd look on his face.

"You might want to come and look at something," he says.

I follow him down the stairs where he's pried off the bottom tread. A satchel sits on the floor inside the staircase. "Don't know why I never looked under the tread before," he says. "Just kept pounding in more nails. Today, after all these years, the idea to pry it off popped into my head." He slides the zipper of the satchel open. Inside I see money; paper money like we used when I was a girl.

"Pick up a few bundles," Wilson says.

I remove some of the money, and beneath, something glints back at me. "What's this?" I ask.

"Gold," Wilson says. "I counted. There are five bars of gold."

I touch the overflowing bag. "It must have been rubbing against the underside of the tread. That's why the step was squeaking all these years. She was telling us where it is and we didn't listen. Until today."

Acknowledgements

I'd like to thank Stonehouse Publishing, and Netta Johnson for once again believing in me. She had a vision for this novel, and her edits made it far better than I could have done on my own.

Thank you to Heather Macdonald for listening to me go on and on about the story-line, and the word count, and whatever else I ranted about as I worked my way through. And thank you to Heather for reading the ARC and, as usual, finding far more typos than I could ever find.

As well, thank you to Kathy Seamer for reading the ARC and finding different typos than either Heather or I.

Thank you to Susan Layton for reading a first draft and telling me that she loved the story.

Thank you to Maureen Anderson for also reading the ARC, and finding typos.

Thank you to my husband, Tom, for allowing me to sit and write for hours on end.

Thank you to Maria Meindl, author of The Work, for reading the story and writing a blurb.

Thank you to Anthony Bidulka, author of *Livingsky* and many other novels, for reading the story and writing a blurb.

Thank you to my son-on-law, Aaron Anderson, my daughter, Maureen Anderson, and my son, Scott Jackson, for being there when I needed technical help, as my knowledge of computers is non-existent.

More about Joanne Jackson

Joanne Jackson is an award winning author of three novels. Her most recent, 'A Snake in the Raspberry Patch,' was the winner of Best Crime Novel set in Canada for 2023, and short listed for Saskatchewan Book Awards 2023. Her first novel, *The Wheaton* was released in 2019, and her forthcoming novel, *Sunset Lake Resort*, is set to be released spring of 2024. Joanne lives in **Saskatoon** with her husband, Tom, and an old border collie named Mick. If you keep your eyes peeled you will see Joanne and her dog walking come rain, shine, snow, or whatever weather Saskatchewan throws at them.